The B side

LILLY K. CEE

Version: Limited Edition   Print ISBN 979-8-9929941-3-1

Line Edit by Jeanine Harrell, Proofread by Nay Merrill at www.indieeditswithjeanine.com

Limited Edition Bonus Chapters edited by Nay Merrill at Nay's Notations Editing, www.naysnot ations.com

Cover and interior images by Lilly K. Cee with Canva Pro and Depositphoto standard licenses

Author photo by In Her Image Photography https://www.inherimagephoto.com/

Contents

Author's Note / Content Warnings

Hello! Thank you for your interest in *The B Side*. I look at this one as Beckman's story, although it is just as much Lucy's and Killion's.

This is not a romance. Is there love and are there steamy scenes? Yes, but the HEA doesn't follow the prescribed definition. However, this is the story Beckman wanted me to tell (along with a surprise guest).

Please be aware that this story contains the following content warnings: *graphic* depiction of suicide by hanging, suicide and suicidal ideation, death, chronic illness, depression and grief, sexually explicit scenes, reference(s) to crime and murder, natural disaster, reference to firearms, reference(s) to kidnapping and child SA, reference(s) to nonconsent.

Dedication

To Jess Elizabeth, friend and fellow author. Thank you for planting the seed to write Beckman's story.
Without you, his story would not have been written.
And thank you for being game to read anything I write.
I hope Beckman, Lucy, and Killion meet your expectations.
XOXO

For anyone who needs to hear it.

It's not your fault.

Prologue

Lucy

"I want love. I want more love than I can handle. I want to be overwhelmed by it." Lucy tossed her dime into the fountain. She used a dime to double her luck. The coin arched into the air before plunking into the clear water, slowly sinking to the shallow bottom.

"I don't think this is a wishing fountain."

Lucy side-eyed Jonah. "They're all wishing fountains." She rephrased. "All fountains are for wishing. And I need every bit of help I can get."

"You'll be fine, Luce." Jonah pulled her away from the J.C. Nichols fountain. "You're smart, beautiful, generous, and kind. Love will happen for you."

She scoffed. But she allowed him to lead her away to continue their journey toward their favorite coffee shop on the Plaza. "You keep saying that, but here I am, in my thirties, and I have no one."

"I'm the same age," he pointed out.

Lucy pushed her lips to the side as she considered it. "We're both old maids. At least you've been married before."

"There's no such thing as old maids. There are only independent women, like you, who've figured out we men are accessories, not necessities. And I wouldn't recommend marriage for the sake of it, something to check off your bucket list."

She knew he was speaking from experience regarding marriage. But she shook her head anyway, her blond hair catching the wind as she did so. "It's not about that. There's so much in me to give. And I want to know what it feels like to be loved; to inspire it, to be adored."

Jonah chuckled. "Be careful what you wish for."

CHAPTER ONE

Beckman

Ellie's screams. They ripped through his soul. Chilled his skin. Panicked his nervous system and stunned his brain.

There were different types of screams: a short, quick, surprised squeal; a howl embraced by laughter; an excited whoop; a drawn-out yowl; a cry of ecstasy. Hers was none of those. Hers were the wails of the tormented, and he'd never forget them.

He'd stood on her deck, smoking his morning cigarette, watching her carefully make her way to the warehouse farthest away. The unique crunching of boots compacting the frozen layers echoed her progress.

Scree-unch. *Scree*-unch.

Sleet and snow had fallen the previous night—early morning, rather—turning the area into a blinding, glistening skating rink.

It hadn't been snowing when she'd given up her two-day vigil outside the tiny room of warehouse number one. The warehouse where her brother was holed up in the back. She'd slept on the cold concrete for both nights, pleading through the door. Crying. Begging forgiveness. Making promises to do better, to be better.

Beckman had tried to coax her away to no avail. Next, he'd tried feeding her and encouraging her to wrap up in blankets, but she refused. She wanted to be punished, so she punished herself.

He didn't know what had spurred her into the house last night, but she'd slunk in, not meeting his gaze, as though ashamed to have given up her watch. She'd been shivering, her nose running. He'd prepared a cup of hot tea for her while she'd taken a shower.

When she rejoined him in the kitchen, they didn't speak. She drank the tea. They moved around each other like ghosts, the heaviness of the situation strangling their words.

As exhausted as he assumed she had to be, she didn't sleep. But neither did he. She sat at the tiny kitchen table tucked under the front window, staring outside and sipping the tea. Guarding from afar. Most likely berating herself for having given up.

Ellie kept watch at the window, although he knew she couldn't see the building next to them. The front deck on the raised house blocked her view. She would have witnessed the sleet and snow as it blanketed them.

He kept watch from the living room, the open floor plan meaning they were mere steps from one another. Emotionally, it was miles away. Her back was to him, her face turned away. The silence crushed, daring interruption.

This morning was no different, with the exception of the whiteness shrouding them, both illuminating and casting a gray pallor to the day. Going through the motions of making coffee, they'd both startled when Ellie's phone had chimed with a text.

She frantically grabbed the device, deflating when she read it. Her hand went to her forehead. "Donna."

She was talking to herself, not to him.

Donna was the event planner for Easy Street Events, Gage's business venture after being discharged from the military. The property was sizable, housing the event center, three warehouses, and this home Ellie and Gage shared. Gage had designed and built it all, including the house they were in. Uncommon for the Midwest, it was on stilts, similar to homes along coastlines.

Ellie shifted her silver eyes to the windows and sighed.

Beckman knew her. Despite the turmoil embracing them, a job needed to be done. A little bit of snow or a lot of personal drama wouldn't deter plans. She had to get to work, to step in where Gage couldn't—or wouldn't.

Shrugging on his coat, he headed toward the door while she muttered to herself the tasks she needed to attend to.

"Rock salt, thermostat, propane heaters—"

He was out the door before he heard anything else. He'd thought he would find relief with her back in the house, knowing she was warm, secure, fed, and—yes—out of Gage's reach, considering the last time Gage was near his sister, he'd held a gun under her chin.

But her presence was damning. He just wasn't sure who she was damning more—him or her.

He looked down at the snow-covered deck and dragged his boot through an untouched area, and then stared at the blemish until he heard the door open.

When she'd exited the house, their gazes clashed for the span of a second. He narrowed his on her, watching her through tendrils of smoke and frosty breath. She deprived him of closer study by ducking her head and rushing past him to the stairs, slipping on the top step in her haste to get away from him, his scrutiny, his presence—he had no idea.

He lunged to catch her, but she'd already caught herself and propelled down the slick steps, knocking snow from the railing in her wake. Her actions were hurried and clumsy with a hint of desperation; she didn't want him to touch her.

So he watched.

Fear roiled in his belly, an all-too-familiar companion when it came to the Rorks. The tightrope he always felt he was walking with them, where one misstep would yank the only family he had away from him. And with Ellie? He'd taken one hell of a misstep. It'd reached fucking catastrophic levels a few days ago.

She paused outside the first building. Her halted steps plunged them once more into deafening silence. The tilt of her head informed him she considered entering the space to check on Gage. Despite being swallowed in a camouflage coat and bright orange beanie over her dark locks, he noted her shoulders dropping. Defeat. Guilt. Fear. He had no idea which emotions were running through her; maybe all. Facing forward, she continued toward the last structure.

Other than her footfalls, the morning was hushed, anticipatory, cocooned in icy, pretty layers, both soothing and terrifying.

She hauled the sliding warehouse door open enough to allow herself entry. A solitary screech of metal on metal rent the air before sounds were once again quieted.

The eerie hush aided the acoustics of her shrieks.

They burst from the building, a banshee's chorus of screams complete with ghostly eyes and claws. They lashed out and snatched at him, sinking into him, shredding him.

He was instantly in motion, fighting to keep his feet beneath him as he raced down the steps. His cigarette hit the ground, dissolving with a hiss.

Before Ellie screamed her brother's name, Beckman knew. Call it instinct, call it intuition, or a good fucking guess after the events of the previous days. But he'd known when the first cry punctured the silence, piercing him.

Gage was dead.

He battled the snow and ice, working to stay upright, trampling the same path she'd taken as he raced to them. Grabbing the handle of the open door, he skated into the room, and screeching metal accompanied his unsteady entry as the door shifted. The concrete did little initially to provide him traction. Purchase found, he took in the scene.

Ellie was struggling to lift her brother's massive body, to relieve the rope around his throat. To give him air, hours too late. She screamed and pleaded with the man as she cleaved to his suspended body.

"Ellie!"

She was hysterical, beyond hearing. And she was focused, determined to lift a man comprised of sheer muscle and literal dead weight. Her adrenaline gave her added strength but not enough.

"Ellie, stop!" Beckman slammed himself against her back, reaching for her clinging hands. "He's gone."

Already frenetic, she turned feral. Gnashing, clawing, attempting to climb the man's swaying body. All the while, tears and snot spilled down her reddened cheeks, lips, chin, and neck. His intrusive thought was to wonder why her tears didn't freeze.

Unable to control her, he placed her in a chokehold—something he'd never imagined he'd have to do to someone he loved—forcing her away. She fought every inch that separated her from her brother, gouging her fingers into his restraining arm, kicking and twisting. Yet maintaining a tenuous hold on the flannel shirt. Until he tore her from him.

Wrenched free of her grip, Gage sightlessly watched the scene, dancing gently from the red rope.

Beckman wrangled her out the door. He slammed her against the steel side of the building, crushing his weight against her. Her hat had fallen away in the struggle, her black hair swirling around them.

She wailed, head back, her grief relayed directly to the heavens on clouds of billowy air.

He braced against her, panting, fighting to maintain his own composure in the face of this loss. She needed him more than he needed to give in to his shock, his pain, his grief, his horror. Cheek to cheek with her, he wasn't sure whose perspiration slicked their skin—both, probably. Or maybe it was tears.

Her fists were furious against him, ineffective against the padding of his coat. He gathered her to him, squeezing her tightly, the hug intended to relieve her nervous system. To let her know she wasn't alone, to ground her. And himself.

Another eerie scream tore through the morning, bouncing off the barren trees, rolling in crystalline waves across the land. She collapsed in his arms before the last echo was silenced.

Yeah, he'd never forget her screams.

Ellie stared at him over the flames. Her visage distorted as the fire danced and smoke rose. Sparks surrounded her, giving her an ethereal appearance, with the wintry night as her backdrop. But she was no faerie, not with her bright orange beanie, yet the magical element persisted despite her pain. Her defiance.

She tossed another length of rope into the firepit. Her expression dared, but he sure as shit wasn't going to stop her from burning it. He'd hated those things for years, was happy to see them burn—wished this ritual could have taken place a long time ago, only not for the reason she was doing it now.

The suicide note he couldn't keep from her, not that he would. But it wasn't something he'd wanted to slap her with immediately while she was vacillating between hysterical tears and grief-induced catatonia.

The police didn't take her emotional state into consideration. Nor had they given grace when they'd scowled at her driver's license. He'd already introduced himself. So their confusion over them both being named Elliott added to the turmoil.

He'd introduced her as Ellie. Her documentation reflected her government name. They'd insisted on calling her Elliott even though he'd explained she was his namesake, but she went by Ellie. No one called her Elliott.

There had been no professional courtesy, no camaraderie that he'd once served on the Kansas City force; these guys were not from his former precinct. They were there to investigate a death. He'd tried not to chafe at their lack of regard. It made him wonder if he was as jaded on the job. As suspicious and dismissive.

Probably.

The police held on to the original letter, but they'd shown it to her through their evidence bag. He'd managed to take a photo of it. Eventually, they would get it back. There was no other conclusion to be made than suicide; the cops knew it, but they were dotting i's and crossing t's. Gage had been too meticulous in his planning. His death wasn't as spontaneous as it appeared to be.

Thanks to Donna, he was able to access Gage's computer. There, he found the organized and practically seamless transfers of property and ownership to Ellie. She was named on everything. Of course, that would raise the eyebrow of any detective—and greedy insurance companies—so it was worth an inquiry, but the investigation would dead-end quickly.

It would have taken time to prepare that amount of paperwork so carefully, telling Beckman that Gage's exit from life was not a reaction to what had occurred a few days earlier, but a goal. Or at least, he was aware enough of his own ideation that he'd wanted his sister provided for if and when he decided to take his final bow.

Not that she'd believe him. Not with that letter. Not when he'd chosen his moment to be the one when she'd left her guard and come inside.

Which, of course, was why it was easy to connect the dots to Ellie standing before the firepit in the middle of the night in Gage's winter military jacket over her flannel nightgown, boots, and her bright orange beanie, burning rope.

Chapter Two

Beckman

Beckman lit his cigarette, side stepping the departing attendees as they meandered away from the graveside. The people talked in hushed tones as they passed by, as one did in a cemetery, respect for the dead and the grieving, and all that.

Taps had been played, of course. Ellie sat stoically and gracefully throughout, tears drifting down her reddened cheeks. He'd wanted to vomit, the tune reminding him of the older Rorks' funeral, the devastation of their loss felt as keenly now as then.

Compounded, actually, as another Rork was being put into the ground. He made a promise that he absolutely would not allow the remaining Rork to precede him in death—as he hadn't before she was born—shifting his attention to Ellie. Whether she'd want him in her life or not after today, he'd do everything in his power to make sure she was okay regardless.

Fear coiled in his belly again, but he didn't have time to pay attention to it.

When they'd handed her the trifold, her lower lip quivered. She had stared at the woman relaying the standard gratitude on behalf of a grateful nation and appreciation for his honorable service. He could tell she didn't hear what the woman said, that she was struggling not to dissolve into a million pieces. But she'd played her part remarkably, thanking the woman for the flag and the words.

Gage had accepted the flag on behalf of their father. Service member to service member. Father to son. Now, brother to sister.

It started snowing again as he stood there, watching her. She remained in her seat beneath the garishly colored funeral tent, wrapped in her black dress coat, hugging the trifold like it was a lifeline. Fixated on the coffin.

He didn't take his eyes from her, even through the fog of breath and smoke. When the coffin began to be lowered, she fell apart. He was frozen, impotent, as he watched her mouth gape in pain, a silent shriek of agony. A perfect representation of torment.

An unnatural click similar to an old-fashioned camera caused him to snap his head around, ready to tear into whomever had the audacity to intrude upon Ellie's grief. Donna stood a few feet behind him, lowering her camera. Her saddened expression gave him pause on berating her, although he silently demanded an explanation by raising an eyebrow.

"Funerals should be remembered, too. Maybe one day, she'll want these. I'll download them on Gage's computer. At least she'll have them." Casting a mournful glance toward the scene, she sighed heavily, the air thick with her breath, before turning and picking her way through the snow toward the waiting cars.

He watched her go. There would be no gathering at the house after the funeral, as was tradition for some families. Ellie wanted solitude, so that's what she would get. Donna had arranged for a light lunch at a local venue—not Easy Street Events, of course—for those who'd come in from out of town, but Beckman couldn't name anyone in attendance. He'd bet Ellie couldn't, either, if she'd paid attention.

There hadn't been a lot of people, which was heartbreaking because Gage had been larger than life and loved others with his whole heart. Then again, suicide—especially of a veteran—wasn't something anyone advertised. Beckman hadn't handled any announcements, and Ellie had been in no condition to do so. He assumed Donna. He'd have to apologize for his glare; she'd stepped up.

Ellie wouldn't leave the graveside until dusk had fallen, and the coffin was covered in dirt. Only then did she stand, clutching the flag to her chest. On wobbly legs, she approached the freshly churned frozen earth, veering at the last minute to go to her parents' headstone. She pushed her fingers through the snow to touch the marble.

"I'm sorry I failed."

Beckman wiped his eyes as he drove back to Easy Street. He tried to be discreet, although he could have been sobbing loudly, and he doubted Ellie would have noticed. Her head was tilted back against the headrest, rolled to the side as she listlessly stared out the window. At any other time, he would have been charmed by the small ice breaks in the Missouri River as they drove by, but appreciating anything right now felt like a betrayal of their grief.

Once home, they trudged up the steps, footfalls as heavy as their hearts.

Inside, they hung their coats on the hooks next to the door. He avoided looking at her, reaching for his tie and loosening it. Walking toward the kitchen bar, he removed his watch and tossed it on the top. Next, he unbuttoned his cuffs. He needed to feel less formal, less restricted, less like he'd put Gage Rork in the ground next to his parents today.

He became aware of her erratic breathing. The tenor of the room shifted, a different kind of fury enveloping him. Confused, having moved from his left to his right cuff, he turned. She glared at him, her stunning silver eyes sparkling with accusation. Desperation.

The accusation was misplaced. It hadn't been *him* who'd ambushed her ten years ago. But it *had* been him who had continued to give in to her. And he'd do it again, now, on the heels of burying their last family member, because he could not lose her, too.

It was their toxic pattern: Ellie crashed emotionally, and Becks fucked away her adrenaline, pain, whatever the hell needed to be assuaged with ropes and the furious clashing of their bodies.

There were no ropes left, so he would improvise. He reached for his belt.

Her lip drew back in a snarl.

She wanted a fight. She wanted to be subdued, to be punished, so that the physical pain matched the internal.

He could never—would never—hurt her like that. But they could pretend. They were both good at that. Unfortunately, it was what he knew he could do to temporarily help her. But this would be the last time.

CHAPTER THREE

Beckman

After they'd brutally and angrily fucked—during which she'd reviled herself as a monster, a demon, and he'd growled in her face that they would never revisit this part of their relationship—she'd fallen back into depression. Rather, she sank deeper into it. The reason wasn't because he'd ended the sex for good—she didn't want it, either—but because her brother had killed himself. He knew that.

For days, she only left her bed to stumble across the hall into the bathroom. The small single-level house began to stink with defeat, sadness, and her body odor.

She refused food, but he was able to wrestle with her enough to get water into her. The dark rings around her eyes deepened. Her skin and hair lost their glisten. She was wasting away in front of him. Her only signs of life were short, angry outbursts that exhausted her.

He couldn't fucking stand it. So while she slept, he cleaned Gage's room, stripping the sheets and cleaning them. Unable to bring himself to throw away or box up the clothes—Ellie should decide what to do with them—he at least cleaned out space in the dresser and the closet. In his mind, this would be her room if she chose to keep the house. He prepared the home for her to occupy as the owner, because she was.

And, despite it being the dead of winter, he called a local sports shop and arranged for a heavy bag to be installed under the house in the open space near Gage's red Mustang. They'd side-eyed him but took his money while giving him tips on how to protect the bag in the weather.

He cleaned the area of snow and assisted them in laying an exercise mat. After they left, he'd gone into Ellie's stinking room and pulled the covers off her. She'd fought him, but he was counting on that fight, her anger. He battled to get her into sweat pants and boots. She weakly fought him when he half dragged, half carried her out of the room, out of the house, and down the steps.

He placed her in front of the bag and ordered, "Hit it."

When she'd merely stood there, he picked up her hand, manipulating her to slap the cold material. He didn't bother putting gloves on her. Not yet. He only wanted to introduce her.

The first day, she allowed him to be her puppeteer. The second day, she caressed the bag on her own. The third day, she fell against it and cried, but she balled her hand into a fist and hit it once, even as she hugged it.

Their progression was slow. Her fugue was hard to break through. He'd placed her in the shower after every session to warm and clean her. At least she'd stopped fighting him. She allowed him to feed her. Color started to return to her cheeks.

On the morning she came out of her bedroom independently, he placed pink boxing gloves on the counter.

She stared at them for a minute before quietly asking, "Can I get another color?"

"I'll get you whatever fucking color you want."

Her question let him know she would be okay. More than how she took to the lessons he provided, how she hit and kicked and yelled out her anger, her grief. The question, while about aesthetics on the surface, was an indication of the future: future use of the gloves in a color she preferred over pink.

It was hope.

He left once her confidence renewed, once the light came back into her eyes. Was she hyper-focused on kickboxing? Yes, but it was an exercise she could control, something in her world-turned-upside-down that she had power over. And he'd rather she obsess over the training than what she'd lost.

"What am I supposed to do now?"

He'd carried his bags to the front door. A taxi would be arriving to take him to the airport, returning to DC, where he was eager to get back into the routine of his job after his extended leave. He turned to her. She was leaning back against the kitchen counter, cradling a cup of coffee. He tried to ignore the flash of uncertainty, the fear that crossed her face. Those were two emotions he'd only recently realized she possessed, and it wasn't like her. His Ellie had always been fearless.

He pointed down the hall. "That's your room now. This is your house. His car is yours. Easy Street Events is yours to continue or sell off."

She flinched when he suggested the last.

"You live, Ellie."

Her lower lip trembled, and her eyes brightened with tears, but they didn't fall. She took in a deep breath and nodded once, determination radiating from her.

Yeah, that was the girl and woman he knew.

They didn't hug, and they didn't say goodbye. When the taxi arrived, he picked up his bags. "I'm only a phone call away."

"Will you answer?"

The uncertainty and fear were back in her voice, only this time he interpreted it as the possible loss of him rather than being daunted by her own path forward. It shouldn't have given him hope, knowing she would miss him, that she was afraid of losing him, but it did.

"Always."

She nodded again, dropping her gaze as she brought the coffee cup to her lips.

Walking out the door, getting into the taxi, and boarding the plane, his stomach churned. Despite her question and the emotion attached to it, he was petrified he'd walked away from the last of his family. After all, the stronger she became, the less she would need him.

At the same time, the weight of ten years of guilty agony lifted.

He prayed it didn't mean it was all over, that his family had been buried with Gage Rork.

Did he give her space after he left? Of course he did. It wasn't entirely intentional. His job was demanding, requiring focus. He also needed to process his own grief. After being relieved of Ellie's demons, of his complicity in appeasing them, he realized he'd put the pain of the last several years on hold. The deaths of his friends were overshadowed by Ellie's grief. He'd felt responsible for both of the kids after that, stepping in as a surrogate where he could. Gage was older, probably had considered him more like a brother than a parental figure, but he'd been struggling, too.

Without the distractions of secrets and death, he'd felt lost initially as he resumed his life in DC. After he'd returned, one of his first cases involved ropes. He realized he was having a PTSD moment from the last ten years—from Gage's death—when his brain superimposed Ellie in the place of the vic. He'd had to leave the scene.

He still had friends on the force in Kansas City, so without being intrusive, he kept tabs on her. And Easy Street Events. The trickle of information kept him grounded. For instance, he'd known when Donna quit, although he hadn't heard it from Ellie. But it encouraged him to know that while he concentrated on drinking less and working more, Ellie was taking his advice. She was living. Or so it seemed.

The sporadic communication was a twist of the knife in his heart. When his phone rang in the middle of the night—an occupational hazard—he experienced a stab of terror that a voice on the other end would inform him she'd joined her brother in death.

That call thankfully never came.

He mailed her birthday cards. He'd wanted to surprise her on her thirtieth, celebrate the milestone with her because he knew she didn't have anyone else. About to board the plane, he'd received a text that a teenager had been kidnapped, so plans, of course, changed. He'd sent flowers but hadn't received a response.

The silence plummeted him back into anxiety over the loss of family. Without her—even if from a strained distance—he had no one.

In his darker moments, he regretted centering his world around the Rorks and blamed himself for not being enough for his wives. There was also the fact that he'd been fucking his pseudo niece.

She'd call to rage and vent. He let her do it, not defending himself—he had no defense. It was a connection to all he had left, her incoherent, grief-filled accusations that were projections of her own self-loathing. Late-night crying jags weren't uncommon in the beginning. She'd needed someone to join her in her grief and guilt, even though she'd hated him for a while. But just as she was all he had, he was also all she had left.

When she'd go quiet, he'd check in with texts and calls. Some she answered, some she didn't. When the late-night calls ended, he knew she was getting better. At least, that's what he'd hoped.

Then one evening, she called and asked him if he thought she was capable of a normal relationship. Beyond her initial trepidation, he'd heard genuine hope and smiles in her voice. She was talking to him again like they'd never stopped, as if more than two years hadn't passed since he'd walked away. It was a new beginning.

He'd been goddamn ecstatic—with a hint of protective caution—that she was falling in love, picking her life back up. She'd hired a new event coordinator, and a handyman—although he hadn't been happy to hear he was a parolee. However, after looking the kid up, Killion Murphy hadn't worried him.

But, true to her nature, she sabotaged the relationship, misled him on the finer details, and ended up in the hospital after a motorcycle wreck. He'd wanted to go immediately, but one, he knew she was okay, and two, it was their habit. If he were honest with himself, he didn't want to go because he was afraid they'd fall back into old patterns.

Another break in communication prompted him to get on a plane—Georgetown cupcakes in tow—to check on her. After all, at that time, he'd thought the man who'd put those smiles in her voice was dead. And his self-preserving, pussy ass didn't want a reprise of the activities they'd put behind them. Keeping away had been the right thing to do, and he was glad she hadn't turned to him for relief. Of course, the little brat had been keeping secrets, which was why she hadn't been devastated by the loss of her man.

Standing on the patio of Easy Street Events that night, a dazzling blond had captured his attention before Ellie. On one level, he was aware of Els, but he'd been entranced by ESE's new event coordinator as she laughed with the bartender, the aforementioned Killion Murphy. The distraction of her presence was why he hadn't taken full notice of the man next to Ellie, Jonah. He certainly hadn't picked up on any undertones between the two, and that's the first thing he normally would have noticed, but he'd allowed himself to be distracted.

Distracted. Nah, she wasn't a distraction. A distraction is equated with something unwelcome, and she was most welcome. He'd wanted to claim her outright, then and there. He wanted to earn and own the smiles she was sharing with Killion.

Instead, he earned her stern, disapproving glare as he took a drag from his cigarette. He didn't mind; her outrage was as captivating as her laughter. He was simply delighted to be the object of her attention.

But something about the scene that didn't have anything to do with her urged him to proceed with caution. And his unease needed to be sorted out. He needed to find the source of it and address it.

Because... Lucy Moore.

Where Ellie was darkness and angst, Lucy was a beacon. And he desperately craved her light.

Chapter Four

Killion

"Hey, Mom," Killion whispered as he entered her apartment at the assisted living facility. It was early, about six in the morning. His mom was an early riser, but on her bad days, she'd stay in bed.

He'd needed the drive to Warrensburg, though, to clear his head. Last night's weirdness at the party cost him some sleep. If he'd ever wondered how Lucy saw him, he had his answer. She didn't. Especially not after Detective Beckman entered the room.

Since he was already awake, he decided to visit his mom. At this point, his parole officer only requested texts when he came to see her, so last-minute visits weren't a problem.

His mom's rooms were small; the term "apartment" was generous, not that he was complaining. He was thankful she had a safe place where she was being cared for. But the suite itself was only slightly larger than a hotel room. She had a kitchenette and a small sitting area with a cozy window well. Her bedroom and bathroom were on the other side of a half wall.

Instead of a foyer by the elevators, though, there was a nurses' station.

Come to think of it, her space wasn't too different from his own room in the back of the warehouse at Easy Street Events. Again, he wasn't complaining. Elliott Rork had plucked him from homelessness, given him a job *and* a home. She hadn't known it at the time; she'd been looking for a general handyman, and he'd been brooding in the church basement looking for a break.

"Son! Why are you here?" Her voice came from the bathroom.

He paused by the front door, straining to hear if she was dressing or doing something else. The shuffling he heard made him assume dressing. "Do you need help?"

After a couple puffs, sounding like frustration, she answered, "I wanted to wear something other than a sweat suit, but I can't get the buttons lined up."

"I'll help." He headed toward her.

"I'll just wear something else."

Killion didn't like the defeat in her voice. Walking into the bathroom where the closet was, he noticed she was half dressed. The yellow skirt she wore reminded him of Lucy.

"You shouldn't have to do this," his mom mumbled.

"I'm happy to help. How many times have I told you it's fair play? You dressed me when I couldn't, now it's my turn."

"You were a baby," she pointed out. "Are you calling me a baby?"

Killion snorted a laugh, reaching for the white buttons on her yellow blouse. "Are you telling me that the food they serve you *isn't* baby food?"

She chuckled, playfully swatting his arm. But she stood still while he lined up the buttons and fastened her in.

"It's the circle of life or something like that." He grinned.

"If you start singing that song..." She playfully warned him.

"I'm a helluva singer. You love my singing voice."

She snorted. "Your voice was precious until your—until puberty."

His smile broadened. She was about to say until his balls dropped.

Anyone on the outside looking in might raise an eyebrow at a bald, tattooed man dressing an older woman. Not old, older. She was still in her fifties. Her health was shit. And he couldn't take care of her. He barely had a roof over his own head after a long stint of being homeless.

These small things he could do for her were his way of trying to give back. She'd stuck by him when he'd joined the military (she'd cried) and when he got into a fight that sent a man to the hospital (she'd cried harder). But she hadn't deserted him.

So there was no fucking way he wouldn't do everything for her that he could. But despite the visits, or whatever she needed, like dressing her, it never felt like enough.

Finishing his task, he stepped back. "There." Then he frowned. "Who are you getting dressed up for?"

He was immediately protective. Had one of the old men around here been making passes at his mother?

"No one. I wanted to feel pretty." She took a hold of his forearm, indicating he was to lead her out of the small space.

"You are pretty, Mom."

It was true. She'd maintained her beauty despite her ailments. He wished she knew that, but he was also aware that she thought she was the sum of her illnesses. She wasn't; she was so much more. Beautiful, funny, and loving. Despite his many fuckups, she still loved him. She rode his ass about it, but she loved him. It made disappointing her again something he strove not to do.

When she didn't respond, he added, "I mean, I look just like you and I'm a stunner."

She laughed. Then coughed. The shuffle from the bathroom closet had worn her out.

He helped her settle into her chair and assisted her with the cannula that delivered oxygen. That irony that she was the one who struggled to breathe when she'd never smoked a day in her life, while he was a smoker, wasn't lost on him.

Watching him, she asked again, "Why are you here? Why did I think I wouldn't see you this weekend?"

Killion sat in the window well, which was his usual spot because it was close enough for her to see him without straining her eyesight. "Yeah, this was spontaneous. There's a wedding this weekend. The rehearsal party was last night. The wedding is this afternoon. I can't stay long because I need to help Lucy set up."

His mom smiled. "I like her."

Killion smiled back. "I like her, too."

So much. But the stars Lucy had gotten in her eyes when she'd met the detective stung more than he'd expected. And not only because there was something weird going on with Elliott and her whatever-he-was. "Uncle" was thrown around, but they weren't related.

"I'd like to see you settle down with someone like her."

Or... with her, Killion added in his head. But, "I'm not exactly a catch."

"Killion Scott Murphy, you are a wonderful man. I know because I raised you." Reaching out, she grasped his hand. "And I wouldn't raise a shithead."

Killion laughed, and it felt forced, although he recognized that he'd indeed inherited his humor from his mom. But images of Lucy continued to flash through his brain.

Lucy, his friend and technically his supervisor. She was also in charge of the church's parolee program that landed him his gig and accommodations at Easy Street.

He couldn't pinpoint when he developed a genuine hard-on for her.

Sure, her kindness and beauty had knocked him out when he'd first met her. And she'd been so proper and earnest in her desire to make sure his involvement in the program was successful—that *he* succeeded. He hadn't wanted to disappoint her. That was still true.

Over time, though, her expressions of sympathy became increasingly grating. She regarded him with a mixture of pity and hope. Pity because of his circumstances and past; hope that he'd pull through and land on his feet.

But those weren't the expressions he wanted from her, like he was the B side of a vinyl album: okay but not exciting.

He'd been working up his courage to ask her out, seeing as things were going better for him. Better than when he'd met her, anyway. Even if his doubts echoed what he'd said to his mom, he'd held onto hope.

But last night, she'd been stunned in a good way. Just not by him.

It could be fleeting, her fascination with the man. After all, he lived in DC. And it could be that the detective wasn't interested in her—which would make him the dumbest man alive.

Killion would have to keep an eye out while the man was in town, see where those chips fell.

Chapter Five

Lucy

Lucy hated the clichés and platitudes people spouted off whenever she bemoaned her middle-aged singlehood. Thirty-five was middle age, right? It didn't matter. What mattered was that she was mid-thirties with a string of *meh* boyfriends when she'd been love-crazy since she was a kid.

Her first—and most memorable—crush happened when she was in second grade. Isaac Rice had picked her up and half carried her to the nurse's office after she'd been flung off the merry-go-round. Bleeding knees and sobbing hadn't deterred him from helping her. In fact, he'd kept asking if she was okay and blamed the older kids for not looking out for her. He'd been caring and protective.

She hadn't known his name at the time, so she'd pestered Jonah to find out. Despite only being six months apart in age, Jonah fell into the upper class. And although he was two grades below Isaac—who was therefore three grades above her—he knew of him. She'd savored the tiny morsel of information despite it not going beyond Isaac's name and grade.

It hadn't stopped her from daydreaming that Isaac would swoop in again, that he would appear out of nowhere, once again her knight in shining armor. She even allowed herself to be flung from the merry-go-round a few times in an attempt to recreate the moment. She was devastated every time she was left to pick herself up and hobble to the nurse's station for cleaning up and bandages.

The one-sided love affair was ill fated, however. Soon after she'd met the love of her young life, her parents packed up and moved to Kansas City.

She'd wished for a fairy-tale romance ever since. To no avail. No one measured up to Isaac's heroic efforts that day and his care for her.

With every letdown, someone had to drop those useless sayings on her. Patience is a virtue. Good things come to those who wait. It'll happen when you aren't looking for it.

The last one was the worst because she was always looking for it. Which meant she'd never find love.

So when she'd walked into the Easy Street Events warehouse office and seen Gage Rork on the wall, she'd fallen hard. It didn't matter that she knew he was dead. Her imagination and heart ran away with what their reality could have been if he'd been alive.

He'd quickly replaced Isaac in her daydreams.

Did she know it was silly? Yes, but silliness was expected of her. She'd always been a dreamy child. A head-in-the-clouds girl who lived up to her name and that infamous song, sans the drugs.

After all, it was easier living in the clouds than being forced to face the reality that she wasn't ever going to be loved. That all the love she had to give would go nowhere. And though she was happy Jonah found the woman he loved, she lamented her own bad fortune in that arena.

Until Becks. Elliott Beckman. A silver fox with haunted blue eyes he hid behind an asshole-ish veneer. She'd been smitten when his attention had shifted to her and he called her pretty.

And she hadn't been looking that night.

"You held out on me." She accused Gage as she entered the office. "I should be mad at you, but he's freaking handsome, so I forgive you."

Lucy pulled her tank top off without hesitation, braless underneath, needing to change into proper clothes for the wedding. She'd been naked in front of Gage before, and she liked the idea of him seeing her, that this was the moment he peeked through the veil and his steel-gray eyes could see her. Admire her. Desire her.

Like how Elliott Beckman looked at her, a look she felt all the way to her core complete with flutters and yearning. When he'd complimented her—done. She was done. Everything around her had gone fuzzy as she'd stared. Older. Graying blond hair. He was adorably disheveled in appearance—she blamed the flight from DC to KC—and his blue eyes pierced. She didn't even mind that he was a smoker. Heck, Killion smoked and she put up with him.

She was prone to falling quickly into infatuation—hope—but she'd known with certainty that she wanted him. Similar to her intuition that Easy Street Events had been destined for her, so, too, was Elliott Beckman—Beckman. She didn't think she would ever be able to call him Elliott.

It didn't matter to her that Killion and Jonah disliked the man for no reason. Well, she sensed Jonah's reason, considering Beckman had shown up and whisked Elliott away. Jonah had planned on rekindling his romance with Elliott that night, and Beckman had interfered with those plans. It hadn't warranted Jonah leaving the rehearsal party early in a depressed and angry state.

And the imaginations of the two men were crazy. Killion snapped at her to read the room, but Lucy didn't see anything untoward. Elliott was taken off guard, sure, but she was also excited. Beckman was the only family Elliott had left. So Killion's snide remark that the two Elliotts were having sex was ridiculous.

Jealousy, that's all it was. She'd called them out on it. Jonah was jealous because he had to share his woman's time. And Killion... Well, she didn't know why Killion would be jealous. He wasn't interested in Elliott.

Seeing Becks today, after she and Killion finished setting up the outdoor tables for the wedding, further excited her.

The previous night hadn't been a fluke.

He'd been sitting on one of the outdoor loungers, looking yummy. Refreshed from his flight. Not even the cigarette dangling from one hand dampened her enthusiasm. She didn't like it, but it wasn't a deal-breaker.

He'd been talking to Jonah, but when he noticed her, his attention diverted. She'd basked in the smolder of his regard. Not even Jonah's angry stare when he turned to find out what had distracted Beckman's attention could calm her racing heart.

Killion nudged her with his elbow, breaking her concentration. She'd demanded what his problem was, but she hadn't cared about his answer. Instead, she'd called out, informing the men she had to change for the wedding. She'd noted Beckman's regard grew warmer.

He smirked as though he could read her mind.

She *had* been thinking about getting naked for him, after all.

Instead, Gage stared sightlessly at her from the wall.

Might as well give him a show. Her gaze locked on the photo, she fondled her breasts, squeezing and shivering, setting off a thrum in her pussy.

She could get herself off from playing with her breasts. It was a thrill she'd discovered years ago, the ability to give herself a tit-gasm. It resembled an orgasm, one that started with her very sensitive nipples. The climax resulted in the tensing of her muscles behind her breasts and trembling, leading to a crescendo of pleasure.

As she tweaked and pinched, her breath ragged, her attention remained fixed on Gage. But she imagined Beckman watching, too, wondering if he would be pleased with her.

It was a thrill, thinking of them and how they'd respond.

Her clit took up an urgent beat, but before it could beg insistently to be attended, a thump on the other side of the wall startled her.

Killion, in his room behind the warehouse office.

Her eyes flew to the side door; she hadn't locked it. Killion could walk in on her.

The mental image of him catching her elicited another delicious tingle.

Maybe she was an exhibitionist.

Maybe she was desperately lonely and any attention was welcome, no matter who.

That wasn't true. She didn't want strangers gawking at her. But Killion wasn't a stranger. And there had been times when they'd exchanged teasingly heated glances. They just never acknowledged it. Or rather, she shoved aside the notion of his interest in her.

Not wanting to push her luck by getting caught, she snatched up her silk shirt and tugged it over her head. The outfit of a shell-pink shirt and pastel floral skirt wasn't as sexy as last night's evening gown, but this was a wedding she'd coordinated, so she had to appear respectable and responsible.

Even if her brain was flashing images of three men watching her get off.

Chapter Six

Lucy

The wedding had been beautiful and romantic and everything a couple would want. She was pleased they were happy and that everything had gone off without a hitch—except for them getting hitched—not only because she'd planned it, but because they were her friends, and all of their friends were in attendance. More than half the congregation had shown up to support and celebrate the day.

That evening, after a quick dinner at Elliott's place, Beckman gave her a ride home. Cue her excitement and anxiety.

She could have taken an Uber—had mentioned she would—but he wouldn't hear of it. Jonah was supposed to be her ride, but he'd bailed early again, not staying more than ten minutes at the reception.

Killion had sulked off after dinner, being in a mood all evening. He'd been grumpy and quiet as the two had cleaned up and broken down the tables. Whatever his problem was, though, it hadn't affected his appetite as they'd eaten the lasagna Elliott prepared.

The atmosphere at dinner had been tense. Elliott neither ate nor spoke. But the food was drool-worthy. And Lucy wasn't going to pass up the meal, or the opportunity to remain in Becks's presence, even if the vibe was off.

Elliott eventually retreated to her room, which prompted Killion's departure. He'd hesitated at the door a minute, looking back at her like he wanted to say something. His gaze shifted behind her to Becks. With a slight shake of his head, he left.

Her nerves were jacked. She was finally alone with him, and she felt like a tongue-tied schoolgirl. To distract herself, she started cleaning. She babbled about how she didn't want to leave until she knew Elliott was okay. That's when she mentioned taking an Uber home.

"I'm taking you home."

The tone of his voice, his response definite rather than an offer, made her tingle. He'd taken control, and she loved it.

On the drive, she sneaked glances at him. Rather, she thought she was sneaking, but every time she tried to side-eye him, he grinned and glanced back. Striving to appear calm, cool, and collected—the exact opposite of what she was feeling—she asked about Elliott, about his job. He answered every one of her questions patiently.

Upon entering her little apartment, she turned to him. "I can give you a tour, or go straight to where we both want to go."

Lust made her brave.

His chuckle sent a bolt to her pussy; it wasn't amusement but satisfaction. He wanted her, too. She swore she was already in love, hearing his low laugh heated with promise and desire.

"The tour can wait."

Correct answer!

She threw herself at him. He caught her, lifting her. She wrapped her arms and legs around him. His enthusiasm matched her own. She'd just met this man, but being with him felt natural. Wanting to get naked with him, even more so.

Besides, he was Elliott's uncle and a detective. She was safe.

Instead of heading to the bedroom, he went to her Ikea futon that served as her sofa. She grinned, spreading her legs wider as she straddled him, rubbing herself against him. He was already hard, his pants jutting obscenely. She stroked him through the fabric, eager to have him inside her.

"I want this." She squeezed him.

He grunted. "I want you to have it."

Without further ado, she ripped off her tank top. Tiny tits meant no bra. It also meant, well, tiny tits.

She shrugged. "This is all I got." She cupped her small breasts with their upturned nipples.

"You're perfect."

"Why, thank you, detective."

With a hungry growl, he yanked her against him, anchoring her on his lap with one arm around her. He lowered his head and sucked her nipple, his mouth hot, his tongue flicking.

She gasped and threw her head back, her long hair dangling behind her. Reaching back, she braced her hands on his knees and thrust her chest forward. "More!"

He obeyed, of course. Pinching and sucking, licking.

She squirmed and gasped, digging her fingernails into his pants. She frantically dry humped him as he sent her spiraling into orbit solely with the attention he gave her breasts.

Her muscles locked, her nipples the conduit of wave after wave of giddy pleasure. When the spasm of delight subsided, she threw herself forward against him. Her uber-sensitive nipples were tingly and throbbing in the wake of the stimulation.

"What was that?" he asked, his blue eyes sparkling with wonder and appreciation.

"It's a tit-gasm," she panted. "It's like having a clit on your nipples. Just as mind-altering and intense, I swear."

Beckman grinned. "You've converted me into a tit man." He dropped his appreciative gaze to her meager offerings. "Of these beautiful breasts only."

Lucy matched his grin. Sometimes the level and intensity of her sensitivity freaked men out. Like their dicks had to compete with her nipples, as stupid as that was. Not Becks, though. He looked like he'd be content to send her over the edge again and again with breast play alone.

But she wanted—needed—more. She needed the hard length beneath her to be unclothed and sheathed inside her. She wanted to be filled, and from what she could gather, he had the equipment to meet her body's demands.

In silent agreement—another sign of how aligned they were—the remainder of their clothes were shed in between kisses and groping. Well, she groped. He caressed. When his shirt came off, she rubbed her face against his chest while scraping her fingernails along his ribs. His stuttered intake of breath let her know he liked it.

She liked it, too. Mens' chests were her kryptonite, and Beckman had a strong, wide chest. And after they had sex, she was going to plaster herself to it and rest. Now, however, she needed him inside her.

He was nude beneath her, his gorgeous cock between them, a drop of pre-cum on the tip. She wanted to lick it off. But she'd have time for that later—she hoped. Instead, she ran her thumb over the bead before sliding her fingers downward. Reaching the base, she gripped him tightly.

"Oh fuck," he breathed out, his gaze riveted to her hand on his cock.

She lifted up on her knees to position herself over him. He tangled his hand in her hair, tugging slightly to tip her head back. She looked into his eyes, and her heart tumbled at the emotion reflected there—more than lust, reverence. He closed the little distance between them and kissed her softly, sweetly, and gently. Unhurried, as though her pussy wasn't poised over his straining and eager cock. As though he wanted a tender moment before she sank onto him.

Holy damn, two days and one tit-gasm and she was a goner.

Before he broke the kiss, she dropped herself down. His groan into her mouth heightened all her sensations. His guttural sounds woke something equally primal in her.

He gripped her hips, and every time she impaled herself on him, he pulled her in tighter while at the same time thrusting upward. It was erotic and desperate, and she reveled in it; he wasn't making her do all the work of bouncing on his dick. Although she would have. He could ask her to do anything, and she would have done it.

But he didn't ask anything of her that he wasn't ready and willing to reciprocate. Every touch, caress, and kiss. The best part of sex with this man? His eye contact. Like many others, he could have watched himself disappear inside her, or ogle her tits as they bounced with their movements. But he watched *her*, gauging and assessing, studying, his lips curling up with every sound and shiver. He stared into her so deeply she was sure he saw her soul.

When she started to come, curling in on herself from the intensity of it, he held her tightly to him and took over, thrusting powerfully into her. She'd screamed against his chest; his solid, strong, sweaty chest.

She was still floating in her state of bliss when she felt him maneuvering her. She felt the loss of him as he slid from her. Then she felt the spurt of hot liquid against her abdomen.

Gasping, she sat up. "Why'd you do that?"

His expression morphed from euphoric to chagrined. "I'm sorry about that. But there's no way I could have made it to the bathroom in time to finish. I'll clean you up."

Lucy shook her head. "No, I mean... I'm on birth control."

Beckman smiled. "I wasn't going to assume." He gently moved her off his lap as he kissed her forehead. "Don't move."

He walked away, fully naked. She ogled his firm ass, wondering if his job kept him fit. Not that it mattered; he was all gorgeous man striding from her. She was looking forward to his return trip.

Good lord, she knew nothing about him other than his cock was magical, his blue eyes even more so despite the ghosts lurking in their depths.

Falling against the futon cushion, she ran her fingers through his warm cum on her tummy. She told herself she did it to ensure the liquid didn't drip onto the cushions, but it was really because she liked the feel of it—of him—on her skin.

As she anticipated, his return to her was even more remarkable. He was unabashed in his nudity. Of course, she was lounging on her sofa like a sex queen. Her gaze dropped from his lazy smile to the beautiful appendage between his legs that had thoroughly delighted her.

"Becks?"

"Hmm?" An amused glimmer lit his eyes when he sat next to her. He started cleaning her up, his smile deepening when he lifted one of her hands. He flicked a glance at her before he started cleaning her fingers as well.

"Next time, you can assume."

His quizzical expression lasted only a second before he nodded once, not commenting.

Oh shit.

Sitting up straighter, she took the cloth from him, ducking her head to hide her embarrassment. "Although, sorry, I didn't mean to assume, either."

He tucked his knuckle under her chin, lifting until their gazes caught.

"You can assume."

Relief flooded her. Grinning, she wrinkled her nose. "So, we just did that."

His own grin and smoldering glance sent tingles through her. "Yes, we did."

They sat for a few seconds, making googly eyes at each other before he laughed outright. "I'm interested in doing that again tonight."

"I have no objections." She assured him. "But first, can I ask you something?"

"Of course you can."

She hesitated. Subtlety wasn't her strong suit. She'd heard more than once she had no filter. So she blurted out, "Why are you sad?"

He startled, his brows drawn together in question.

Most would retreat from the conversation when he didn't respond, but she was curious. And he hadn't denied it. "It's not obvious, but you fuck me like you're trying to dispel demons." She grinned. "Not that I mind."

And she didn't, not at all. She felt like his salvation, and she reveled in being the one someone else needed.

Pointing to her pussy, she added, "Demon dispelling is its specialty."

He chuckled, eyeing her display. The admiration and appreciation in his gaze made her giddy. It was a thrill to have her cunt so obviously coveted.

Closing her legs, she moved onto her knees. She combed her fingers through his graying blond hair, leaning against him. "I really am curious."

His eyes roamed over her face, assessing her sincerity. He must have been able to gauge it, because he nodded once.

"The last time I was in Kansas City, Gage died." Now he was the one to duck his head, taking the cloth back from her. "I'll put this away. What do you need?"

Her heart ached for him. At the same time, it tumbled over his consideration, his care for her.

Shifting into a cross-legged position, she noticed his attention flick to her pussy before he intentionally turned away.

She answered his question with her own. "Can you tell me about him?"

Beckman's head and eyes shot up. He didn't appear angry, though; he looked… What? Like he was afraid he hadn't heard her correctly.

"I'd like to listen, if you want to…" She faltered.

Hopefully hesitant, that was the expression on his face, in his eyes. Like he'd been waiting a long time for someone to ask.

He swallowed, and his blue eyes misted. But he nodded. "Yeah. I want to."

And he did. All night, he poured out stories of Gage and his memories of both the boy and the man. He was animated, rushing through tale after tale as though he'd never had the opportunity to share them and was afraid he wouldn't have this opportunity again. Or like he had to share them before the memories disappeared.

And Lucy soaked it up. Between midnight snacks and more sex—lovemaking, to be honest—the past surrounded them. She liked to think his stories fed both their souls, and she fell harder for a man she'd never met while seeing the possibilities with a man she'd just met.

That night, the world ceased to exist beyond the confines of her apartment, his arms, each other, and Gage.

He went to church with her the next day and spent that night with her, too, before he returned to DC.

She was prepared to be devastated, another dead-end, short-lived romance.

But before he left, he tipped her chin up. "I'll be back. For you. In the meantime…" He held up his phone.

He didn't ask if she wanted him to come back because he already knew the answer. And she loved that, too, his confidence. He knew what he wanted—her!—and he wasn't going to let whatever it was that they'd started end.

She fell even harder.

Chapter Seven

Lucy

A long-distance relationship wasn't something she imagined she would be able to maintain. It wasn't that she was needy—although, maybe she was—it was because she saw the world differently when she was happy. And Beckman in her life made her giddy. She wanted to share every experience with him, even things she had done before, because it was better with him around.

It was why her crush on Gage Rork endured despite never meeting him. But being on his property made her feel close to him. Her imagination conjured his presence. Everything she did was intentional, wondering if he approved—hoping that he did. It comforted her.

She moved easily with his ghost accompanying her. So easily that, before meeting Beckman, she used him as a stand-in when men attempted to pursue her and she wasn't interested.

"I have a boyfriend," she'd say, an image of Gage floating in her head. "He's a successful businessman, a veteran." All true.

Or that time when she'd been rummaging around in the second warehouse and found a box of old Christmas ornaments. One was of a gray clay cat, the tail broken off due to age or use. On the back, his name and a year were handwritten—she assumed the year represented when it had been purchased.

Laughing, she'd held it up as though he was watching from the rafters. "You were a cat person."

Little nuggets like this were enthralling. Gage was *here*.

Beckman, however, was not, but he still felt near. He made the distance disappear. For her, he made it easy. Part of that was how enamored she was with him. How natural she felt with him, how immediately at ease she'd been with him.

Clearly. The second day they'd met, they'd gotten naked.

The distance also provided them the opportunity to step back and discover the little things about one another. To start where most couples did. Interests, likes, philosophies on life. Was Beckman also a cat person?

Beckman did all the right things. Flowers. Gifts. Never leaving her on read. That was what was important to her: his attention, his time. She loved the flowers, but she loved his interest in her more. His grin as he'd mimicked her question about a favorite animal.

Both. They both had said both. It immediately set off her daydreams of them with their cat and dog. House, kids, pets.

DC to KC was one flight away. Even though he wasn't on it often, he made the times that he flew to her memorable. Like her birthday, when he took her for a couple's massage.

It'd been her first professional massage. She enjoyed the pampering, his thoughtfulness, and the knowledge that he was naked under his towel just feet away. They both ignored the face cradles, preferring to look at one another instead of at the floor.

When instructed to turn over, she was so busy ogling her sexy man—who appreciatively eyed her exposed chest as the blanket slipped—that she didn't pay attention to elbow placement. The next thing she knew, the face cradle flew forward before dropping to the floor.

She'd gasped. "Oh my god, I decapitated the table!"

Beckman's laughter filled the room. The sound made her more warm and tingly than the heated oil.

She'd repeatedly offered to be the one to fly to him, but he didn't want her inconvenienced.

"My family is in KC," he'd say. "Come to DC in the spring, when the cherry blossoms are blooming."

Despite what he'd said about his family—referring to Elliott, of course—when Beckman was in town, they didn't spend a lot of time with Elliott and Jonah. On the occasions they did, it was rarely at the Easy Street Events property. Dinners out (pizza, because... Jonah). An occasional sporting event. A walk through the Crown Center Christmas display over the holidays, although Becks could only join after the festive days.

That wasn't a big deal for Lucy. ESE was where she worked, so being away from it while Becks was in town didn't strike her as odd. Besides, Killion always got into a mood when Beckman was around, moping like someone had kicked his dog.

It also meant she had Beckman all to herself, which was the best thing ever, because she was falling for him. Hell, she'd fallen the moment he'd turned his eyes to her the night they'd met.

So the distance didn't matter. Her fantasies filled the gaps in time, and she dreamily moved from one visit to the next, on a cloud of happiness.

And then, one day, it was spring.

Her head full of expectation and anticipation, images of romantic romps and heart-stopping declarations, she finally went to him.

CHAPTER EIGHT

Beckman

Betrayal is tricky yet straightforward at the same time.

Lucy stared in quiet shock. There was pain in her pretty blues, devastation wrapping its arms around her tighter than he had that morning. The fact that his actions to which she was reacting had occurred years before he'd met her didn't matter.

Her response was expected, thus straightforward.

The tricky part came with how immersed she now was in that past. What he and Ellie had done contributed to what he'd call a Judas kiss, one they'd both delivered.

He turned away from her confused and hurt expression to consider the Potomac River rushing by the Georgetown Park bench they'd secured on a warm May afternoon. They'd walked here from Arlington, pausing on the Key Bridge so she could take pictures. He'd taken a photo of her there, too, her soft beauty outshining the view. White shorts and a yellow tank top were like high fashion on her. But she was even classier wearing heels and nothing else.

They were on their third day of bliss, him showing her around his home.

It was her first time visiting him in DC, and he wanted her to love it as much as he did, to enjoy herself. Although he saw the ugliest parts of the area as a detective, beauty remained.

Of course, they'd walked the mall and the monuments and museums. She'd marveled at everything that had changed since she'd last seen it as a child. At Arlington Cemetery, she walked slowly, her expression mirroring respect and sadness as she read some of the headstones.

He'd taken her to the Exorcist steps, to the Georgetown cupcake shop that was Ellie's favorite. There, Lucy defiled the delectable treat by removing the frosting. She'd unapologetically declared, "I don't like frosting." But she'd pronounced the cakey part "addicting."

Halfway through her trip was when he decided to drop the truth of his and Ellie's past. Halfway, because he'd wanted those perfect couple of days of reconnecting. Talking, fucking, holding one another.

Halfway, too, because he didn't want to give her news like this only to wave goodbye at the airport. If she needed two days to be mad at him, he wanted to give her that opportunity. He'd already put it off long enough. Ellie rode his ass in texts and phone calls, pointing out that the longer he waited, the worse the hurt. As annoyed and adamant as she was—and Jonah, in the background—that couple was honoring his wishes to be the bearer of this news.

"Does Jonah know?"

Her question surprised him even though it shouldn't have. He knew how big her heart was, but it reinforced her caring nature that her first concern would be for her friend. He turned back to her. She was still sitting on the concrete bench, only now, she had her feet up on the bench as she hugged her legs. Protecting herself.

Beckman nodded. "He knows."

Realization brightened her gaze. "Of course he does. The wedding.

That's why he hates you." She quickly shook her head and rolled her eyes at herself. "I mean, he doesn't like you. Jonah isn't capable of hating anyone."

Beckman smiled, but he didn't voice his opinion that she had it right the first time. As much as he respected Jonah, Ellie's new man did not like him. They both knew Ellie was madly in love, would never do anything to jeopardize her relationship—now—and that Beckman wasn't a threat. However, Jonah could not get past... Well, whatever it was he wasn't letting go.

"So..." Her gaze traveled to the river behind him.

He watched her do the calculations in her head: A few months shy of a year, they'd been trying this long-distance thing, and he was only now telling her. He tried to justify it by pointing out that, combined, they'd only seen each other about three months' worth, but he was full of shit. It'd been nine months.

Ellie was right. The longer he put it off, the greater the pain. He'd wanted to spare her this, to not see the bewilderment on her face. He didn't want her to look at Ellie differently, either, or to blame her for any of it—or him, if he was going to be honest.

What Luce was grappling with was the information that he and Ellie had a more intimate past than simply family friends. He didn't want to go too deeply into the details of that past if he didn't have to. Again, it was to spare all of them.

Her next question also surprised him. "Did Gage know?"

Fucking hell.

Beckman reached for his cigarettes, shaking one out. He was aware of her scrutiny as he took time to light it. "Toward the end, yeah, he did."

She looked even more perplexed. "Toward the end of what? The... arrangement?"

"Before he died."

Her eyes widened, stricken. More stricken, he amended. She was caught off guard every time he opened his mouth. Beckman continued to watch her. Her wheels were turning again, putting puzzle pieces together.

"I read the letter," she said, dropping her own bombshell. "The part about wanting to punish her, choosing her, didn't make sense until..."

Beckman raised a brow expectantly.

"Until now." Her gaze chased to the river.

He wondered how and when she'd seen Gage's suicide letter. Now wasn't the time to take her to task over it. He was the one in the hot seat, and it would only be a means to distract from his own discomfort and, yes, shame. He wasn't proud of what he'd done. It didn't matter that both he and Ellie had been consenting adults. Ellie was still beating herself up over her ambush of him, though, insistent that he hadn't consented.

True. She'd shocked and horrified him, but he fell in line quickly. Too quickly, considering he shouldn't have touched her to begin with.

Beckman remained quiet, drawing on his smoke, waiting for the next question or the judgment—or both. He'd once told Ellie to have faith in Lucy and her capacity to understand and forgive. At the time, he'd only met the woman, was smitten with her, but her strength of character led him to that initial impression. He'd also said it for Ellie's sake in an attempt to relieve her of the burdens of her secrets and the past she insisted on self-flagellating herself for.

The relationship, Lucy didn't seem to give much weight to. Gage's discovery, the letter, his death... That was what Lucy was grappling with. It was the same thing he and Ellie had faced once. Still faced. It would never go away for them.

"How did he find out?"

Lucy had a fascination with Gage. Beckman was aware of it; everyone was, to some extent, whether they thought she was curious, trying to honor his memory by keeping the event center alive and booked, or sad about a life that ended early.

Beckman knew it was a deeper interest. She was more than merely interested. With him, she pressed for stories, pored over photos, and watched home videos of the man singing. It wasn't something that bothered him. Instead, he found liberation in sharing memories that were both dear to him and heartbreaking at the same time. He was easier with Lucy when reminiscing than with Ellie. Els read too much into every word, every inflection, looking for the blame. It was because she still blamed herself.

But Lucy's appreciation and inclusion of Gage in her everyday life extended to and influenced her care of the event center and things that were his. For instance, the laptop she used had been his work computer—handed over to her when she'd been hired by Ellie. It was still encased in Gage's leather satchel. Though large, unwieldy, and manly compared to her daintiness and preference for pink, she refused to switch it out. She rubbed the leather whenever it was slung over her shoulder. Beckman wasn't sure she was aware that she did it.

Blowing out a stream of smoke, he remembered the last time he'd seen the other man alive. The anger, the yelling, the gun pointed first at Beckman, then at a terrified Ellie. The accusations that broke her, the actions that culminated in death.

"In the worst possible way."

It was the truth, and there would be no glossing over it.

Lucy raised a hand, rubbing her chest. To soothe herself? Imagining the ache Gage must have felt?

"Ask me anything." He encouraged her, even as he thought to himself, *Please don't.*

"So, he caught you two having sex."

Beckman nodded once, bringing the cigarette to his lips for another draw. It'd been more than that, but he didn't want to reveal all of Ellie's secrets, her personal demons, the ones he'd fed. Lucy would need to get those details from the woman herself.

He almost laughed at the mental image of Lucy challenging Ellie, but he checked himself. Lucy was intimidated by Ellie for some reason. She wasn't going to be confronting anyone, and it shouldn't be a confrontation. This happened long before he'd met Lucy, before Ellie had met Jonah.

"How long did it last, your unconventional relationship?"

Best way to put it, actually.

"Ten years."

Her gasp nearly killed him. She'd thought a couple of times, not a prolonged period.

"Let me be clear, it was sporadic. There weren't booty calls every other week. Toward the end, it was only occasionally."

And that was because Ellie had returned to Kansas City, eventually to live with Gage as her brother's mental health deteriorated.

"Do you think he would have... if...?"

Could Gage have been saved? That was the question she was asking. "Gage struggled constantly. Ellie refused and still refuses to see it; she worshipped her brother. She thought her love could save him, that her need for him to be okay would make him okay." He ashed the cigarette, which gave him a momentary excuse to look away.

Despite the number of times he and Lucy talked about Gage, his suicide hadn't been up for discussion. "Gage came back with a lot of guilt, a lot of problems. He had no reason to feel guilty for doing his job, but he'd always been a teddy bear. He loved everyone. He was creative; you know that. You've heard him sing, and he designed both the event center and his house. And he was gregarious, which is why the event center was a success so quickly.

"But he was a time bomb. We tried everything to keep him grounded. Ellie moved in to help him out, but"—he sighed—"the timing was unfortunate. For Ellie. For all of us, but specifically for Ellie."

"Jonah really knows all of this?"

"He knows everything. This isn't something to keep from your partner." He gave her a pointed look. "You can call him if you like."

"I will in a minute."

Beckman didn't know if that was a good sign or a bad one. But she was still here, engaging with him, and he was thankful for that. She chewed her bottom lip, speculative as she watched the water flow behind him. He'd stand here all day in the sun until she was satisfied. He only hoped she would also walk back across the Key Bridge with him.

"Is this why you didn't come for the holidays?"

Again, the woman surprised him by asking that as a follow-up question. "Partly. I did have to work. Holidays are a special time in my line of business."

After another space of time, she asked quietly, "What, or who, do you see when you look at her now?"

This was more along the lines of what he'd expected. The query didn't come from a lack of self-confidence or fear that Lucy wasn't enough. She knew she was; at least, he told her constantly how much he appreciated her presence in his life. It was curiosity, and it was a valid question.

After another long drag and expel, he answered, hoping she'd understand. "I see Ellie. The little girl, the teenager, the sister, the daughter, someone who is special to me. I see the temptress she was, on a destructive path. I see the badass in her and the woman she's become." He shrugged. "I see Ellie."

Lucy narrowed her eyes. It hadn't been the answer she wanted to hear.

"She isn't one thing, like you aren't one thing. What we did doesn't define her or me. Now, I see a woman who is wildly in love, who is finally happy, and I'm fucking grateful for that and proud of her."

Her disappointed expression persisted, so he pressed. "What are you asking me?"

"Do you imagine her naked? I mean, you've seen her naked. When you look at her—?"

"No." It was true. "Of course I know what she looks like naked, but it's not a visual I carry around with me. Do you picture me naked all the time?"

A spark of amusement glinted in her eyes, which thrilled him.

"Or your ex-boyfriends? It's not a conscious thought; it's something I know about her and don't dwell on."

"Is that why you two don't hug? It's noticeable."

Damn, she was taking him to task. But he wanted her to do so, to continue to demonstrate how invested she was. "We're attempting a reset to the time before. It's also respect for her and Jonah's relationship."

That was sort of a bullshit answer. They'd hugged throughout her life. But now, it was weighted. Again, there was personal stuff meant to remain between himself and Ellie, although he doubted she kept anything from Jonah. Personal for him, then. Maybe one day he and Ellie would be comfortably back in the relationship they'd had before she'd tied herself to his bed, looking for something. Pleasure, safety... She'd trusted him. Epitome of the fucking double-edged sword.

Lucy nodded, her wry expression reinforcing Jonah's less-than-favorable view of him. "I thought he was being super judgy about the age difference between you and me. He and Killion both."

Killion Murphy, Ellie's on-site, ex-con maintenance man, was another of Lucy's protectors who would prefer to see him out of the picture. Of course, to be fair, he was certain Jonah wouldn't have an issue with him and Lucy if there hadn't been the past with Ellie. Jonah was one of the most accepting persons he'd met, except when it came to himself.

"Jonah and Killion have their reasons for being against us."

She scoffed. "Killion doesn't. He has no interest in Elliott."

Beckman rubbed his forehead. Nah, Killion thought of Ellie as a friend, almost as a sister. He was former military, after all, so she'd low-key adopted him into her life as a surrogate for Gage. Hell, maybe even for her father. Killion's issues were along the lines of self-preservation: He was an ex-con while Beckman was a detective. It was a natural wariness, he supposed, although he didn't have a problem with Killion.

No, Killion wasn't happy because of Killion's affection for Lucy, which was superbly hidden. But he was jealous as all fuck of him and Luce. Probably no one suspected, but Beckman had seen the daggers shot in his direction when he'd visited and placed an arm around Lucy. Or kissed her.

"I have no interest in Ellie beyond taking care of my best friend's kid. We're all each other has left of her family—my family. That means more to us than..."

Neither had had that foresight then, but the other Rorks had all been living at that time. Now, he wouldn't give up his only link to them for anyone, and neither would Ellie. He suspected that was why Jonah tolerated him, to preserve Ellie's memories of her family.

"Tell me what you're thinking? Where are you at with this?"

With us?

Lucy took in a breath, held it, then let it out slowly. "It might take me a minute to wrap my head around this."

His heart fell, but it was understandable.

"But"—she gave him a small grin—"I'll get there, I will. I mean, it's the past. She and Jonah are rock solid."

"Pixie." His voice was low, intimate, using his pet name for her. "Even if she and Jonah weren't solid, Ellie and I are never going back to that place."

Despite the timeline, he hadn't particularly liked the way he and Ellie had fucked. She'd needed it, and he wanted her safe. But if he never saw another rope in the bedroom again, it would be too soon.

Lucy was a refreshing and glorious addition to his life. She brightened his otherwise dull existence; he looked forward to being in her presence. He really appreciated her more vanilla nature in bed—not that it wasn't spicy or imaginative. It was a true connection with her.

She nodded, accepting his words at face value—another one of his favorite things about her. She wasn't suspicious or looking for an angle. Biting her lip again, her gorgeous eyes filled with apprehension and anxiety, as though the past several moments paled in comparison to what she was currently thinking.

"Let it out, pix."

Instead of looking at him, she chose to toy with her shoestring. "I want to assume that since you're telling me this, we're exclusive now?"

Fuck.

Chapter Nine

Lucy

Lucy paced the wooden planks of Georgetown Harbor, waiting for Jonah to answer. Beckman was sitting on a barstool at a nearby riverside bar. Whenever she glanced over, his attention was on her, whether he was drinking his beer or taking a drag from his cigarette. It wasn't overbearing; it was watchful, and she appreciated it. He was also probably freaking out—she hoped so, at least—that after this conversation with her best friend, she would get a plane back to Kansas City and forget about him.

She might do it anyway.

Jonah answered. "Hey, Luce."

Turning toward the Potomac, she snapped out, "I retract permission for use of my name for any of your children. No kids, no dogs, no cats, no freaking turtles!"

He sighed, immediately guessing, because Jonah was weird like that. "You're years ahead of yourself still for that possibility. But this wasn't my truth to share."

"I am so sick of that answer from you!" She'd held it together remarkably well while talking to Beckman, but now, with the one person who knew her better than anyone, she allowed herself to feel all the feelings. "You were so busy protecting your girlfriend that you forgot about your friend!"

"That's not true."

"Where have you been the past several months while I was falling in love with a man who won't commit to me because of what he and your girlfriend did? Where were you, Jonah?"

His voice took on his authoritative tone with her. "First, stop referring to Elliott as 'your girlfriend.' She's *our* friend. Second"—he released another breath—"I didn't know about his commitment issues."

"Yeah? Well, now you do."

"That's his decision, not Elliott's. You know he's been divorced a few times."

"Was that judgment?" she sneered.

"Was that defense on his behalf?"

Lucy checked herself, modulating her tone. Damn, Jonah knew where to punch. But he'd known her all their lives, so yeah, he knew. "On my behalf, too. I know you hate the idea of him and me. What I didn't know was why."

He was quiet for a moment. She could imagine him bending his head, a hand on his hip as he considered his next words. "I have my prejudices when it comes to Beckman. But if you're happy, Lucy, I'd never try to take that away from you."

A tear slipped down her cheek. She let it fall. "I don't know if I'm happy right now."

"Then I'll tear him apart myself. He can love you, but he does not get to hurt you."

"Hasn't everyone done that?" More tears fell. She swiped at one cheek, irritated. "And he doesn't love me. He's never said it, and he probably never will."

"I am not a fan, you know that, so you know how hard it is for me to say that I know he cares about you, for you. We all do, and so does he." He cleared his throat. "Elliott and I both wanted this out sooner, for everyone's sake, especially yours. He did finally tell you. He could have pussied out and cut things off, but he's facing the music."

A little late. She scuffed the planks with her shoe, feeling surly.

"Why do you think he won't commit? What did he say?"

"I asked him if his telling me meant he wanted to be exclusive." She rubbed her chest, attempting to soothe what couldn't be soothed right now. "In short, he said no."

"He's seeing other people?" Jonah sounded pissed off, like her friend was about to crawl through the phone to get to Beckman.

"No. He said no, that he didn't need anyone else, but he wanted us both to have our options open, just in case."

"Okay, I'm a guy, and that's a bullshit line."

His statement put her on the defensive. "Like you said, he has been through a few divorces. And with the Elliott thing..." She shrugged to the river, because Jonah couldn't see her. "He's put off right now on formal relationships. He didn't say it like that, but what else could it be?"

"How did he say it?"

"He didn't want to lose me, he's not interested in anyone else, but the label wasn't something he was comfortable with right now." Her bottom lip quivered. "Label. I'm only a label. Or not—I'm not even that!"

"What do you want to do, Lucy? I can be at the airport to pick you up. Decide if this is a today fight, or a forever fight."

Another Jonah response, but it gave her pause. Did she want to be upset for a little bit, or walk away completely? Uncaring about the spectators, she plopped down on the boards. "I want to go back to an hour ago."

"Realistically. Do you want to come home?"

Did she? She looked over her shoulder to where Beckman was sitting—correction, to where he was now powering toward her with an expression of concern.

Her heart squeezed. "No. I want to change his mind."

"I'm here."

"I wish you'd been there nine months ago." It was a pissy thing to end the conversation with, but she hung up and watched Beckman approach.

God, she was in love with him, and it tore her apart. She'd been his whole world their first night together, and he, hers. He hadn't noticed that she had Ikea furniture, including her bed—or he didn't care—fucking her first on the futon where they'd combusted. At least, that's how she'd felt. Touching, kissing, and getting naked had been a race, and neither could get there fast enough.

That feeling with him never went away. From their first time to this morning, whether they took their time or it was a quickie as he bent her over the breakfast table, it always felt desperate and new and electric. Her body was nourished by his, and she hadn't realized how hungry she'd been, or even that she'd never tasted real food before. His responses, reactions, made her assume he'd felt the same.

Their first night, they'd fucked, then made love, and also lain in each other's arms and talked. Gage hadn't been the only topic of conversation. They'd talked about Jonah, as strange as it would seem. Becks had wanted to talk to him. He informed her that he liked Jonah for Ellie—only Beckman called her Ellie, but she knew it would be weird for him to call her by his own name—and he wanted to do what he could to help the man win her.

And she'd loved that, his concern for Elliott and his respect for Jonah.

Now, he crouched in front of her. "Pix."

She loved the nickname he'd given her. He'd tried Tinkerbell, but she'd glared once and thankfully had never heard it again associated with her. Pixie, she liked. She liked it even better when he shortened it.

Shaking her head, she wiped at the last of her tears. "I feel like everyone was in on the joke except for me, and aren't I stupid not to have figured it out?"

"No." He quickly assured her. Reaching out, he grasped her chin, and she gave him her full attention. "Your innocence—"

"Ugh!" She ripped her chin from his grasp. "That's another way of calling me gullible."

"It's not. I love your perspective on the world—this fucked-up world—and the way you see beauty. That makes you a diamond, strong, faceted, stunning, and precious. A treasure. Not gullible."

"But not your treasure, your diamond," she mumbled.

His sigh was heavy with regret. "You are. I want to give you what you need, but right now, I can't."

"What about tomorrow? Next week? Do you have a timeline?" She wanted to cry again. "Never mind."

She didn't want to hear him answer 'never.' If she left it open, there was a possibility that she would be worth something to him some day. Knowing she wasn't good enough hurt.

"I don't want to lose you."

She made a face. She didn't want to lose him, either, but what did he think would happen? He'd basically told her she wasn't special while also informing her she *was* special. Her heart was rending in two.

He reached out and ran a knuckle down her cheek. "You don't owe me anything. You can walk right now."

"Do you want me to walk away?" Her throat almost closed up as she asked, terrified of his answer.

"No, but I can't expect you to wait for me."

"Maybe that's what you've been needing all along: someone to wait for you." She said it impulsively, but she meant it.

If nothing else, she was determined to be the someone who didn't fail him. Perhaps it was her romantic side, or her masochistic side, but she wanted to be the winner in the end.

His expression at her words was one of resignation more than admiration, maybe even sorrow. But he underestimated her if he thought she wasn't strong enough to stick by him.

Chapter Ten

Beckman

Instead of turning and running for the hills, his pixie dug in her heels. Goddamn, he didn't deserve her. And he hated hurting her. He'd landed blow after blow, and she'd stood in the face of it all, absorbing the emotional hits.

His fear that she wouldn't accompany him back across the Key Bridge was for naught, because she was naked in his bed, one gorgeous leg out of the covers. It was a habit of hers to keep one leg out. He didn't need to look to know. She said it regulated her body temperature as she slept. He'd been in bed with her enough to know that being fully covered led to a middle-of-the-night kicking and thrashing fit until her leg was uncovered.

It thrilled him to have this intimate knowledge of her. Maybe others knew it, too, but he was grateful to be included in the Lucy club. That and her giggle when he licked her clit, like he was tickling her, before she arched her back and moaned, digging her fingers into his hair. He found the giggle more satisfying than the moan; it got him harder.

Leaning against the railing of his tiny balcony, he studied her through the sliding glass door, pulling on his cigarette. No, he wasn't worthy of her. But she was stubborn, and he fucking loved that about her. Stubborn, determined, and hopeful.

His clenched stomach conveyed that her hope in him was misplaced. He had a track record: several divorces and even more failed relationships. After all, what longevity could one expect when he couldn't be honest about his extracurricular activities with his friend's kid? He'd dated, of course, but he was the prick who knew nothing was going to come of it other than a few weeks of sex, if he was lucky.

After Gage's death, he hadn't bothered. Relationships hadn't been a priority. He'd been reeling as much as Ellie. He was ashamed to be relieved that Gage's death put a stop to his and Ellie's fucking around; it shouldn't have taken something that extreme. He should have been man enough to end it sooner. But he hadn't been. Not even after Gage's death, the funeral. She'd been spiraling, and because of the dysfunction they were in, it happened again. It'd been a short, violent act meant to jar.

He left her with a different outlet. He taught her how to rage against the heavy bag. She was a fucking natural.

There was a shit ton of unresolved issues between them still. It was evident in the way they never found themselves alone for too long. Lucy had called it out, their lack of touch.

Nothing was spoken, but there was an elephant in the room they were desperate to escape. Until that elephant was gone, Lucy and he didn't have a shot. He didn't want the answer of his hesitancy to move forward to be Ellie. But it was one of his reasons. The other reasons would lead him into a deeper self-reflection he wasn't prepared for.

It wasn't fair to Lucy, not that she saw it that way. She wanted him, wanted to belong to him, and she felt rejected.

As if sensing that he was thinking about her and staring at her, she stirred. He watched her reach for him, patting the blankets a few times before she lifted her head to presumably gauge where he had gone. After a minute, she shifted and peered through the glass doors at him. She smiled sleepily as she untangled her other leg.

Beckman watched with appreciation as she vacated the bed and tippy-toed her way to the door, her tiny breasts bouncing with her choppy movements. He flicked his cigarette into the alley below while she was sliding the door open. Gloriously naked, she hurried across the short expanse. He held her close when she wrapped her arms around his waist.

"You're indecent." Not that he minded, not at all.

"You're half indecent." She snuggled closer, rubbing her nipples against his chest, emitting a guttural sound of pleasure before she settled in.

Beckman grinned, catching sight of their reflection in the glass. His smile looked as goofy as he felt. He'd never before encountered a woman whose nipples were so sensitive. He was awed by the phenomenon and enjoyed giving her tit-gasms almost as much as he enjoyed bringing to orgasm with his cock buried inside her.

"My dick is covered. For now." He was wearing low-slung light cotton pajama bottoms that he could drop with a tug on the drawstring.

She smiled mischievously. The top of her head reached his chin, and he wasn't a tall man, average. That's how short she was. But they fit together perfectly. This was a unique experience as well. His exes had been his height or taller, making cuddling like this awkward, to be honest.

"Will you fuck me on the balcony?"

Beckman chuckled, scanning the other balconies and windows to ensure they weren't providing midnight entertainment. "No, I will not."

She pouted.

"But I will pick you up, take you inside, and fuck you." He wiggled his eyebrows in invitation.

Smiling, she shook her head, and tucked herself back under his chin. He ran his hands over her slender back, dipping down to grasp her butt cheeks. Her hips rocked forward against him, and she squeezed him tighter, but the gesture wasn't filled with anything more than comfortable intimacy.

If he could freeze this moment with her sleepily content in his arms, he would. He could stand here all night with her, despite the late-night spring chill. No past, no tomorrow, only now. Closing his eyes, breathing in the scent of her lavender shampoo, he became his own worst enemy and burst the bubble. It was going to end anyway. He might as well have some control over when it did.

"You okay, pixie?"

The air shifted, surrounding them with tension.

"I want to be."

"I want you to be, too."

"There's something you can do about that."

He caressed her lower back. After a couple of weighted minutes during which he convinced himself he could hear the ticking of a second hand, he offered, "I'll work on it. I promise you that. What I can't do is ask you to wait for me to get there."

He felt and heard her sigh, the soft breath ghosting over his skin.

"This isn't a rejection, Lucy."

She rubbed her cheek against him. "I know that, but it doesn't make it hurt any less, like you don't want me."

"I do. What I don't want is me for you. Not right now. I wasn't prepared for you, a brilliant, kind, and gorgeous woman who knocked me on my heels." He was sincere. It was true. "You deserve more than what I can give at the moment."

Her silence was rife with contemplation. Then she surprised him, as she always did. "You can make it better by letting me rip your hair out. It's only fair."

His grin returned. "I agree. And I plan to make you rip out every strand."

"Promises, promises."

He walked her backward through the door she'd left open. She tilted her face up, an expectant smile on her pretty pink lips. Shuffling toward the bed, he caught her bottom lip with his teeth, tugging gently. Instead of kissing her, however, he dropped to his knees.

"Wha—?" She laughed, looking down at him. "What are you doing?"

He placed an open-mouth kiss on her abdomen, then licked her. She shivered. "Leg on the bed," he ordered, even as he grasped her behind her knee and started lifting her leg. "And hold on."

As instructed, she dug her fingers into his hair. With her leg lifted and foot braced, she was open to him, the evidence of her arousal filling him with deep satisfaction. He'd barely touched her, and she was wet, her clit erect and demanding his ministrations. And he wanted to lick it, suck it, and revel in her giggles and gasps.

But he checked himself. He owed her more than a quick orgasm. This was penance and apology wrapped in worship. Hair grew back, after all. He began with a small massage of her labia, tiny circles at first, working his way up and around her eager clit, not giving the reaching bud the attention it was demanding.

He licked up her wetness, slowly tongue fucking her. His scalp bore testimony to how much she enjoyed that, along with her moan. Attempting to direct him where she wanted him, she squirmed in his grasp, rotating her hips and lifting on her tippy toes. He chuckled, dodging her.

"Suck my clit, Becks! Please!" she begged, her breath catching.

He glanced up at her body, her nipples hard and puckered, begging to be sucked and tugged until she thrashed and screeched in pleasure. Her head was thrown back, showcasing her sleek neck. The mewls and whimpers she made that accompanied her rocking hips were music to his ears. Her desperation for his mouth on her clit boosted his ego.

Not until her legs trembled, both the one supporting her and the one braced on the bed, did he give her what she wanted. He flicked his tongue over her clit, and she giggled. He grinned. On his second pass, though, she moaned. He sucked and flicked while continuing his massage of her labia, occasionally slipping his thumbs inside her.

"Becks, Becks." She bent forward, her long hair dancing along his back, and wrapped her arms around his head like she'd imprison his face in her cunt for eternity. Fucking fine with him. But she wasn't going to be able to stay on her foot once she started coming, so he lurched forward, grasping her under her thighs, and turned.

Her body was shaking with the first wave of her orgasm when her back hit the mattress. She bucked and tossed, alternately gripping the sheets and his hair while he sucked her through her orgasm.

"Stop, stop," she panted, wriggling against him.

Her clit would be overly sensitive. But the words weren't said in earnest and were the typical prelude to her double orgasm, which had her arching her back, shaking, her mouth open in a silent scream, suspended in time before she screamed out and collapsed, exhausted.

He climbed onto the mattress with her, admiring her sweaty and flushed skin, her parted lips as she sucked in air. When she opened her beautiful blue eyes, she looked drunk. Love drunk, she'd once called it.

"You still have hair," she said drowsily.

"We have all night."

Chapter Eleven

Lucy

She was opening herself up to another heartbreak. Well, he'd already broken her heart. But in a way only Beckman could do, he was able to hold her together despite it. She tried to channel Jonah, questioning whether or not she was holding on to Becks because she was terrified of being alone, afraid that no one else was going to want her. After all, she was thirty-six and so far, no living person interested her enough beyond a few orgasms. Until Becks. Was she taking the crumbs because she was sure she'd never be offered the whole pie?

Sitting back with as much dramatics as the economy window seat of the airplane would allow, she fiddled with her cell phone until she found her favorite playlist: Gage Rork singing country music. Lucy wasn't crazy about the genre, but she was addicted to Gage singing it. This was her private playlist from home-recorded songs she'd found stored away on her laptop. Well, it'd been Gage's laptop first, which is how she found them. Backing up the songs was necessary, she'd justified, because the laptop was old, and it would have been a shame to lose Gage's music if—when—it crashed.

Watching white fluffy clouds whiz by as she hurtled toward Kansas City, she brooded over Beckman's revelations. His past with Elliott, she shoved aside. She wasn't sure how to approach that, or the woman herself. Jonah would be no assistance, defending his woman, so Lucy was feeling a little adrift: best friend's loyalties divided, and her... Well, she couldn't call him her boyfriend now, telling her he didn't want to commit. He'd denied it being about Elliott, but she wasn't stupid.

It was a good thing she had hours to think about it, isolated on this plane and trapped with her erratic thoughts... Said no one ever.

Becks had left her at security with a kiss that begged her to stay. A few people catcalled and whistled. It'd been a knee-knocking, please-don't-make-me-say-goodbye kiss. The kind of kiss that continued to have her reeling as she boarded the flight, head so in the clouds that she rammed into the back of a man with her luggage. He'd swiveled, pissed, until he saw her. His expression and mood instantly changed, and he offered to help her.

Pretty blonds were catered to in that way, despite her lack of cleavage. A bat of her lashes with a vapid, helpless grin, and men fell over themselves to assist her. Of course she'd needed the help, being short, and she'd need it again when they deplaned.

Panty-melting kisses be damned, maybe that handsome man would help her out in another way. His smile had been warm and polite, even if a touch condescending. She didn't care if he'd thought her a helpless damsel in distress—she quite literally had been. With a wink, she'd be able to hook him. Yeah, yeah, she was being egotistical, but she could do it. Maybe she should try it—test the strength of Becks's conviction that she be free to do as she wished and fuck at will. That was her wounded interpretation, anyway. She could text him, or FaceTime him, and let him know she'd taken his advice to heart with a rando who'd helped her with her carry-on.

Ducking her head, she peeked through the veil of her long hair and studied him. He was concentrating on his cell phone, probably watching a movie he'd downloaded. Not for one second did she think he was reading.

Gage continued to serenade her as she studied the stranger. Not only had Gage been a massively gorgeous bear of a man, he'd been talented. He sang and played guitar. On top of that, he was a successful businessman. If she'd been lucky enough to meet him, it was a foregone conclusion that he'd have fallen as madly for her as she had for him.

Her crush transcended time and death. He might not be a physical presence, but he was always on her mind. She felt surrounded by him when she was on the Easy Street Events property, like his ghost stalked her. And she wanted him to accompany her. Gone he may be, but her imagination brought him to life, and he was as real to her as the other men in her life.

Thoughts of those men and their respective reactions to her musings about a strange man floated across her mind's eye. They chided her: Jonah, Killion, and even Gage, although she'd never met him. Based on his videos, she had a pretty good idea that he would be side-eyeing her with loving admonishment. Jonah would be more direct with his disappointment, and she hated it when he gave her that look. Killion would shake his head at her, partially amused, but ready to run interference.

No, she wouldn't fuck a stranger because she was a little hurt. Turning her attention back to the skies, despite Gage crooning to her, her anxiety kicked up with every mile that passed. The farther this contraption took her from Beckman, the harder the tug on her heart. Was she doing the right thing by leaving? It'd only been planned for her to stay a week, but her leaving felt permanent, like their bond could break at any moment.

It was a strange sensation to experience, especially because when Beckman would visit Kansas City, then leave, she didn't feel this way. Was it only because of what she'd learned?

Trying not to cry, she concentrated on Gage's voice, taking comfort from him. If the man was alive, things would have been so much easier for her—she knew it was a shitty thing to think—but she and Gage would have been the perfect fit.

Why did she have to walk into Easy Street Events two years too late?

Chapter Twelve

Killion

"F*uuuck*."

The word came out strangled, as choked as his cock in his fist, cum spurting over his hand and stomach. Her giggle pushed him over the edge. It cascaded over him through the office wall like a physical caress.

It didn't matter that she was speaking to Beckman—a man too old for her, who didn't deserve her. Of course, neither did he, lying on his bed, jerking on his dick to the sounds of her voice. But at least he was *here* instead of hours away.

Pushing off his twin bed, he walked a few steps to the corner shower and turned it on. The noise of the water drowned out her voice. It was a relief as well as a torment, being cut off from her.

The past week had dragged while she was in DC. He couldn't stop imagining that man fucking her, making her laugh. He also—meanly—imagined Beckman couldn't keep up with her, taking frequent naps and experiencing performance problems. Killion had no evidence that the man's age slowed him down, but it made him feel better.

He'd tortured himself all week. He knew how dreamy her expression became when she talked about her boyfriends. And he wanted the looks she gave to the undeserving like Greg (he was short-lived), Gage (a dead man, but was still pulling her better than himself), and Beckman.

He thought he'd gotten one of those looks from her once. But other than their flirty banter—all innocence on her part—it'd never happened again. He convinced himself he'd imagined it, especially since she was already with Beckman at the time it occurred.

Lately, her expressions around him had been amused. Merry. Brighter, like her project was going well, the pound puppy was adjusting; a favorite plant was thriving. The B side of the album was surprisingly good.

He preferred pity over motherly pride, though. He had a mother. He didn't want or need that from Lucy.

Killion left his room and walked through the darkened warehouse. He went to the side door that led to the office and rapped his knuckles twice before entering. It was all the warning he gave before entering. It was more than he'd normally provide, considering this was their working space, but he hoped it helped wrap up her phone call.

"Morning, sunflower."

Sparkling blue eyes narrowed at him from her seat at the desk. She was so pretty this morning. She was pretty every morning, but especially this morning, in a thin yellow sweater that clung alluringly to her slight curves. He was a man who appreciated all types of women, all sizes, but he'd become fixated on this one.

Beckman called her his pixie; Killion didn't like it. One, it was too cliché, and Lucy wasn't a cliché. Second, Killion had read once that pixies were mean. Lucy didn't have a mean bone in her body. So, it didn't fit. She was petite, that was it. Beckman had no imagination.

To Killion, she was a beam of light, her energy infectious. With her blond hair and penchant for wearing yellow, well, sunflower fit.

"You know I hate sunflowers."

She'd told him that a million times, but she hadn't told him to stop calling her that. He thought she secretly liked it.

Grinning mischievously, he leaned against a filing cabinet, removing his packet of cigarettes. "Nice greeting."

Lucy eyed the pack in his hands, huffed, and turned away. "You know, the church has a program for that."

Killion frowned. Her church had a program for everything. He'd once joked with Elliott that the church was the Amazon of programs. One of those programs had landed him this gig, so he wasn't going to push back too hard on the nonsmoking program.

Instead, he asked, "Did you get your boyfriend to enroll?"

She snorted. "No. And he's in DC. He's a detective. You know this. His job is stressful."

Her statement stung, but he teased her. "Dealing with you is stressful."

She jerked around, eyes wide. "Killion!"

He was taken aback. She appeared offended. Normally, what he'd said would be an excuse for her to snark back—they were playful like that. They liked to tease one another. He tried to think of it as the longest foreplay on earth, but she probably thought of him as (hold in the vomit) a brother.

He held up a hand of atonement and surrender. "You know I'm messing with you."

She blinked, then visibly deflated, slumping back in the chair. "I'm sorry. Weird week. Weirder morning."

Weird was right, because hadn't she been giggling about twenty minutes ago? Enough to get him off. He couldn't make out the words—the walls weren't that thin—but she'd definitely been laughing. Also weird because the week to which she was referring had to be the one with Beckman. The thought of trouble in paradise gave him a charge, but he was quick to reprimand himself. He didn't want Lucy hurt.

Then again...

"How is Beckman?" he asked, and he hated asking. He hated when her face lit up and she chirped happily in response.

She lifted a shoulder and pushed her lips to the side. "Good. I haven't talked to him since I got home last night, and he's back at work, so I assume he's okay."

Killion hoped his expression remained neutral. The giggles had sounded intimate, the type you share with your partner. She and Jonah would have a laugh or two—even a giggle—but not like that. Nor could he imagine that kind of interaction with Elliott, the two of them discussing anything intimate. They were friends, sure, but Lucy remained cautious when approaching anything serious when it came to Elliott.

He pressed. "You're sure everything's okay?" Because he couldn't ask "Then who were you having a giggle with this morning that was so sexy it got me off?"

"Why wouldn't it be?"

Killion shrugged. "You seem snippy." He amended his statement with a smile, trying to elicit the same from her. "Snippier than usual."

"I'm rarely snippy with you." She chided him, her good nature back in place. "And if I am, you have wholly deserved it."

"Never. I'm an angel." He grinned.

"You're naughty," she said matter-of-factly as she spun back around.

Good thing, because his jeans grew tighter. She hadn't meant it as dirty talk, but his dick chose to hear it that way. Goddammit, he was going to have to jerk off again. It was becoming an occupational hazard. He wondered if he could turn in a workers' comp claim for carpal tunnel for as many times as he had to beat off because of her.

"I'm going to stick with angel." He forced out a lighter tone than he was feeling, straightening from the filing cabinet.

"You're delusional."

He smiled as he left the office through the front entrance. It was too early to hit Elliott's boxing bag hanging beneath her and Jonah's house because his boss was still asleep. Elliott was a late sleeper. Jonah had probably already hiked ten trails and was at his shop in Parkville.

So he walked the property, his morning and evening ritual, careful now to keep away from the back corner where Jonah had designed... Well, it was what it was: a sex adventure land of ropes for himself and Elliott. Killion had accidentally found it—thankfully, *not* while it was being used—and had given Jonah a baleful stare over the lack of a heads-up.

Jonah had smiled, unapologetic.

Killion didn't begrudge him. The man had worked his ass off getting Elliott to come around, and Killion was happy they finally got together. But what if he'd been strolling one night and had seen something that scarred him for life? Elliott was a knockout—who could deliver a knockout—but she was his pastor's woman. He did not need a visual of his pastor stringing her up. Even now, he gagged a little bit. Any other couple, and he'd pop the popcorn and take a front-row seat. Those two? He knew them. They were toeing the line of family, so no, thank you.

Which brought his thoughts back to Detective Beckman. He was the only person Elliott had left of her family but also the man she'd had an affair with. Sexist as it was, Killion put the blame on Beckman for what transpired between them—she'd been young—even though she'd deck him for taking away her power in the situation. And she had one hell of a cross. He'd prefer to steer clear of it.

Now that same man had his sights, hands, and intentions set on Lucy. It was mutual. Lucy was as enamored with the detective as he was of her. The man wasn't Lucy's type, which was shocking and a bit unnerving because those were the relationships that typically stuck.

Example: Jonah and Elliott. Pastor and atheist. Early riser and late sleeper. It created a chemical reaction that threatened to set off smoke detectors.

Typically, Lucy liked bad boys, the massive biker types, like her previous boyfriend, Greg. Or the deceased Gage Rork, although he was only massive, not a biker. Big, bald, bearded, and tatted up—Lucy's preferred type all day long.

Killion wasn't too far off the mark being bald and tattooed. But he wasn't bearded, he wasn't huge. He was sinewy, strong, but not aggressively muscular. Gage Rork had been a tank of a man; he'd have overshadowed Killion when it came to bulk.

Running a hand over the material that covered his firm stomach, he assured himself that physically, he was enough. He knew he was, without being arrogant. He was a good-looking man. Pretty hazel eyes. Decent cock.

He smirked—it didn't hurt to be humble.

Job.

Home.

His lips twisted to the side as he felt a twinge in his chest.

About that. Yeah, he had a home. He was grateful for it, that room behind the office. He wasn't going to take it for granted that he had a permanent address for his driver's license, his mail, and could, with confidence, fill out random forms with a *home address*.

It also kept his parole officer off his ass.

But it was a room in a warehouse. It didn't even have a sink.

Detective Beckman had an entire apartment. Lucy did as well. Jonah used to have one in the River Market neighborhood until he moved in with Elliott. Everyone had a *home*.

No wonder Lucy looked at him the way she did.

Walking the property (skirting the ropes course) took two cigarettes. Killion properly disposed of the butts. First, ESE was technically a nonsmoking establishment. He was given a pass because he lived here, and he assumed Elliott wasn't allowed to be that restrictive regarding his lifestyle. The fuck if he knew the rules.

Second, Elliott was a nonsmoker. And a fitness geek, with her kickboxing. She also loathed litterbugs. Now with Jonah on-site and his repertoire of adventure sports, Killion was more conscious of his habit than ever.

And of course, there was Lucy. She wasn't sporty, and she was dating a smoker, but he knew she wasn't happy about it. Like, what nonsmoker would cheer to land a partner with a bad, stinky habit? He was well aware of the side effects that had nothing to do with health. He kept spearmint gum on hand.

He rounded the front of the event center, both seeing and hearing Elliott and her bag, the *thump, thump, thwack* echoing. Watching her routine as he approached, he determined she was in the warm-up phase.

"Mind if I join you, boss?"

Chapter Thirteen

Lucy

The steady rhythm of thumps and an occasional jangle of the chain was background noise Lucy was accustomed to. Usually, it was Elliott. Sometimes Jonah joined her. Lucy never watched those two, because hitting the bag together was sort of foreplay for them—of course, everything was foreplay for them—and Lucy didn't need to witness that.

Today, however, it was Elliott and Killion. The blows were easy for her to distinguish. She considered herself highly in tune and able to decipher Killion from either Jonah or Elliott. A special, useless skill of a highly intuitive person.

She flattered herself. She knew Jonah was already at work because they'd passed one another on the long driveway. Even without having seen him, she knew it was Killion because they laughed every few minutes. Elliott and Jonah were mostly quiet, serious competitors.

Lucy peered out the window. Killion hit the bag, causing it to jump under the power of his punch. His lithe, muscular body was covered in sweat, making his tattoos shimmer. She admired his form, his clean strikes, his control. He looked edgy and sexy. Just because she was with Beckman didn't mean she couldn't admit Killion was very lovely to look at.

Elliott said something, causing him to pause and step back. She patted her thigh, shifting her hip, clearly instructing him. Killion corrected his stance. Elliott continued her silent critique, her rapt attention reminding Lucy of a clinician.

She settled her attention on Elliott, beautiful and shapely. She had her black hair pulled back in a ponytail. Clad in a black sports bra and Lycra shorts, all her perfect curves were accentuated. Jonah had taken one look at her a year ago, covered in sweat and projecting an aura of *fuck-around-and-find-out*, and he'd been hooked.

Tilting her head, Lucy stared. A pang of resentment shot through her when the two shared a laugh. She felt both left out and envious that Elliott was living her life seemingly angst-free.

Lucy stared harder, trying to picture Elliott and Beckman having sex. It was a painful exercise because Elliott was passionate and gorgeous. If she and Becks had even an iota of the chemistry that she and Jonah did, their affair would cause more envy. The saving grace for Lucy's sanity was that she'd never seen an attraction like Jonah and Elliott's. And there was no chemistry between Elliott and Beckman on the occasions they were together.

According to Beckman, the sex hadn't been about passion but about mechanics; a means to an end. But observing Elliott's ease, her beauty, her effortless sex appeal, Lucy found it hard to believe that it was only "mechanics."

How could they have done that, anyway? How could they have one day decided to look at each other that way? Honestly, if Jonah, after knowing her their entire lives, had made a pass at her (which he wouldn't), she'd have dramatically made a gagging gesture and shoved him away. She might even kick him in the balls. Because... gross.

Beckman hadn't provided a lot of details even though he'd answered every one of her questions. How it started, she hadn't asked. Why it ended, she understood. And it shouldn't matter anyway. Beckman had ex-wives, all of whom he fucked. Lucy herself had past boyfriends on whose dicks she'd bounced.

So why did the thought of Beckman and Elliott bother her so much? Because she knew them?

Fixated on Elliott, sweaty and strong and gorgeous, Lucy recognized jealousy had something to do with it. She'd never have a body that lethal. And although she didn't want Jonah, she wanted a love like theirs. She'd been a romantic all her life, but all she seemed to get was disappointment, like a boyfriend telling her to fuck around. Jonah would never allow that for Elliott, nor would Elliott be tempted.

Lucy grimaced even though no one could see her—other than Gage, who saw all from his spot on the wall. She and Elliott weren't the same in that, being tempted. Elliott would never, not now, at least, but Lucy had daydreamed about it on the flight home with a rando.

And there had been that slip a few months ago with Killion. It wasn't anything to feel guilty about. Of course, that she was recalling it now made her feel guilty because it should have only been a one-off that didn't make an impression.

And it hadn't been that big of a deal. A little eye fucking and mutual appreciation of one another. After all, Killion was a gorgeous man in his own right. And now that he was coming into his own, his confidence and swagger were on point. It'd been innocent. Innocent eyeball sex.

They'd been at church—because of course, they were—and someone was telling them a story. Okay, the other person was gossiping. Lucy was listening intently (now peeved that she couldn't remember the drama). Killion was leaning against the door jamb, arms folded across his chest.

At one point in the story, Lucy snickered and looked over at Killion. He'd smirked, striking her as hot and yummy at that moment. His casual lean was sexy as hell, and his hazel eyes caught hers.

As the person droned on, they continued to stare at each other. For a beat too long. Then it was for several beats. Her heart banged in her chest, her cheeks heated—matching the embers of heat in his eyes—and still, she didn't look away.

When he dropped his gaze down her body in frank assessment, not hiding his appreciation, she realized they'd been eye fucking. She was warm and tingly and... Oh god, she was a faithless bitch.

She'd quickly turned away before his attention had a chance to come back to her eyes. She felt bad. And excited in an energizing way by his admiration. It hadn't felt weird. It should have felt weird. Although she'd had that fantasy in the office (and a few more since), this was real life. Shouldn't the reality be alarming that she would respond that way?

She couldn't help but wonder if Becks sensed that she wouldn't or couldn't be faithful to him. Could she be? Because her brain had been whirling and her imagination had taunted her since he'd given her permission to see other people.

Was it the circumstance or the way she was made?

Chapter Fourteen

Killion

"Hey, I'm heading to that fancy over-priced hardware store to pick up those gaudy lanterns you ordered last week. Wanna keep me company?"

He'd entered talking, and Lucy almost came out of her skin she jumped so hard and high.

"Damn. You okay?" He was genuinely concerned and curious. Her mood was still off.

She stared at him blankly, taking him in, then turned away. "I have a lot on my mind."

Two events were coming up one night after the next, but she'd never batted an eyelash over anything like that. At a loss as to what he could do to help her, he repeated his offer. "Wanna clear your head by hanging it out the side of my truck window while I speed down the highway? You can howl, I won't mind. It might move some cars out of our way."

His sassy ask was rewarded with an amused glance and a small smile.

"Is that a yes?"

She shook her head. "I'm probably not the best company right now."

Disappointment washed over him, but he strove for nonchalance. "Sure, okay." He reached for his pack of smokes in his shirt pocket. "Elliott said something about coming down to review the numbers anyway. The business shit of the business."

Lucy perked up. "If I go with you, can we go to that new specialty tea place?"

Warmth spread over him, a little bit of giddiness, too, when it looked like she was agreeing. "We can go anywhere you want."

Standing, she grabbed her pink purse from the desk overhang. "My lanterns aren't gaudy."

He backed toward the door. "Not if you're someone who likes seventies Sears-style decor." He continued to tease.

She bantered back. "Ah, how cute that our widdle Killion knows about Sears."

He was only five years her junior. At least he wasn't— He stopped his line of thinking, because it went immediately to the biggest age gap he knew: Becks and Elliott, the bookend of ages between the lot of them. He shied away from continuing on the topic.

"I've got a mother. She mentioned Sears more than once." It was probably where Beckman had bought all of his unimpressive suits at one time.

"Then she has spectacular taste."

"She had the good taste to birth me, so yeah, she's pretty spectacular."

Lucy approached, but he remained in the doorway grinning at her. His grin widened when she rolled her eyes. His heart stopped when she reached down to wrap her fingers around his hand. Only it was the hand that held his cigarettes. She redirected them back into his pocket. Still, he appreciated the contact.

"No smoking if I'm in the truck."

"Yes, ma'am."

She rewarded him with a pat on his chest in approval.

If he thought he'd have a snowball's chance in hell with her, he'd try his damnedest to kick the habit; take her up on her offer of enrolling him in the church program. She'd be pleased if he did so, and he liked her praise.

Stepping aside, he opened the door for her. "Your chariot awaits."

The chariot was a rusted, dented truck with a surprisingly comfortable bench seat. Which he knew because he'd had to sleep on it when he couldn't find a place to crash.

Lucy breezed past him, and he caught the scent of her shampoo. She smelled so good, light and floral, like a walk through a garden. He followed, resisting the urge to scent the air like a dog.

He was a dog, though, sniffing—literally and figuratively—around a woman who had a man.

They walked the short distance to the vehicle, and he opened the passenger door for her. It was a habit he'd fallen into with her, opening doors. Chivalrous, his mom had informed him.

Once Lucy was settled, he headed to his side, casting a glance at the raised home where Elliott and Jonah lived. Elliott was stepping off the bottom step. She'd changed into jeans and a white T-shirt with Jonah's alma mater across the front. Killion saw her sporting Jonah's university more than her own, or maybe she was simply wearing his clothes. Of course, the shirt looked like it'd been made for her.

Paused, one hand on the railing, she watched them with a sorrowful expression.

Killion called out, taken aback by the sadness. "Hey, boss, want to come with us?"

She flicked her attention behind him, to Lucy, before she forced a smile. "No, I have work to do."

"We're working."

Walking toward them, she waved them off. "Then get to it."

Killion nodded and slid onto his seat. He tossed a look at Lucy as he shut the door, but her attention was on their boss. Normally, Lucy would be all smiles and waving, but she was subdued. In the seconds he watched, she dropped her gaze away and pretended to fuss with the seat belt.

"What's going on between you two?" He wasn't dumb. He knew tension when he saw and felt it.

"Nothing. Why would anything be wrong?"

He started the engine, looking back at Elliott. She had also turned her eyes away, although her gait was steady and her head held high. "The chill is in the air. You've been back a day, how much could you have pissed her off already?"

"Why would it be my fault?"

Killion grinned as he reversed the vehicle. "Okay, sunflower, out with it. You're grumpy and have beef with the boss." It suddenly struck him, the puzzle pieces adding up, and he shifted the vehicle forward. "Oh. You know."

She gasped. In his periphery, he saw her turn toward him as she slapped the bench between them. "You knew?" The pitch of her tone further indicated her outrage. "Why am I the last person to know that my—whatever he is?—had an affair with my boss?"

"She's not only our boss, she's our friend, too," Killion pointed out. But he fixated on something else. "What did you mean by 'whatever he is'?" He hoped it was an indication of trouble in paradise. "You don't know what he is now?"

She flounced back in her seat. When he looked over, she was staring forlornly out thc window.

"Do you want to tell me what happened?"

There was a pause before she asked sarcastically, "Do *you*?"

Not really, but he understood she was hurt. And probably pissed off. He'd been angry, too, instantly disliking Beckman in defense of his friend, Jonah. Well, that, and Killion's relationship with the law hadn't always been stellar. It's plausible he never would have liked Beckman anyway, but the relationship with Elliott had taken center stage. And more egregious, the man's relationship with Lucy.

"If you'll remember, Jonah and I called it that night he'd shown up. You said we were jealous."

He hated throwing her words back at her, but it was the truth. Everyone had seen the intimacy—everyone except Lucy.

Silence met his words. He glanced at her occasionally as he navigated the highway toward the Country Club Plaza. She was lost in thought as she stared at the scenery. Although he doubted she was seeing the city pass by them.

Trying to offer some comfort, he added, "It was long over by the time he met you."

"I know that," she responded softly. "But it still smarts."

He grimaced. He should have said something sooner. But they'd sort of had a pact, to protect Elliott, that either she or Becks would be the one to break it to Lucy.

"I'm sorry I didn't say anything."

"It's not your fault."

Until she'd said it, he didn't realize that he thought it may have been, through keeping secrets. At least now she'd understand why he and Jonah never warmed up to Beckman, despite the man's importance to Elliott.

And to Lucy, he begrudgingly added.

He parked in the parking garage and shut off the engine. Instead of looking at her again, he stared straight ahead, giving her as much privacy as possible while they remained in the cab. Honestly, he'd sit here all night in silence with her, if that's what she wanted.

Several minutes passed before she murmured, "He doesn't want a commitment. Not with me, anyway."

Killion looked at her in disbelief. He imagined his eyes popping out of his head. Who the fuck wouldn't want her? He wanted to ask if they'd broken up, but then again, there had been those giggles of hers that morning.

She shrugged, ducking her head. "He said he didn't want us to be exclusive."

It didn't make sense. They'd been game on since seeing each other that night. As much as it pained him, Lucy was over the moon about Beckman. When he was in town, they were inseparable. Beckman stayed with Lucy instead of in the spare room at Elliott and Jonah's. Of course, that would be weird, he supposed. He wondered if Beckman would stay in a hotel if he and Lucy hadn't paired up. He'd never know.

"He wants us to keep our options open, whatever that means. I was tempted to fuck a guy from the plane to test his resolve." She sighed. "But I couldn't do that. Randos never interested me. And I'm sure it would've only been to hurt him."

Killion wasn't random.

He was trying to suppress the giddiness racing through him with the news that Lucy was free to date around. It meant he might have a shot.

Thank you, Elliott Beckman, you fucking fool.

If that man's actions led Lucy to him, then he'd send him a bouquet of roses. And some tissues.

Now wasn't the time to broach the subject. But he wasn't going to make the same mistake twice by letting too much time pass before he told her how he felt.

"I'm here if you need me. I mean it, I'm a good shoulder to cry on."

She forced a smile, her words at odds with her strained expression. "We'll get there, he and I. I have faith in him."

Selfishly, Killion hoped they would not get there, and that her faith was misplaced.

Chapter Fifteen

Lucy

Retail therapy hadn't helped. They'd wandered her favorite tea store far longer than necessary, but she walked out without anything. That had been a first.

The items she'd ordered had been waiting for pickup at the hardware store, so technically, she hadn't needed to go. But when Killion mentioned Elliott would be in the office, she panicked and bailed. Elliott had always intimidated her—something about her self-confident badassery—and Lucy didn't want to face her. Elliott wanted to talk, and working was her way of trying to break the day-old ice. Based on her defeated expression when she'd seen her sitting in the truck, an expression Elliott rarely sported, Lucy knew the silence was bothering the other woman.

But she didn't want to discuss Beckman and their past. If it were up to Lucy, the subject of Elliott and Beckman's past relationship would never again come up so she could blithely ignore it like everyone else had been doing.

How would a conversation like that go anyway? There was no way they would share an intimate chuckle over the lover they had in common. Lucy didn't even know the questions to ask. And she didn't want to hear the story all over again.

Nope, not happening.

After she killed as much time as she could in the second store, she headed toward the exit.

"Ladies first." Killion opened the door with his hip and invited her to precede him with a wave of his hand.

Still stewing in her mood, she halted on the threshold. "Why?"

"Why what?"

"Why ladies first?"

He looked confused, but he answered, dropping words like he was trying to pass a pop quiz. "Tradition? Polite? So I can have your back? Chivalry?"

"Well, maybe we ladies don't want to go first. Maybe we don't want men walking behind us."

He was quiet, watching her as though he was trying to figure her out, and why it was important.

"I mean, maybe a lady needs to fart, and she doesn't want to hold it in."

For one second, he looked stunned, then he fell against the door, opening it wider. Laughing.

"Killion!"

"Jesus, Lucy, if you have to fart, just do it!"

Huffing, she stomped through the door. "I don't! I'm just saying that it isn't as chivalrous as you think sometimes."

He chortled after her, his fit of giggles following them to the garage. She wondered what he was tickled over the most: the word—because men—or him imagining her trying to sneak a toot.

When they'd returned to the property, Lucy mumbled a goodbye, jumped in her little yellow car, and sped home. She took a hot bath, cried, and then climbed into bed, pulling her weighted blanket over her.

Jonah began sending text after text. She stared at the messages coming through: *I haven't seen you since you returned. Are you okay? Do you want to talk? I'm here for you, Luce. I love you.*

The last made her cry even harder. She wanted Beckman to send that message. She was afraid he never would.

Mornings bring clarity and a new outlook on life.

Well, that sentiment was a pile of shit. All morning brought her were puffy red eyes and a crying hangover.

Toting her phone like a good luck charm, she went to the kitchen and turned on her kettle for tea. She was determined not to read the messages—fearful they would all be from Jonah—until she'd showered and consumed a cup of Earl Grey.

The shower was skipped, but she did make her tea. Sitting on her sofa, she considered the message count on her phone. Fifteen. Certainly, Jonah hadn't fired off that many texts after she'd left the first few on read. Right? Bracing herself against the disappointment she knew she would experience, she opened them.

Jonah. Killion. The church group chat for the parolees program.

And there, nestled among the others, were two messages from Beckman.

Clasping the phone to her chest, she sent up a quick prayer of thanks. Her heart was beating out of her chest. It shouldn't surprise her. They hadn't broken up; he was scared and wanted to take the slow road.

Meanwhile, he offered her up to a buffet of men.

Not really. But kind of really.

She read his message first, of course: *Miss you, pixie.*

It made her smile. The second message predicted she was already asleep, but he wished her a good night anyway.

Well, at least she wasn't out of sight, out of mind.

CHAPTER SIXTEEN

Beckman

Dipping his razor in the sink, he rinsed the foam and scruff before returning to his cheek.

Stupid was his *modus operandi* when it came to women. Four divorces. *Ellie*. And now, the best fucking woman who had walked into his life, he couldn't give what she wanted, needed, or deserved. Well, he could, but he wouldn't. It wasn't her—fuck no, she was perfection—but in a sense, it was her. Because she was perfect. Her giggles, kindness, intelligence, and quirks that included a crush on a ghost.

To that point, if Gage had lived, Beckman wouldn't have had a chance in hell.

He was overwhelmed that he'd had a chance with her at all, and although he berated himself hourly about not locking her down, his hypervigilance or instinct urged him to be cautious. Instead of racing to put a ring on it, desperate to create for himself what the Rorks had had—a family—he wanted this to be right with Luce. He couldn't bear the thought of, first, using her to fulfill his own desires, and second, that she wasn't as ready as she thought she was.

Or as ready as *he* thought she was. Her friendship with Jonah was not the relationship that had him hesitating. It was the one with Killion. Those two were tight, and he was aware of—suspected—Killion's feelings toward her. Regardless of where he and Lucy ended up, Killion was going to be part of the package.

Beckman wanted to see it play out. Because when he committed himself to Lucy, he didn't want any surprises for either of them. Worse, he didn't want any regrets. Maybe it was masochism or striking before he got struck.

He'd like to think he was magnanimous, but that was bullshit. He had a shipment container's worth of baggage. She had a relationship he wanted her to figure out—not blaming her one bit—and he was in no position to begrudge her that discovery.

Meanwhile hoping there was nothing to discover.

Did it feel like a kick in the balls? Yeah.

He told himself he was overreacting to ancient history, allowing his failures to make him willfully ignorant of the fact that Lucy loved him, and only him. It was how he got to sleep at night.

Only one of his ex-wives still talked to him—his last ex, Abby. She'd also refused alimony, bless her.

"I didn't marry you for your money." She'd teased him, adding, "Because you don't have any."

Given that they were signing divorce papers when she'd cracked that joke, he'd wondered why she *had* married him. She'd rattled off the usual: steady job, handsome and charming, she appreciated his family values that shone through with his relationship with the Rorks; she wanted that, too.

"Then why are you divorcing me?" He'd quipped.

Although citing his long hours was typical amongst his wives, she included the complaint of how he'd disappear right in front of her when he was working, he'd get so lost in it. She didn't blame him, she'd assured him, but she sensed he held back from her. Maybe she was greedy, she said sadly, but it turned out he wasn't *enough.*

"It's not intentional on your part, babe."

Considering his relationship with Abby had been easy—so he thought—and his best marriage, her words hit hard. He wasn't enough. And that had been before Ellie. During and after Ellie, he was even less.

He didn't want that for Lucy. He wanted her to have everything, to give her all he had, but he was afraid his all wouldn't be enough. Especially when his all came with a CONEX box of unresolved strife.

Chapter Seventeen

Killion

"I haven't stopped thinking about what you said. About you and Beckman."

Lucy stepped back from him, scrunching her nose and twisting her lips, her posture deflating.

Dammit. Seconds ago, she'd been laughing as he spun her around the event space. She'd come to investigate the music that was making the ground shake. He'd installed a new sound system, and it worked. So well that she'd entered with her eyes wide and hands over her ears.

"Killion! We're going to get a noise violation from Kansas!"

He'd laughed and instantly broken out his best dance moves, running his hands over his body as he slowly gyrated his hips. Strippers would be proud—or jealous—of his swagger. His exaggerated moves brought a reluctant smile to her lips as she clearly tried to hold back laughter.

Okay, maybe he was more comical than sexy, but her shining eyes were worth it.

She shook her head at him as he approached her, trying to give him a stern face but failing miserably. The facade crumbled completely when he swept her into his arms, swinging her around to the country banger. Her resulting laughter was worth a hundred violations—although the music wasn't that loud—and Elliott's disapproval of the music choice; she had something against country music. But she and Jonah had gone off on an adventure together, so she wasn't here.

After his comment, however, her enjoyment fizzled. Her defeated posture wasn't the response he wanted. Her gaze uncertain, she stared at him, waiting for him to continue. The upbeat tune was now out of place.

He walked over to the panel and lowered the volume.

"Thinking about what?"

When he turned back to her, she had her arms folded.

"The open door policy, I suppose you can call it."

Her nose scrunched even more. "I wish I hadn't said anything. It's embarrassing. I admitted the man I'd fallen for doesn't want me. I mean, not exclusively. I'm sorry it's bothering you, too."

Her gaze fell away as her features softened. She was hurt. But she'd also misunderstood. He was going to ignore that she'd said she'd fallen for Beckman. It wasn't a secret. She'd gone starry-eyed for that man the night she'd met him.

"It's not bothering me. It gives me hope."

Her expressive eyes snapped back to his, confused, like she was trying to figure out how her rocky relationship could give him hope when it was breaking her heart.

Killion cleared his throat. His heartbeat jacked up. It was now or never, and he wasn't going to choose never. Even if she rejected him, he would have an answer. That was always better than not knowing. "I want a shot."

She looked perplexed and darted her gaze over to the bar. "You want a shot?"

Damn, he was fucking this up.

Ducking his head, he rubbed his bald scalp. "Nah, I mean, kind of. I want a shot at you." He peeked up at her.

She slapped her hand over her heart as though guarding from a literal bullet. As she regarded him and his bashfulness—because, yeah, he was—her expression morphed from confounded to incredulous. Then angry.

Shit.

Her brows came together sharply, and her lips thinned. Stomping forward, she reached out and slapped his arm. He flinched, not expecting the sting. Then she hit him again.

"Hey."

It was all he got out before she became a slapping machine.

"Hey, hey, I'm sorry!" He dodged, trying to catch her flying hands.

"You oaf! You jerk! I am so mad at you!"

"Yeah, I'm getting that vibe." He jerked his head back to avoid a blow to his face.

She wasn't being violent; she was merely annoyed. There wasn't a lot of force behind her smacks. Rather, her flapping gestures were to make a point.

He realized with a start that only Lucy and his mother slapped him. And he didn't mind it from either of them.

Suddenly stopping, she gasped as though her tantrum had consumed too much energy.

"Why, Killion? Why now?" Her voice cracked. "Why when it's too late? Why out of the blue like this?" Stomping her foot, she demanded once more, "Why now?"

"Why would it be out of the blue?"

It was, of course, for her. In the back of his mind, he reminded himself that she only saw him as a pet, a beloved plant, *a project*. There was no way she'd ever wondered about a relationship with him. And Lucy fell in love quickly. But not with him. Fuck, she was mooning over a dead man.

But he'd stuck his dick out, so he was going to keep going. Nothing to lose now. He'd already made shit weird.

"For you, maybe it is. Not for me."

Her stare was intense. Her silence, even more so. He could see her thinking, though, perhaps running over all their interactions and wondering what she might have missed—what clue had gotten past her.

After what seemed like an eternity, which was only minutes, she asked cautiously, "Is this because of what I said about the guy on the plane?"

It was Killion's turn to be perplexed. "What?"

"Fucking a random dude to get back at Beckman."

"Wow." He wasn't doing well if she thought he wanted to help her get revenge. He rubbed the back of his neck. "I'd forgotten about that, but if you want to piss off Becks, I'd be the quickest way to do it." It was true. "But no, I don't want to be a random fuck to make your boyfriend jealous."

She dropped her gaze at the word 'boyfriend.'

He hated seeing her sadness, and he was afraid she blamed herself for the man's decision. "I don't know what's going on in his head, but he's giving me an opportunity, if you also want it. So, it's not too late. You aren't committed—and that's a good thing for me. It gives me a chance."

"I don't know what to say. I mean, as mad as he made me, I don't want to lose him." Her expression pleaded for him to understand.

"Call him. Call him and ask. Be up front about it. He'll either stick to his guns or this will be the thing that makes him realize he's being a douche."

At the insult, a flicker of annoyance crossed her face, but it quickly went away.

He legit saw her brain process the possibilities, her eyes traveling over him as though he'd appeared before her for the first time. Although, he was aware there'd been moments and exchanges of heated looks before today. He wasn't new to her, nor was their attraction. They'd been real fucking good at hiding it, is all.

So good that he was sure he'd imagined it from her. But the speculation in her eyes...

Then her expression closed off.

He grimaced, his own insecurities surfacing. "I'd understand if you said no. I mean, I've already fucked our friendship by saying this shit, and I have a record—on parole—with no real home." He forced a grin. "I'm not exactly a catch."

"You're the douche if you think I'm that shallow. And it shows that you don't know me at all if you think I would hold any of that against you."

"I know."

"Do you? Because you're resourceful, you're determined, you're dedicated. You're funny and kind and loyal. You're a good son and a good man, Killion."

He held his breath, waiting for her to end this quest of his with more placating words about his attributes—all good, but not good enough to gain her interest. He was almost wishing for it, to give him a definitive answer and put him out of his misery.

She didn't do any of those things. Instead, she took a few steps away from him. The conflict on her face was his fault entirely, and he didn't know what to say to fix the mess he'd made. Well, he blamed Beckman, too, for providing him with hope. But he kept his mouth shut as she turned and walked to the door.

There, she paused.

He held his breath as he watched her. Hoping she would turn around and say something. Anything.

But without looking back, she walked out.

“Way to go, genius.”

Chapter Eighteen

Lucy

Lucy curled up under her weighted blanket, hiding from the world like a little girl. Only, she was an all-grown-up woman with bigger issues. Not even the pressure from the blanket calmed her nervous system.

What was she supposed to do? Seriously, what?

Killion's proposition hadn't offended her. It hadn't shocked her in that way. She was more shocked by the charge of electricity that had raced through her. She wasn't supposed to feel that way toward another person now that she was with Beckman. Right? She was the steadfast one, fighting for her relationship with him. Determined to prove to him that he was worth the wait.

Now this. And the knowledge that Killion's advances hadn't been unwelcome. The lack of guilt over her initial excitement is what made her feel guilty—that wasn't right, either, was it?

Moaning into her pillow, pulling tighter into a fetal position, she wondered if her lack of a committed relationship with someone she wanted was skewing her perspective. Of course, she wouldn't know. If Becks had committed, she knew Killion wouldn't have said anything. She knew Killion well enough to know he wouldn't fuck with her mind that way.

But that door was open.

And she was curious.

Killion was someone she adored, another man she felt completely safe around. Whom she'd always been herself with, no pretenses. In some ways, he knew her better than Beckman; differently, for sure.

But what if it didn't work? What if they tried, but it was misplaced affection? She'd lose her friend.

What if Becks broke things off for good with her?

What if it all went wrong and she lost them both?

Her keenness was real enough. She wanted to discover if the excitement of Killion was real. And she wanted Beckman. She wanted them both, without consequence or risk.

But once she started down this path, there would be no going back. She couldn't say "just kidding" and expect that they'd revert to their original roles and relationships without a hitch.

Killion was right about one thing. She needed to call Becks.

Chapter Nineteen

Beckman

"Pix. Hearing your voice is what I need right now."

He was walking from the metro toward his apartment. It'd been a shit day, but thankfully not because of any crime. It had been an administrative day, and he hated paperwork. So hearing her voice was a reward, answering mundane questions about his day (he was honest about it) and hearing about hers (she was coordinating a local, exclusive film premiere).

He tossed aside his cigarette, mentally registering Ellie's disapproval somewhere in the universe over his littering. "Can you tell me about the film? Anyone famous?"

She laughed, and his nervous system instantly calmed. The woman was magical.

"It depends on your definition of famous, but they are local heroes. An Irish rock band. They're hosting an advance showing of their film for friends, family, and a few of their most loyal fans. At least, that's the pitch they gave me. Killion upgraded the sound system. I'm surprised you didn't hear it."

He smiled. If he hadn't been holding a phone to his ear, he'd look goofy. He probably did anyway. "I'll bet Ellie and Jonah loved that."

"They aren't here. The Jeep was loaded up, so I'm assuming they'll be away a few days. They don't check in with me, so I'm not sure."

His smile fell. "Have you and Ellie talked to one another?"

He knew they hadn't. One of the two of them would have said something, but he'd heard from neither on the topic.

"No." She said it like he'd asked if she liked pineapple on her pizza.

"Do I need to fly there and get you two in a room?"

Of course, where was Jonah in all this, and why hadn't he pressed for a conversation? Although, he suspected they were waiting for Lucy to feel comfortable with broaching an uncomfortable subject.

"They haven't been here, I just told you they're gone."

Her wounded defensiveness checked him. "Sorry, Luce. And I'm sorry I put you in this position."

She was quiet for so long, he thought she might've hung up on him. It was a habit of hers when she was frustrated, ending a conversation without the proper sign-off. But a glance informed him the line remained open, so he waited.

Eventually, she asked quietly, "Do you want to make it up to me?"

Was she about to ask for phone sex? Hell yes!

"You know I do." He assured her with a low growl.

"Will you be mad if I go out with Killion?"

The words were rushed, which is what caused his brain to glitch, because she did *not* ask if she could date Killion. "What was that? Sorry, pix, I didn't hear you."

A car honked, providing him with a bit of truth behind the words.

Her "shit" was spoken away from the phone, but she sighed heavily and asked again, "Can I date Killion? You said—"

"I know what I said."

He paused on the street corner, no longer registering the vehicles, the roundabout monument, or the people, because his words came back to bite him in the ass. Damn, that was fast, but he should have expected it. Killion's speed, not Lucy's. He hated being right.

"I mean, it was your allowance, I suppose you could say. Seeing other people?"

"Is this a test?"

"No."

He was slow responding to her query—who the fuck wouldn't need a moment?—focusing on the sounds of her breath, which were uneven. She was nervous. Meanwhile, he was busy trying not to have a heart attack in broad daylight on a street corner.

"Yeah, I'm the asshole who can't commit right now, and I told you that you could. I'd be an even bigger asshole if I expected you to wait until I figure out you're all that matters."

He should have placed boundaries on that: *except* for Killion. But that would have been an even bigger dick move than the one he'd made.

There wasn't a sound like relief or celebration from the other end of the line. All he heard was breathing. If he had to assign an emotion to the silence, it would be stunned. Or hurt.

"I kind of don't want you to say yes. I don't want you to be okay with it."

"Pix, I am anything but okay with it. But I'm not going to stand in your way for something better."

"I'm not looking for anyone better, Becks. This isn't... I don't know, I think I wanted to feel like it's a major thing and you were wrong."

"I probably am wrong." If she'd been standing in front of him, she'd see the heat in his gaze as he said it, his certainty. Reaching for his cigarettes, he shook one out. “What do you want me to do here?”

Tension radiated through the ether.

“Don’t tell me I matter and then make me feel like I don’t.” She hung up.

Damn it.

Chapter Twenty

Lucy

To be honest, she was a little pissed at Beckman for being—in her opinion—cavalier about her dating other men. She honestly had expected him to reverse his stance and declare they would be exclusive, because she knew he didn't like Killion. Or rather, Killion didn't like Beckman. She didn't think Becks had an issue with Killion. Until now, that is.

But because Becks didn't put his foot down, she decided to say "fuck it." Maybe it had been a test; she hadn't intended it to be that, and she did like Killion. She liked that they had the foundation of a friendship to lead them into whatever this was. And she'd spent the previous evening trying to decide whether it was anything.

She'd sat on her balcony overlooking a parking lot, not that she paid attention to the comings and goings beneath her. A car could have been broken into and she wouldn't have noticed. She'd been going over the past couple of years' worth of interactions with Killion. From the moment he'd shown up at the church, newly paroled and hoping their program could find him steady employment. He'd been angry and nervous, understandably, but he'd been courteous and patient with her. He'd been brusque and reserved with others, but he always had a smile for her. And eventually, a nickname.

She'd noticed. Her first reaction to him had been Lucy-esque: She'd seen a beautiful, tattooed man, and her infatuation was instant. Like seeing Gage's picture, she was immediately attracted.

But she swiped her impressions away. It wouldn't be professional of her to form a relationship with him. He needed time to find his balance. And the church didn't need a scandal of her having sex with their parolees; it could harm the program.

Looking back, she realized she'd noticed everything about Killion, not all entirely because of her initial attraction. His moods were easy for her to read. And when he was down, he allowed her to cheer him up. He rarely grumped back at her. And he didn't want her to worry. When she'd ask about his housing situation, or where he would sleep that night, he was quick to reassure her. He'd rub his scalp, duck his head, and say evenly, "I'm good, sunflower. I've got it sorted."

Only for her to find out through others that he'd slept in his truck in the parking garage.

Did his eyes linger more than once? Sweep over her in appreciation? Yes. But it hadn't occurred to her that it was an attraction that matched her own. Because they'd become friends.

If Killion had approached her a year before, what would her response have been? If Beckman hadn't been in the picture, would she trust herself more with the decision to try to date Killion? Because she was sure, employee-employer relationship aside, she would have agreed to date him if he'd asked. Hell, the amount of time they spent together now—shopping, eating—could be considered mini dates. Right? And knowing he was interested in her as more than a friend or a boss—she'd never been that—was flattering.

Could the slightest indication of interest from a man turn her head? Yes. Did it mean she acted on all those indicators? No. But this was Killion. There was a coziness with him. He had a gentleness she'd recognized from the beginning, and it baffled her that he'd gone to prison for beating up a man. That he had to attend anger management as a condition of his parole.

She hadn't been lying when she'd rattled off his attributes. She guessed that she might be the only person who knew the depths of how good he was, and she'd always been aware of how special that knowledge was, like he trusted her with the tender parts of himself.

Walking toward the office, knowing Killion was on the property somewhere, she sent him a text: *Let's do it.*

Only after she hit send did she realize how he could interpret those three words.

"Shit," she said as she entered the office, quickly tapping out a clarification.

But she never got around to sending it, because Elliott was in the office.

"Shit," she said again.

Elliott leaned back against the desk, arms folded. "You can't avoid me forever."

It sort of had been the plan, though: dodge Elliott until she felt like she could have this conversation. But, like Jonah, Elliott didn't like things to fester. Ugh, they were made for each other.

Lucy ignored the comment. "When did you two get back?"

She wanted to smack her forehead for not noticing the signs of life. But Jonah's car wasn't here, although it rarely was when she got in because he would have already left for work.

"Last night."

Struggling for nonchalance despite her heart pounding so hard she heard it in her ears, she asked inanely, "Where'd you go?"

"Ozarks."

Lucy could tell by Elliott's tone that she knew Luce couldn't give two flips where they'd gone. Still, she responded, "Cool."

It did explain the brevity of the trip.

She sidled by her, placing her purse in the desk overhang, trying to ignore Elliott's stare, the anticipation making the air heavy. She wished she'd pushed for an earlier conversation with Jonah to prepare her for this moment. Too late now! So she mirrored Elliott's stance, crossing her arms as she leaned against the far wall.

Elliott's expression was guarded, but there was a resignation to her as well, like waiting for the other shoe to drop; hoping it wouldn't but knowing it would.

Lucy looked down, scuffing her shoe against the floor. "I don't know what's in my head. I mean, it was a long time ago, it didn't affect me, but it's weird to know about... it."

She tossed a glance to the picture of Gage on the wall, returning as quickly to the contemplation of her shoe. "You were both consenting and—"

"No." She interrupted. "Becks didn't consent, not initially. That, you can't put on him. This was me, I started it."

Lucy peeked up. He hadn't mentioned that. "But why?"

She smiled, but it wasn't a happy one; it was the response someone gave when they were covering up pain.

"That's a longer answer than you might expect. The word Becks used was hubris. I didn't care about, or understand, the consequences; I had a selfish need and I trusted him." She looked away, shrugging. "I was ruled more by my libido than my brain, but I knew he wouldn't hurt me. I thought I was being powerful and breaking men to my will; I thought it was exciting to get them to cave, then walk away—or rather, they got pissed and walked away first. Using my body to get them to do what I wanted, I interpreted it as control. I wasn't a good person, and Becks hated everything about it, but..." Another shrug.

"Ten years of not understanding the consequences?"

Elliott nodded, her silver gaze steady even if haunted. "I hurt a lot of people. I'm not proud of that. And Becks and Gage..."

Lucy didn't say anything as Elliott trailed off, fighting the need to seek out Gage's picture again. "Beckman told me Gage had found out."

"Yep." The word was tortured, but she maintained eye contact. "I killed him. Gage. He was already standing in the gasoline, but I lit the match and handed it to him."

The words were jarring, as was the emotion behind them. Lucy could tell that Elliott believed she'd been responsible. A flash of impotent fury burned through her at the thought she'd been robbed of Gage by Elliott's selfishness, but it dissipated as quickly.

The image of Elliott standing at the gravesite, the perfect representation of grief she'd portrayed in that photo, surfaced. The anger was replaced with sympathy. The burden of guilt Elliott carried—might always carry—squashed anything other than sadness.

As much as she wanted to comfort the woman, though, she had to ask, "What about Jonah? I mean..."

How did she ask if he was in danger of being pushed too far? After all, Gage was dead and Beckman was gun-shy about commitment, so she felt she had reason to be concerned for her best friend.

The hint of a smile lifted Elliott's lips, and she glanced up briefly. The expression reminded Lucy of when the two had started dating and how Elliott—the baddest of bitches she'd ever met—would appear shy. Lucy had called her smitten. Clearly, she still was.

Of course, Lucy had seen evidence of the love she and Jonah had for each other, but when Elliott melted at the mention of his name, it soothed her. Now, that bashful expression was accompanied by Elliott encircling her wrist and rubbing affectionately.

Lucy frantically shoved away the mental images of how those bruises came to be. She did not want to dwell on what Elliott and Jonah did together. Originally, Elliott had tried to be discreet about the marks. Now, she wore them as proudly as expensive bangles.

And damn Jonah. But Lucy noticed he was pleased with the marks, as well. He'd run his thumb gently over her bruises, the all-encompassing heat they generated together scorching those in their vicinity.

"You know Jonah. He can hold his own. Besides, that's not me anymore. Is he aware of everything? Yes. If I veer, he'll course correct me."

Lucy decided to silently agree instead of allowing her imagination to run rampant with how he'd accomplish that goal. But it was true. Jonah was solid as a freaking rock.

"And Beckman?" she prompted.

It wasn't jealousy or fear that Elliott and Becks would slip back into what they'd once done. Lucy couldn't place the emotion she had, but she was anxious. She also wasn't sure what she wanted to hear.

"I love Beckman."

Lucy tensed, but Elliott was concentrating on her encircled wrist.

"But I love him the way I always have. It was never romantic, what we'd done—what I did. Desperate, maybe. For me, at least. And yes, on one level, I knew how much he despised doing that for me, and hated me in those moments, but that was as enticing to me: getting him to do it against his will. Like I said, it made me feel powerful."

"And now?"

"I don't need that. Or want it. Jonah is quite literally my match." Again with a small smile accompanied by the self-soothing gesture of rubbing her wrist.

Elliott met her gaze again, straightening up, one leg shifting behind her. It was her defensive fighter's stance, ready to absorb the blows. "I wouldn't blame you for hating me."

Lucy frowned. What was going on with people that they felt comfortable assigning emotions to her she'd not expressed? Of course, she'd avoided Elliott for a few days and couldn't look at her without feeling hurt. But it wasn't Elliott's actions that had cut; it was Beckman's rejection.

"I don't hate you. I would think you'd know I'm not capable of hating anyone."

"Sorry."

Lucy hadn't seen this side of Elliott before: vulnerable. For some reason, she was shocked that it made the other woman appear stronger. Owning it, so to speak.

Elliott's stance and features softened. "I am glad he has you. He deserves happiness, and you make him happy. So thank you for that."

Pleased adrenaline rushed through her. Was this it? Had she been wanting—needing—Elliott's approval of their relationship, even after all this time? As she reveled in the elation, her phone buzzed, the alert one of an incoming text. And her heart plummeted into her stomach. Heat burned her cheeks with embarrassment as she realized she had her own secret now.

Guilt pushed her to blurt out, "He doesn't want to make a commitment."

Like it was an excuse, a justification for what she was about to do, even with Beckman's permission. As if Elliott's approval was premature or misplaced.

Elliott's expression turned painful and pleading. "I have no right to ask for it, but please don't give up on him. I'm sorry to have contributed to his reluctance. It's not because of you, not at all."

"How do you know? Has he said anything?"

She shook her head. "We don't talk to one another like that anymore. But it's the only thing that makes sense."

Anymore. Lucy's heart wrenched in her chest. Elliott made mistakes, but she was also aware of everything it had cost her.

Her phone buzzed again. She clasped it to her chest, as though that would silence the thing.

Elliott nodded to the phone. "I'll leave you to that." She forced a smile. "He'll want to know how this talk went."

Shit. She thought it was Beckman. But Lucy nodded. "He will."

She asked leadingly, "And how did it go?"

Lucy smiled. "Better than he expected, I'm sure."

Elliott nodded once in satisfaction. "If anything about this bothers you or you need more details—whatever it is—ask. I don't want the past to get in the way of you moving forward with him."

"I will. I promise."

"For what it's worth, he's never looked at any woman the way he looks at you, and I've met all of his wives." Elliott indicated the phone once more. "Tell him I said hi."

Lucy watched until the other woman left, closing the door behind herself. Falling back against the wall, hugging the phone, she whispered, "Shit."

Chapter Twenty-One

Killion

Killion tugged at his collar. It felt tighter tonight than the times he'd worn a dress shirt for church or check-ins with his parole officer. Of course, he never attended the service, preferring to hang out in the basement with the other parolees. Now, instead of being the one looking for a job, he assisted others in getting one. Volunteering for the program counted toward community service credit, too. And while check-ins with his parole officer didn't require formal wear, his mother had said it showed respect.

This evening, however, he was out of his element. More so out of his element, he mentally amended. Churches and parole offices weren't his idea of a good time, but he was accustomed to them. A fancy restaurant in Union Station was out of his comfort zone. But he wanted his first date with Lucy to be perfect, because she deserved it.

He invited her to precede him as the host escorted them through the place, fighting a smile as he remembered her comments at the hardware store.

Rolling her eyes at him, she walked ahead. She fit in with the elegant grandeur of the place. Her soft shell-pink dress and heels matched the decor. She moved with ease, comfortable with the surroundings.

He was the oddball, a bald man with tattoos peeking up from his collar. He wasn't normally self-conscious, but this place was upper echelon and he felt like he was pretending to be someone he wasn't. But Town Topic for burgers wasn't a first date befitting a goddess. Although, because she was Lucy, she would have rolled with it.

Once seated, a waiter stepped up to the table, asking for their drink order. The man's attention was on him, expectant. Even Lucy beamed across their little table at him, waiting for his response.

Fuck. What did she drink? As many events as he'd served as bartender, he had no idea what she drank.

Clearing his throat, he watched her expression as he ordered. "Chateauneuf du Pape." They'd recently served the vintage at the event center; he'd liked the name. Thank god he remembered it because she grinned.

"Bottle or glass?"

"Glass. I'll take a tonic with lime." His eyes on her, he noticed her brows dip in slightly, curious.

When they were alone, she leaned forward. "You're going to make me drink alone?"

She was teasing him, but the answer was yes. The reason he wasn't drinking should be obvious to her, but he shrugged. "I'm driving."

"Uh-huh." Her amused look remained in place as she perused the menu. "Trying to get me drunk. I see what you're doing, Mr. Murphy."

He chuckled. She didn't sound opposed to the idea, although that wasn't his plan. "Fancy restaurant, fancy wine."

Her look scrutinized him. "I appreciate the effort, and I do like the menu here, but I wonder if we're here more for me than us?"

"Of course this is for you," he answered quickly, his heart missing a beat at her use of the word *us*. At her dismayed expression, he added, "I want to make you happy."

"I love that, I do, and the effort you're putting in tonight. But spending time with you is what makes me happy. Do I like the menu here? Yes. Do I need it?" She shrugged. "No."

Killion was unsure how to respond. Was she saying it for his benefit, because she knew this was out of his price range and his comfort zone? He knew he couldn't keep this up, and he knew he couldn't compete with whatever Beckman was doing for her. But he wanted to try.

"I'm concerned you think I'm superficial."

"We know each other better than that. I know who you are. I never—and have never—had that opinion of you. I just want to show you that I can give you nice things sometimes. It won't always be ramen noodles in the back of a warehouse."

"I love ramen noodles in the back of the warehouse." Picking up her knife, she brandished it at him. "Don't get it into your head that you need to compete for anything. That'll piss me off and turn me off faster than anything."

He blinked. Nope, she could never be confused with being superficial when she was so intuitive.

"Thank you for treating me tonight. I really do appreciate it. I'm hoping for a little less starched Killion and more bad-dance-moves Killion in the future, though."

Future. His head swam a little.

"I'm a phenomenal dancer."

She made an exaggerated face that said "Okay, think what you want," then grinned.

"You do have sexy moves. I wonder how far those sexy moves extend?" She winked.

His heart nearly exploded from the shot of adrenaline her words and expression gave him. Before he could marshal his thoughts enough to say anything—an odd moment of speechlessness—the waiter returned with a glass of wine and the tonic.

After the waiter left, their orders safely marked down, the moment for teasing her felt as though it had passed. If she wanted to continue to flirt, he'd pick it back up.

But he had another question, curiosity driving him to ask, "Is everything good with the boss?"

Honestly, he'd been wondering how that conversation had gone, because there'd definitely been one. Her follow-up text the other day had begged him not to say anything to Elliott about "us."

He would cling to every time she used that word. For a while, at least. Because it made everything seem possible. Like she and him could work. How they worked, with Beckman in the mix, was a crazy unknown. But all systems were a go from that end—stupid motherfucker—and he was endlessly grateful for this opportunity.

He wished he'd had the nerve to approach her before Beckman had entered their lives, but wondering about what-ifs was wasted energy. And he knew Beckman had signed off on this foray, this liaison; otherwise Lucy wouldn't have entertained his request.

That was another conversation he was dying to hear about, but first things first.

Answering his question, she shrugged. "Sure, why wouldn't it be?"

Because you asked me not to mention anything to her about us dating. Because you'd run away from her the other day. Because your boyfriend had banged her for years.

"Everything got cleared up, then?"

She wrinkled her nose. "Pretty much."

"Okay. Good."

He didn't believe her. Well, if that wasn't an awesome start to a relationship.

CHAPTER TWENTY-TWO

Lucy

Despite her enthusiastic consumption of a delicious meal and Killion's enjoyable company, the atmosphere made the evening stilted. They'd both ridden it out, but when a shoe doesn't fit right, it's noticeable. She and Killion weren't fancy dining. They were more authentic with one another than that.

Thankfully, the date didn't end after dinner.

When he escorted her to the streetcar, she almost jumped up and down and clapped her hands with glee. No matter how many times she'd ridden up and down the line, it was always an adventure.

"Where are you taking me now?" She linked her arm with his and leaned into him, beaming up at his gorgeous face.

"There's a concert at Power and Light." He grinned, looking proud of himself. "It's a Charlie Daniels Band cover group."

Her jaw dropped. He'd noticed her obsession with a specific song by the band—sung by Gage—and was now taking her to hear it live. Although, not really, because her love of the song was only because Gage was singing it. But the fact he'd paid attention made her heart pump harder.

"I love that."

A thrill zipped through her when she glimpsed his bashful smile before he turned to look up the rails at the approaching streetcar. Gah. Giving in to impulse, she threw her arms around him, hugging him tightly.

He removed one arm from her grasp to wrap it around her, pulling her against his side. She buried her face into his chest. He smelled good, cologne and man with a hint of spearmint but no detectable cigarette smell. Like he hadn't had one.

He kept his arm around her as they jostled onto the streetcar. He only let go to pull her onto his lap since seating was limited due to the crowd.

"This certainly worked out in your favor." She teased him as she wriggled her butt.

Killion's expression morphed into comedic longing. "Sunflower, I'd suggest you don't do that again unless you want me to scare these people with the impressive size of my cock."

A giggle slipped from her. This was a joke Killion would have made regardless, and it relieved her. But there was an undertone this time that she hadn't caught on to before, and she reveled in his unabashed attraction to her.

Knowing others found her fuckable was something she'd always been aware of. Reciprocating it was another thing, because she didn't. She knew Jonah would argue with that, thinking she fell for anyone who paid her attention, but it wasn't true. With Beckman, and now Killion, she treasured their admiration of her. She loved that she could inspire desire from them because it was what she wanted. From them.

But from anyone else? No way. Not unless Gage miraculously came to life. So at least she wasn't a total whore, lusting after two men instead of everyone. She wasn't going to count Gage for the obvious reason: She couldn't act on her attraction to him.

As the streetcar progressed up the hill toward Power and Light, they both ducked and looked out the windows to admire the passing scenery. She pointed out the direction of a jazz club she liked, restaurants and wine bars that had made an impression.

"I need to use the streetcar more often," she declared. "Jonah used to live at the end of the line, in River Market."

Their eyes met at the mention of Jonah. She could read the question in his eyes, whether or not she had told her best friend about her and Killion. No. They hadn't spoken since she'd returned from DC.

She shifted her gaze away.

Until there was something to tell, she justified, there was nothing to tell. And she wasn't in the mood to have another conversation about Elliott and Beckman's past, so yeah, she was ignoring him. A text here or there was enough to provide him with proof of life, and he'd been good enough to give her space.

The living room at Power and Light was decently populated. The open-air venue surrounded by bars and restaurants comprised the living room. Killion led her past the stage to the bar. "What can I get you?"

Lucy shook her head. "I'm good. I want to go up there."

A platform opposite the stage was situated at the back of the living room. A few people were up there, dancing or leaning against the narrow side bars, watching the band perform.

Without hesitation, he took her hand and led her to the platform. Still holding onto her, he morphed into the silly dance he'd been doing at the event center. His grin was self-effacing. She laughed and matched his crazy moves. The heat in his eyes as he studied her movements sparked a fire in her belly. And everywhere else.

As one unfamiliar song after another was played, it confirmed for Lucy that it wasn't the band she liked, or their music, but Gage's version of it.

But she had a good time dancing with Killion on the platform. He was an awful country line dancer, and she fell against him in hysterical fits of laughter more than once.

"They need to add something livelier to their set. Taylor Swift, maybe," she teased him.

"I don't think these people could handle my awesome moves if they drop that beat." He proceeded to move like he was shaking something off.

Lucy threw her head back and laughed. Killion was fun; she'd always known that, and he didn't lose his silly nature even as he courted her. Why had she thought he would change?

Oh yeah, taking her to a fancy restaurant that wasn't his style at all.

Here, though, he was in his element. He'd unbuttoned his dress shirt to expose his neck and tattoos. His sleeves had also been rolled up, displaying inked forearms.

Lucy bit her bottom lip as she bounced along with him to the music. He was sexy without trying, and she didn't think he was trying, but the swing of his hips and shimmy of his wide shoulders had her heart in palpitations and her pussy throbbing to a beat faster than the band. He moved fluidly, and she could imagine the smooth roll of those hips as he thrust into her.

The sweat on her forehead wasn't from dancing.

He grabbed her hand and pulled her in; she went willingly, hoping she didn't melt down from the contact. When their bodies collided, the suggestive movements setting her aflame, she realized they'd never danced together like this before. Why would they have? But it was still an oddity considering how many events they'd attended—worked—together.

Killion grinned down at her, his eyes so pretty, spiking her already elevated pulse. They moved together so well.

So… fucking… well…

But when he glanced at her lips, holding her closer, and lowered his head, her heart leaped for another reason entirely. Because she panicked.

"Stop, I can't. I'm..."

Chapter Twenty-Three

Killion

"I'm scared."

Killion lifted his hands and backed away. Her admission rocked him, and he was instantly as fearful as she. For different reasons, maybe, but it was a shared emotion. "I'm sorry."

Had he misread anything? Was he making assumptions he shouldn't have? He'd never have tried to move on her if he wasn't sure she was feeling it; that they were both feeling it.

But Lucy frowned, her expression telling him he was overreacting.

"I'm not afraid of you." She pushed her lips to the side, clearly reconsidering. "Well, in a sense, I am scared of you. I'm afraid of this entire situation."

He struggled to maintain a neutral expression even though his stomach bottomed out. He'd known it was too much to ask for, for her to reciprocate his feelings, to see him as anything other than a friend. Shoving his hands in his pockets to prevent himself from grabbing her to him and begging, he managed a nod.

"You are so bad at hiding your feelings." She called him out, a hint of intimate amusement in her voice. "It's one of the things I adore about you."

Adore. Ugh.

"You can't hide from me." That was accompanied by a mischievous grin.

He smiled back, braced for the blow. She was right, though. They were friends, and as such, had been more honest with one another than a newly dating couple might be. There hadn't been a need for the "getting to know one another" phase, no need to impress for fear of rejection.

Until now, when he wanted more than she apparently did. And the night had been going so well. He could have sworn she'd been sizing him up lustily. Obviously it was wishful on his part, and she'd only been having fun.

Rubbing the back of his neck, he assured her. "I'm not interested in hiding from you."

The situation, on the other hand, he'd prefer to run from.

"Look at me, Killion."

Her heart-shattering blue eyes implored him.

"I'm looking at you, sunflower."

She cocked her eyebrow at the nickname, but didn't berate him. Instead, she took a step back and held her arms out to her sides. "What would you see if you didn't know me?"

"If I didn't know you?" He ran his hand over his mouth in an attempt to stop from blurting out his answer; it came to him too quickly. But she nodded in response to his question. "The truth?" he mumbled through his fingers.

"Only the truth."

As she'd pointed out, she'd know if he lied. So, he answered despite the alarm bells in his head that it was the worst thing for him to do.

"A hot blond. The sweetness is a facade and you're a bitch. Maybe frigid, but more likely uses men to get what she wants."

Her expression fell.

Fuck!

"But I *do* know you, Lucy. None of that is you, at all. Not possible. Well"—he amended—"you are hot."

"Is that what you thought when you first met me?"

Killion frowned. Had that been his opinion? He'd definitely noticed how gorgeous she was—not a soul alive could argue her beauty—and how nice she appeared to be. He wasn't sure how his almost kissing her led her to ask these questions, but he'd already entered the water.

"I think I was more afraid that you would be a bitch—especially to a parolee—than thinking you were. Maybe that your involvement with the program, with us, was fulfilling a savior complex. I wanted you to like me, and I was afraid you wouldn't."

The latter was still valid.

Dropping her arms, she nodded, a look of resignation on her face. "I'm a stereotype, I know that."

He shook his head when she put up a hand to halt his denial.

"I am. Because of my appearance, people assume that I'm a flirt or a user—or both."

Killion ground his teeth together. She wasn't any of those things.

"So when I kiss you and I like it, I'll be playing into the stereotype. When I have sex with you, I'll be proving everyone right."

He strove to move past the promise of "when" and focus on her words. Her fear.

"Blonds haven't cornered the market on unique relationships. You aren't playing into anything. And call me selfish or stupid, but who gives a fuck what—" He cast his gaze around and landed on a couple two-stepping nearby. He pointed to them. "*They* think? Strangers?"

"It's not about people I'll never meet. I'm scared about the ones I could hurt most. That includes you."

"I swear to fuck, Lucy, I'm not saying this to pressure you or manipulate you, but he said okay. If he can't handle that, that's on him."

"But I don't want to lose him."

So he—the possibility of them—was to be the sacrifice her fear demanded. What did he expect? His dumb ass had come to the party way too late.

"I don't want you to do anything that hurts you. I'm sorry to have contributed to it."

"Killion," she implored.

"I know this is fast. But I know I can give you what you want. A commitment. Not now, not before you're ready, but I want it to be me. The man who makes you happy. Because you make me happy, sunflower."

Forcing aside his devastation, ignoring her stricken expression, he grinned. "I mean, it's probably for the best because you would have really liked sex with me."

"I don't want to lose you, either."

He waved a hand, dismissing her words. Walking over to the railing, he jibed, "Nah, not possible. Who else is brave enough to collect those gaudy lanterns for you from the hardware store?"

"Stop."

Leaning back, crossing his arms over his chest—he needed a barrier to protect his heart—he sobered. Lucy rarely dropped her tone in an authoritative manner, so he knew she was serious. Not that she hadn't been before, but this was another level.

"Those are the best words I've heard, I swear. And I want to be selfish enough to have you both. Despite everything I'm afraid of."

He hated to see her struggling. Did he hate the idea of Beckman in her life? Yeah, of course. Was he so put out that he was going to piss this chance away? Fuck no.

Opening his arms, he said with all the gravity he felt, "Have me. In whatever role you need. I'm already yours no matter what."

It was the truth. Even if she walked away tonight, Lucy would always be a woman he admired and respected. There wasn't anything stereotypical about the way she helped people—had helped him—her empathy for others was unmatched. She was genuine, even if she did sometimes lean into others' expectations of her as a shallow blond. She wasn't, not at all.

It was her empathy that had her obsessing over a dead man. It was her empathy that had given *him* hope in this fucking world, another cheerleader in his corner besides his mother. It was her empathy that was causing her distress.

Dropping his arms, he added, "Be selfish. Because I'm going to be. I want a chance. I want to see what we could be." Correcting himself, he added, "What we *will* be."

Call him crazy, or conceited, but he knew their bond of friendship was their greatest strength. But this was her choice. Now, he waited for her decision.

Chapter Twenty-Four

Lucy

The longer she stared at him, her brain crowding with the assumptions and judgments of others, the more his confidence waned. He dropped his gaze, appearing to be running as many thoughts through his head as she was running through hers. Or only one. He didn't think he was good enough.

He'd already told her his fears.

"Look at me, Killion."

His hazel eyes snapped up to hers. She saw him brace, his body tensing, ready for the blow. Walking up to him, she placed her hands on his folded arms. Pushing herself up onto her tiptoes, she said quietly, "Don't be weird."

His brows drew together in confusion, but she closed her eyes and leaned in, brushing her lips over his. She didn't know what jolted her first, or the most: the spark that raced through her at the contact or Killion's lightning-fast reaction. Both were electric.

Rational thought fled as Killion took over the kiss. She was pulled flush against him, his fingers gripping her hips, holding her solidly in place. It was sexier than being swept up in his arms. And damn, he was a fantastic kisser. His tongue played softly with hers, lips moving deftly over hers. His body moved languidly against hers, making subtle love to her, tongue and body moving in unison.

Everything inside her combusted in the best way.

Throwing her arms around his neck, she leaned in closer, needing more of him, needing to be closer, to feel him everywhere possible. She wrapped a leg around his, not caring if they were causing a scene. If her raised skirt was giving anyone a show, let them watch. In truth, their location, the music and people, faded away into a black void. It was only she and Killion on the raised platform. Her heart was beating out of her chest. Her pussy was wet and throbbing. The sensitive tips of her breasts were delighting in the contact.

Killion eased her back, and she made a verbal moan of protest. He chuckled, playfully nipping her bottom lip. "Look at you throwing yourself at me." He was breathing heavily, his eyes bright with wonder and mischief. He rested his forehead against hers, watching her. Cheeky words, but he knew; it was obvious. To him and to anyone who cared to watch.

"Uh-oh. I think I'm in trouble," she breathed. "Because I don't want to be your friend anymore."

He grinned, the smile lighting up his eyes. "I don't want to be your friend, either. There can only be one pretty friend. Otherwise it never works out."

Lucy's jaw dropped, but she huffed out a laugh. Pushing up on her tippy toes, nose to nose with him, she fired back, "Thank goodness you're the ugly one."

He snorted. "The way you were trying to climb me tells a different story. I'm a delight."

It was true. He was a delight, and she'd be more than happy to climb him again. Naked.

"Why did we wait so long to do this?" she asked.

Killion snaked his fingers into her hair, tilting and cradling her head. She wanted to swoon at his romantic gesture, at the Hollywood-level posture he was placing her in so he could continue his knee-buckling assault on her lips and heart.

"We have some catching up to do, sunflower."

CHAPTER TWENTY-FIVE

Beckman

"Hi. What are you doing?"

Beckman hit pause on the VCR, freezing an image of Vince and Charlotte Rork in mid-barbecue prep. Flames distorted their faces. The blurry freeze-frame image reminded him of Ellie as she'd stood in front of the fire burning rope. She had Charlotte's hypnotic silver eyes, after all.

He shook away his thoughts, dispelling the mental image. "Hey, pix. I'm watching home movies."

He shifted on the sofa, realizing he hadn't moved in a while, engrossed in reliving the past. At the sound of her voice, though, he was propelled into the present. His stomach knotted. The last time he'd heard from her, she'd hung up on him.

"Really? Like, Gage and everyone?"

"Yeah. Gage is fifteen in this one; we're at the lake."

Beckman hadn't shared these videos with her yet; it wasn't intentional, but she'd only been to DC once since they'd started seeing one another. Mostly, he took advantage of his time off to be in Kansas City. He also hadn't felt a need to connect with his old friends for a while. These days, however, he needed to immerse himself in the comfort the memories provided. Even if it was accompanied by grief and regret.

"Oh, I want to see. Let me FaceTime you."

And she hung up. He chuckled. He was smiling when she called back. She was in her apartment, sitting on her sofa; he recognized the pattern of the material. "Hi, gorgeous."

Her cheeks pinkened in pleasure, and her smile intensified in wattage. "Hey there, sexy man. I miss you."

"I miss you, too." He was trying to read her expression, to see beyond what she presented, bracing himself.

"I wish I could crawl through the phone and snuggle on your lap. I miss snuggling with you."

He missed it, too. "One plane ride."

She wrinkled her nose. "Stupid jobs."

"You love your job." He reminded her.

"I do." Leaning close to the phone, looking conspiratorial even though she was alone—he assumed—she said in a loud whisper, "I talked to Elliott."

That wasn't the news he'd expected, but he was eager to hear about it. Ellie hadn't mentioned anything, but they'd fallen out of the habit of doing anything more than checking in. Her phone calls to him for advice were a thing of the past.

"How did it go?"

Putting distance between herself and the phone again, she shrugged. "Okay. I mean, maybe I was making too much of it?"

Beckman narrowed his eyes, suspicious. "What do you mean?"

"I mean, in the grand scheme of things, and in life, it's not that big of a deal, right? I was shocked, sure. I was hurt that I was the only one who didn't know, but that's all done now. People need to be more understanding of things that don't affect them. I mean, if anyone thinks it was a taboo relationship, well then, they aren't taking into account that you aren't actually related. Right?"

He had the sense that she was trying to comfort herself for something else. As though negotiating with herself that if she was cool about his and Ellie's past despite the questionable taboo angle, then Ellie would be cool about her and a different, possibly taboo relationship.

Deciding to cut to the chase, he asked, "What happened with Killion?"

Her expression fell, her cheeks reddening.

Busted.

"Luce, I told you it was okay."

"We haven't done anything," she blurted out. "Just talked about, you know, logistics. Not about *that*, but of—"

"Stop." He interrupted her. "You don't owe me any explanations. I only ask because of your lightning-fast about-face over me and Ellie. One conversation with her is pretty fast to move on from. I know you're hurt."

"I'm just saying that I don't have a right to be. I wasn't here, I didn't know either of you."

"Tell me it doesn't hurt."

Everything he'd done to her had to be smarting. Keeping his and Ellie's past from her, not giving her the commitment she needed and deserved, and telling her it was okay to date Killion. Well, not specifically Killion, but he knew there was a repressed attraction between them. Curious as she might have been to explore that interest, it had to be a blow that he'd let her do that.

"What am I supposed to do about it? Quit my job? I don't want to do that. Stop talking to her forever? When her boyfriend is my best friend? I'd have to give Jonah up, too. So all I would end up doing is losing everyone. And that won't work because I'm pretty certain I'm to be his best man at their wedding."

"Wedding? Did I miss something?"

"No, I meant someday. I imagine it will happen, and I imagine myself as his best man." She batted her lashes at the camera.

"And?" he asked, prompting her.

She eyed him warily through the screen. "And what?"

"And maybe if you give her this pass, she'll give you one?"

Her blue eyes dropped away, guilt coloring her expression.

"It's okay, pix. I'm okay with it."

Liar. It was fucking killing him, but these were the consequences of his actions. "If you're happy, I'm happy."

That, at least, was true. His wish was that she wouldn't find happiness with Killion. Again: He'd done this to himself.

"I'm..." She pushed her lips to the side as she contemplated her words. "I'm weirded out. I don't know what I'm doing, I'm not sure what it means that you would be okay with this, and I'm curious about what might happen, but also afraid."

Lucy's unfiltered honesty was one of the things he loved most about her. Well, he'd take that any day over subterfuge.

"What do you mean you aren't sure what it means?"

"Do you really care? Am I holding on to you tighter than you want me to, so you're trying to push me away? I don't understand why any man would be okay with his girlfriend dating other men."

He leaned into the camera, trying as much as possible with the electronic gadget to stare into her eyes. "I care. I'm obsessed with you. I'm asking you to hold on tight. To me. I fucking pray you can keep holding on. The last thing I want to do is to push you into another man's arms, because you belong in mine. But I'm not where I need to be to give you what you deserve." His fear was that he would never be able to give it to her. Not because of her, but because of himself.

"Tell me not to date Killion."

"I won't do that." He put his finger in the screen. "You're curious. I suspect how he feels."

"What if I fall in love with him?"

She asked it like a challenge.

Here was the gut punch he'd been expecting.

But he answered as honestly as he could. "Then we figure it out. But I'm not letting you go, Lucy. I will fight for you."

"Then fight for me now."

"I am." He assured her quietly, knowing she didn't understand.

"I don't know what I'm doing," she repeated.

"Trust your instincts." He stared her down through the screen. "Trust how you feel."

She looked tortured, not because of the choice, but because she didn't want to hurt him. It's all he needed to see, to know, that she did indeed want to pursue whatever it was with Killion.

He suspected there had been more than a discussion, but that was hers to share when she felt safe enough to do so. And he wanted her to explore whatever she needed to with Killion. Not really, but yeah—really. He needed to know how Killion was going to fit into their lives. Would he be a burst of excitement and adrenaline—a walk on the wild side—to quickly burn out? Or would it go deeper?

His instincts told him it would be the latter.

Beckman wouldn't contemplate a scenario where he himself was no longer in the picture. That was an outcome he couldn't think about because he'd have no one to blame other than himself.

"You wouldn't be in this position if I hadn't placed you there. I also think Killion would have remained unrequited in his feelings if I hadn't given him this opening. But here it is, both of you are admitting to an attraction. See where it takes you."

Her stare burned through the screen. "Even if it takes me away from you?"

"Will it?"

Her chin trembled and her eyes watered. She shook her head. "I don't want it to."

The declaration eased the knot in his stomach, the one that jacked his adrenaline with anxiety over losing someone he cared about. He should name the sensation the Rork reflex.

"Then it won't." Wagging his eyebrows, he teased, "It doesn't have to be one or the other, you know."

Her watery eyes widened, but it wasn't with shock over the proposition, but that he had discovered something about her—she'd had the same thought. "That's very progressive of you."

He laughed, although his heart lurched in dread at the thought. "Look at me. I'm proof an old dog can be taught new tricks."

These weren't tricks he wanted to learn, but he'd do what he had to do.

Except commit. Jackass. Literally something that simple. Grab her up, make her his wife, have babies. A family. He could have a family with her tomorrow. Except now, he'd given her the space to admit to herself she needed and wanted more.

What was the saying? If you set something free...

She sniffed, then wiped her nose, returning a small smile.

"But some old tricks, this dog can't give up." Shifting on the sofa, he flipped the camera on the phone so she could view the television. "VHS."

Her laugh filled the room. Apropos of her nickname, the sound sprinkled magic and happiness. "That's so cute. So vintage! It still works?"

"Of course it still works." He reached for the remote and hit play.

They watched, and he narrated the moments of his life, answering her questions. His attention, however, was no longer focused on the past.

Chapter Twenty-Six

Lucy

Being apart from Beckman sucked. That feeling wasn't new, but every day away from him made their long-distance relationship harder.

Dating Killion wasn't intended to be a replacement, a filler for her absent boyfriend, nor was he. Despite her disappointment over the physical distance from Becks, their new ritual of watching his home movies was something she loved. They'd perfected it so he streamed on his phone and she watched on her computer. She'd eat popcorn, curled up on the sofa, and watch his, Gage's, and Elliott's lives pass before her eyes.

Of course she recognized Gage and Elliott's parents. It was still jarring to see the difference in their ages. When Beckman talked about the older Rorks, Lucy imagined them as his contemporaries, but they were at least fifteen years his senior. When Becks had pulled a pregnant Charlotte from the car the day they'd met, she'd been thirty-six to his twenty-two.

Watching the videos, Lucy was struck by how in the middle he was. In fact, he was closer to Gage's age than to Charlotte's. She'd watch how he'd play around with Gage like a kid, then stand next to Vince at a game or barbecue grill like an adult.

Other women started to come in and out of their recorded memories. Beckman's ex-wives. He'd identified them as they made appearances: Diane, his first wife, who pretended to be someone she wasn't and turned out to be an absolute wretched bitch (okay, Lucy may have expanded on Beckman's description). But he informed her that the woman had had an unhealthy obsession with Elliott. So much so, it concerned both Vince and Charlotte. Supporting his words, every appearance the rough-voiced brunette made on the screen, she was holding a toddler-aged Elliott on her hip like she was her own.

Becks also shared that when Elliott was three years old, she'd gone missing from a petting zoo. He admitted the first person he'd suspected was Diane.

"Oh, wow," Lucy breathed out, eyes wide. "I imagine it was scary to have a toddler disappear like that."

Considering Elliott was fine, she didn't press for the story. Kids had a way of wandering off and terrifying their parents, after all. Besides, Beckman pressed the fast-forward option, shooting past his first ex.

When creepy Diane disappeared from the timeline, she was replaced with Carmen, then Becca (he mentioned she liked the name Becca Beckman more than she liked *being* Mrs. Beckman), and eventually Abby. Lucy realized Becks didn't have a type: Diane wasn't striking in appearance or mannerism and rarely smiled; Carmen was the opposite of her predecessor. Deliciously curvy, she was quick with a smile and a wave to the camera. She was the most affectionate with Beckman on-camera, hugging and mugging with kissy faces. Becca was pretty but appeared reserved in the movies; shy, maybe. Abby was dark featured and sophisticated—definitely the most confident and self-possessed of Beckman's exes. Her eyes screamed intelligence, and her demeanor appeared calm. She was also his favorite ex, he admitted.

Well, she couldn't have an opinion on that because Jonah and his ex-wife remained good friends. And Christy was one of her best friends. Even Elliott was on board with the relationship, and they'd gone camping together in Oregon more than once.

As much as she loved these nights with Becks, it was bittersweet. It drove home the distance and enhanced her loneliness for him. She wanted to be with him, cuddled up in the comfort and safety of his arms. She wanted to feel his warmth, be caressed by his hands, to watch him grin as he played with and twisted her nipples until she convulsed in pleasure from a tit-gasm.

They ventured into phone sex. She loved watching him masturbate for her, to her, as she did the same. His hand moving furiously over his cock made her mouth water. It was her fuel as she finger fucked herself, disappointment flooding her after she'd float down from her high because he hadn't been the one to make her come. It wasn't his fingers inside her, his hands, his mouth, or his body on hers.

She wanted him here, or to be there, to feel him. Her need and desire for Beckman hadn't waned because of Killion, nor would it. Her romantic relationship with Killion was new, but it felt as right and comfortable as her relationship with Beckman. Was that weird? To be certain about a man she'd only kissed?

And shouldn't she feel more torn between the two men? What did it mean that she could find joy being with another man? That she was looking forward to the moment she would get to experience what she and Killion were like together, sooner rather than later—she was hoping for sooner. How he'd touch her, move against and within her.

She loved Beckman; she was certain of that. As surprising as it was, she was falling for Killion, too. How could that be possible, loving two men at the same time? Was something wrong with her that she wanted to bang two men? That she loved her time spent with each one, and didn't make comparisons? They both were amazing, and even though she had yet to be intimate with Killion, she didn't want to give one up. Did she have to? Traditional norms said she couldn't have both, but that was an archaic mindset. Right?

That she was trying to justify it for herself meant there was something about the arrangement that made her uneasy. It wasn't either of the men. They were both wonderful. So it had to be herself. Whether she was with Becks or Killion, she was cherished. She could disappear from the world with either man, be it cocooned in the safety and intimacy that Beckman provided, or the excitement, comfort, and familiarity that Killion did.

No, her discomfort came from something more superficial: how others would perceive her. Or more to the point, Jonah. What would Jonah think? Or Elliott.

Because she wasn't going to obsess over what some random person thought of her for being with two men; a lesson from Killion. But those two? Their disapproval would devastate her. Not that they could force her to make a choice.

Any ultimatum on their part, however, would lead to a rift. Ultimately, that was what she was afraid of: her world being torn apart because she'd found love with two men.

Beckman had been an instant infatuation. She'd known immediately he was the man for her. Beyond his handsome features and crystal-clear blue eyes was someone who needed her. He needed her to have faith in him, to give him time to prove to her that the waiting would be worth it. His hesitation, although hurtful originally—it still stung—meant he was licking wounds, but he was trying to better himself for her. And she wanted to prove that she could remain constant for him. Because she would.

Her relationship with Killion had developed over time, of course. Their new relationship was one that she hadn't known she was missing because they were friends first. But that lent to a deeper level of trust and understanding.

So yeah, her desires could bring about destruction to everyone involved and on the periphery. And Lucy didn't want anyone hurt.

Herself most of all.

Chapter Twenty-Seven

Lucy

Easy Street Events had a state-of-the-art kitchen. Gage had brought in all the top-of-the-line equipment. Lucy had once pointed out that cooking shows with real chefs could be filmed here.

Sadly, it was underused, and she swore only she appreciated it. Whenever she booked an event with caterers, she tried to convince them to meal prep in the kitchen. Sometimes she got her way, like this evening's event.

Not only was the kitchen used, but the caterers left a mess. That wasn't typical. Every other caterer had been professional and left the place as clean as they found it.

The mess meant an additional charge. Because she and Killion had to clean it up at two AM.

"Fuck my life," she moaned, looking around the space. "It looks like they had a food fight. This is going to take forever to clean up."

She could book professional cleaners, but they wouldn't come in the middle of the night, and she wasn't leaving food out. Mice were already a problem in the ceiling, eating wires. Leaving food out was an invitation for a deeper invasion no one wanted.

Killion stood next to her as they surveyed the damage.

"Tell me they're on a ban list or something now."

Lucy nodded. Definitely.

He nudged her arm. "You go home. Get some sleep. I can take care of this."

"No way. I will leave no man behind."

Realizing the double meaning behind her words, she glanced askance at him. He must have realized it, too, because his shoulders were shaking with quiet mirth.

"Good grief." Moving farther into the disaster area, she said, "Let's get started."

They dove in. There was no helping it, really. Without the need to communicate with words, they instinctively moved around one another, taking cues from the other. They worked together seamlessly.

Taking a small break from scrubbing caked flour off the floor, she sat back on her heels and watched Killion. He moved aside the refrigerator as though it wasn't a behemoth of an appliance. At some point, he had switched on the sound system—low enough not to wake Jonah and Elliott—and he was bobbing his head to the beat. Sweeping to the beat, too, but she doubted he noticed.

He had more energy than she did. Or maybe he was pushing himself the same way she felt like she was pushing herself, racing toward a stopping point.

This felt familiar and comfortable—physical depletion aside—and she realized that she and Killion had always worked well together. In sync, sometimes wordlessly. Perhaps that was why it was easy to move from friendship into something more. She still needed a reason, a justification, for opening her eyes to his magnetism.

The most outlandish thought was that the possibility of them was thanks to Beckman. It wasn't a credit he wanted assigned to him, she was certain, but he'd made her and Killion possible. Or rather, she was free to open her eyes, mind, and heart to Killion.

She smiled as she continued watching him. Like when he kissed her, his entire body was in motion; fluid, encompassing, sexy. Full of gusto.

Tilting her head, she wondered if that translated to everything he did. When they had sex, would every part of her be delighted by the movements of every part of him? Would she be surrounded by his touch?

Killion stepped away from the refrigerator, glancing her way with a tired smile. He startled, doing a double take. His tired smile turned mischievous.

Running his hand down his chest, he teased her. "Sunflower, you're looking at me like the snack I am."

Her grin matched his. He was definitely a snack, even tired and sweaty from the manual labor.

"You're making me blush," he said in a low tone.

The smolder in his eyes was in contrast to the comedic fanning of his face. Warmth spread through her from his expression. But when his fanning morphed into a beckoning one-finger gesture, her heart rate increased.

Standing, she sauntered toward him, the promise in his hungry expression dispelling her exhaustion.

When she was in front of him, inches away, he made a show of looking around. "So many useful countertops."

"Where have your thoughts taken you, Killion Murphy?" She raised her eyebrow, fighting to appear cooler than she felt.

But she was aware her nipples were poking against her tank top, evidence of what he could do to her with merely a suggestion. And that look in his eyes.

"My thoughts have placed you on every surface of this kitchen, where I spread you like creamy peanut butter."

Lucy let out a surprised laugh, then snorted when she tried to rein it back in.

He tried, she could tell, as hard as she tried, before they both burst out laughing.

Reaching out, he grasped her by her nape and pulled her to him, the reverberations of his chuckle thrumming through her.

"Too fucking bad we just disinfected this place."

"There's a spot on the floor." She chuckled against the hard expanse of his chest, pointing in the general direction where she'd paused to ogle him.

He quickly spun her around, shocking her again, and grasped her hips, tugging her back to him.

"Look at how this place is sparkling."

Lucy looked around, for the first time that night seeing it as it should have been: clean and shiny. They'd worked hard, and it had paid off.

Speaking of hard, his erection pressed against her back. She stilled, her heart skipping a beat before it picked up a galloping pace of excitement and anticipation. The cadence echoed in her pussy.

"Keep it clean or dirty it up?"

"Cl-clean," she choked out.

Not for any other reason than her curiosity about how he would accomplish what she hoped he was promising, while not destroying their hard work. Although she wouldn't be upset if he did toss her onto a countertop and spread her wide open.

He dipped his head so his mouth was against her ear, and she shivered as his breath caressed her.

"Okay then. The kitchen stays clean while I get filthy."

Holy fudge monkeys.

Her surrender was immediate with those words. She was an anticipatory puddle.

Shifting his right hand from her hip, he slipped it under the hem of her shirt, seeking skin. The ghosting of his fingers along the flesh of her tummy pulled a moan from her. As his hand traveled up to caress the tender skin beneath her breast, his other hand moved up to caress her neck, angling her head back against his shoulder.

She closed her eyes, savoring the sensations; her lips parted with her small pants.

He greedily claimed her lips, hot and demanding.

Lucy's knees gave way. She grasped onto his arms, counting on him to hold her up. Her hands were shaking, her body trembling. She opened her mouth beneath his, allowing his urgent plunder. She didn't know what to feel first: his mouth, his tongue, his body pressing hard against her.

His mouth moved from her lips to her jawline, to beneath her ear. She was putty in his arms. And selfish, giving little in return as she waited for the next sensation from him that would exalt her senses even more.

When his seeking fingers caressed the underside of her breast, she moaned again, eager for his exploration to reach a bit higher to her needy nipples.

But the hand at her breast slipped, forcefully yet slowly running the length of her taut stomach and abdomen. Her breath caught; she almost came with expectation.

Killion slipped his hand beneath the band of her pants, dancing his fingers teasingly above the place she needed him to finger. She raised on her tippy toes to meet him there, but he outmaneuvered her.

"Killion!" She'd meant it as a demand, but her voice sounded desperate. Appropriately so.

"Do you want my fingers in your pussy, sunflower?"

"Yes. Fingers, cock, mouth—something!"

He chuckled, but he also obliged her, dipping his fingers down, the easy slide making him groan. "Oh, fuck yes."

Thrusting against his fingers, she agreed. Oh, fuck yes!

"You said something about my mouth?" he asked.

"I said—"

She choked off her words when he removed his hand, only to grab hers. Leaning forward, he braced her palms on the stainless steel countertop. The cool surface was welcome to her heated body.

"No smudges. Keep your hands there. We're keeping it clean, right?"

Lucy turned her head to berate him for the slightly mocking intonation, but he was faster. Dropping down behind her, he took her pants with him. She gasped as the cool air hit her ass, her pussy.

Again, the chill was welcome.

But it didn't last long.

He took advantage of her vulnerable stance. Without preamble, his tongue was licking her. Hungrily, like he'd be pulled away before he was sated. The ravenous attack on her cunt made her squeak.

He paused. She felt his breath on her ass.

"Did you just squeak?"

Breathless, she nodded, not knowing if he could see the gesture or not. Her hair spilled over her shoulders, dangling down toward the clean floor.

"Fuck yeah," came his pleased response.

Followed by a welcome and aggressive flick of his tongue against her clit. Dancing on her tippy toes again, she giggled.

Again, she felt him lean back. "And a giggle?"

"It tickles." She defended herself.

"Oh, I'm not complaining."

He grasped her around her thighs, tugging her farther back and spreading her more, elongating her body as she fought to maintain her hold on the steel surface.

"I love your giggle. It will be my life's goal to make you giggle at least once a day."

Lucy laughed, then choked on the sound when he resumed his task.

Her brain shut down—forced down—as pleasure consumed her. He licked, sucked, flicked, and groaned. Her body quaked, and stars danced behind her eyelids. The torment of being in a precarious stance heightened the sensations, the excitement. Would he be able to make her come before she lost her balance and face-planted?

She rode his face as much as her position allowed, and he found and teased her into orgasm.

Throwing her head back and then forward again, she chanted, "There, there, there."

His pressure and cadence remained constant, bless him, and her muscles locked as she came. Her fingernails screeched against the countertop, echoing her broken shrieks. He didn't stop as she fell apart, shaking violently. No, he continued to flick and lick, extending her orgasm.

"Killion," she gasped out, feeling her strength fail, her head swimming.

"I've got you."

And he did. As her body continued to pulse with pleasure, he stood, pulling her pants up as he did so. Then she was swept into his arms.

"No." She protested.

"No?"

"Your turn," she panted. Although she wasn't sure where she'd find the strength, she would rally for him. And she really wanted to see his cock.

"This isn't a card game." He was moving, carrying her from the kitchen. "You're staying here, with me. I'm not letting you drive home in the wee hours with no sleep. You're exhausted."

It was true. She was beyond exhausted. And deeply sated.

"What will Jonah and Elliott say?" she asked hesitantly, peering up at him.

Unspoken was that she didn't want them to find out about her and Killion. Not yet. What if this blew up in her face—which it probably would? There was no sense in adding fuel to the fire.

Killion studied her face, a resigned understanding taking over his features, before he ducked his head. The lights turned off, so she couldn't further study him.

"I don't think they'd argue that you shouldn't be driving tired."

She was in so much trouble with this man.

And there was something else about tonight she needed to remember. But as Killion lay next to her in bed, the sense of urgency slipped away.

Chapter Twenty-Eight

Beckman

Sick. That's how he'd felt after he ended his call with Lucy. He'd reassured her everything was fine. He was fine. Peachy keen. He'd encouraged this, remember?

"It's okay, pixie."

He'd said it on repeat. She wasn't beating herself up—no reason to. She was more concerned about him after she relayed the news that she and Killion had taken the relationship to the next level.

No dipping their toes in, no taking it slowly. Of course, why would they? They'd known each other a long time. Killion's feelings had been there the entire time, forced to be put on hold. Hers, Beckman now suspected, had also been repressed.

Their teasing and chemistry were too palpable for there not to have been feelings, whether or not she'd wanted to face it. Or had even recognized it.

He did appreciate that she was honest with him. It meant she was including him, in a sense. No sneaking around. She laid it out on the table so the three of them could navigate this development together.

Standing on his balcony, he shook out a cigarette. He stared at the city, letting the activity and sounds ground him.

It didn't keep his thoughts from racing and warring.

He was to blame.

He was the pissant who'd faltered when Lucy had needed him. He'd been arrogant. And short sighted.

He knew there was something between Killion and Lucy. He'd never wanted to be more wrong than he was now. Because *now* he was having conversations with Lucy about the three of them, how they would—all three—figure this out together.

He wasn't walking away.

She wasn't walking away.

He knew Killion wouldn't.

Lighting his smoke, he narrowed his eyes. His anxiety spiked despite the nicotine racing through his bloodstream.

It was too late now. The train had left the station and was barreling... Where, exactly? Off the rails or to a safe harbor?

Chapter Twenty-Nine

Killion

Lucy's delighted squeal echoed through his small room as he simultaneously thrust and spun, taking their sweaty and naked bodies from his dresser, where she'd been perched, to his bed. Her back barely hit the mattress before he was wildly thrusting into her again.

Her drenched yellow hair stuck to her face and neck, driving Killion even wilder. Lucy disheveled was an unusual sight, but when he'd been the cause of her flush and glazed look, she'd never looked more beautiful. He felt like a beast with her, driving roughly into her like he'd never get the chance again. She thrashed and arched beneath him, her legs wrapped firmly around his hips, panting encouragement.

Being inside her was better than he'd ever imagined, and he never took a second of having her in his arms for granted. Tomorrow, she might choose. So he was going to immerse himself in her company and her body with gusto.

Moans, pants, and begging filled the space. He sucked and pinched her nipples, the sensitivity in her peaks thrilling him as much as her. Before she came on his cock, she tensed and shivered from the breast play.

"Tit-gasm," she gasped in her frozen arch. "Tit—oh god, Killion!"

His name on her lips, her pussy clenching tighter around his cock, almost made him come. He clenched his teeth to ward off the orgasm, watching her, reveling in her flushed cheeks. But when she bucked against him again, violently riding him from beneath, he lost it. Gripping her to him, he jerked his hips furiously until his brain was obliterated, and he groaned and tensed against her.

She rode him throughout his orgasm, her legs wrapped around his hips, determined to get hers a second time—this time from the pleasure he brought her pussy. Ignoring the heightened sensitivity in his cock—the condom helped—he kept fucking her. It only took a couple of thrusts before she once again stiffened beneath him, breath halted as she came hard.

He slipped out of her when she collapsed back against the bed, her body going lax. With her eyes closed, he watched her float in the aftermath. The beat of her pulse in her neck indicated her heightened state. He tried not to disturb her state of bliss when he removed the condom.

When he settled beside her, though, content to hold her, she turned away. But it was only to snuggle back in his arms, wrapping herself up with him by drawing his arms around her. He obliged by holding on tight and wrapping his leg around hers. Her hum of contentment had the same calming effect as a cat's purr.

"But."

He hummed questioningly, burying his face in her hair at her nape. He didn't remember saying or asking anything, but it was possible he'd been babbling in his post-fuck euphoria.

Shifting, she wrangled a leg out from under his and the sheet. "Remember, I need one leg out of the covers or I'll overheat."

"Yeah, you will," came his cheeky reply.

She giggled, and his cock jumped against her ass.

He fucking loved her giggle. He loved it more now, knowing he could elicit a giggle when he sucked her clit. It was a guarantee that he'd be spending more time with his head between her legs; he'd told her as much.

Now properly situated with one of her legs peeking out from the covers, they settled back into quiet contentment. Holding her was surreal, a delight he'd never get over. He wanted to squeeze her, cleave her to him forever. The burst of emotion he experienced, fully aware this moment might never have happened, overwhelmed him.

"Hmmm." The sound from her was contemplative.

"What?" he asked, breathing in the scent of her sweat mingled with perfume. It was the best fucking smell, especially because he was the one to make her sweat.

"We fit perfectly." Her statement was one of wonder, consideration.

He smiled into her hair. It was true, she nestled perfectly in his arms. He held her tighter, giving in to his temptation to squeeze. "We do."

"It's weird."

He huffed out a laugh, her hair shifting with his breath. "Why would that be weird?"

She was slow to answer, but the wonderment was still in her voice. "Because I fit perfectly with Beckman, too."

Kick. In. The. Balls.

Here she was, wrapped in his arms, their bodies warm and naked after they'd fucked each other in a mind-expanding way, and she brought up the other guy.

"You'd think one or the other would be a bit off. But I fit perfectly with you both." She twisted slightly to smile up at him. "It's like a sign."

He smiled back at her despite his balls aching from the imaginary kick—or his heart recovering from the blow. "A sign of what?"

Returning to her original position, snuggling deeper into his embrace, she answered, "That you're both perfect for me."

He nodded. Lucy needed reassurance that having a relationship with—fucking—both of them wasn't wrong. "That's because you're perfect."

She snorted a laugh.

On that note, he patted her hip.

"As much as I'm enjoying this moment, and would happily say this evening can be damned so I can stay here with you, we need to get ready."

Lucy had arranged a fundraiser for the church, and guests would be arriving shortly. Yeah, he was amused that they were banging right before a church function.

Groaning, she rolled over for another snuggle. "It's times like these I wish I could call in sick."

Killion grinned. It was saying something when Lucy would prefer to remain in his arms over doing a job she loved and was excellent at. "I'll make it up to you."

"I'll hold you to that."

Chapter Thirty

Lucy

The event center was jam-packed. The donation corner was piled high. Furniture, clothes, toys, diapers, kitchenware, and so on. She'd had the idea to host a fundraiser to gather items for the families the church supported, which included refugees getting started in a new land and home, as well as those who needed a hand up during hard times. For those without physical donations, Lucy and Killion were both busy with their phone apps, swiping credit cards.

Local wineries and eateries donated their food and time, so this was one of the rare events that Killion wasn't working at the bar. The band outside provided the tunes. The fundraiser was also a great way to promote the event center. She wasn't going to fool herself about that.

As successful as the event was, and profitable as far as donations, there was another reason for the zing in the air. He was why she felt like she was walking on clouds. Every movement reminded her of the afternoon with Killion. But knowing he was in this room, working alongside her—as he'd done for a year—the atmosphere was sprinkled with something extra magical tonight.

When she'd sneak peeks at him, he was usually staring back, a delighted smile on his face. She walked taller, knowing the object of her affection was watching her as closely as she watched him. The stolen glances energized her. Memories of the physicality of their sex, and the shower sex afterward, replayed in her head.

Were they obvious? Probably not. There were too many other distractions to occupy people's attention. And there was no way she and Killion—or she and Beckman, for that matter—had the same level of explosive chemistry that Elliott and Jonah did when they were together.

She was both envious of that and grateful. Envious because those two were dynamite together, and grateful because it meant these moments with Killion were only theirs for now, and not fast-flowing lava that caught everyone up in the heat.

Thinking of Elliott conjured her. Lucy noticed her enter the space from the patio, her sleek panther-like movements gaining the attention of many. Elliott's self-possessed dark beauty was hard to miss. And though she was admired based on her appearance alone, no one was of interest to her except Jonah, even when he wasn't present. Lucy doubted she noticed how awestruck people were around her.

Lucy included.

She was dressed in a simple linen pant suit—an outfit suited for the occasion, as Elliott was most comfortable in workout gear—with her hair up in a ponytail. Casting her gaze around the room, she looked impressed by the number of donations. Then she swung her attention until it landed on Lucy. She smiled.

It was silly to be giddy. But there it was. Seeking Elliott's approval and gaining it always made her feel warm and tingly. If Elliott ever reached out and patted her on the head, Lucy was afraid she'd drop to the ground for a belly rub. That's how much she reveled in the woman's good opinion. If she couldn't be a badass herself, then having the approval of a badass was a close second.

Elliott headed toward the bar. Lucy walked that way as well. It was a habit they'd developed, that some time during any type of function, she, Elliott, Killion, and Jonah, when he was in attendance, all ended up at the bar.

Tonight, however, one of the winery's ambassadors was handing out offerings.

Elliott accepted a glass of red wine and turned to watch her approach. Despite the smile on the woman's face, she could feel Elliott assessing her, trying to read her, to ensure all was still okay between them.

There was a comfort to that, although Lucy knew Elliott valued their friendship. If she hadn't, she wouldn't have cared about Lucy's reaction to learning about her and Beckman. But the searching look on her face told Lucy that it was still a concern.

Lucy only hoped Elliott couldn't read that she had a secret of her own, one that she wasn't ready to share. Beckman would back her, she knew that, as would Killion. But now wasn't the time to share anything considering Lucy herself didn't know the outcome of the unusual arrangement. She needed to have that figured out before she tried to take on the world.

"I didn't think we'd see you today."

Although Elliott made appearances at most events when she was in town, church functions weren't her thing. She knew a few of the people, having attended sporadic church events, including the annual float trip, but those attendances were few and far between.

Elliott reached up to smooth down her already-smooth black hair, bruises still displayed on her wrist. Or were these new ones?

Gah, Jonah. There really were things she didn't want or need to know about him.

Thankfully he wasn't in attendance tonight despite being the assistant pastor of the congregation. Lucy could go unsinged.

"I like this winery." She held up her glass in a salute.

The woman behind the bar smiled at her comment. "We like that you like it." She shifted her attention to Lucy. "Red or white?"

Lucy shook her head. "I'm working. But if you leave a little bit of red at the end, I'll gladly consume it then."

"You got it." The woman promised her.

"Haha, I rhymed."

Elliott chuckled.

"Hey, boss." Killion greeted as he joined them. Tipping his chin to the woman, he requested, "May I get some water?"

His request was quickly answered, and a small water bottle was handed to him.

"Thanks." He accepted it and returned his attention to them.

Lucy wrinkled her nose in faux contemplation. "Why don't you ever call *me* boss?"

He grinned, heat in his eyes that thankfully Elliott couldn't see since she was standing next to him. "Maybe one day you'll give me reason to."

Her eyes widened at the suggestive response.

"Be careful how you talk to her." Elliott teased him, clearly having missed the innuendo. "One day she's going to be my Aunt Lucy."

Killion's amusement disappeared instantly. Her words couldn't have affected his good humor more if she'd slapped him. Smile gone, his attention shifted from Elliott to her, his expression one of expectation.

What he expected her to say, she didn't know. With a small smile and shake of her head, she offered, "Well, nothing's been announced."

Wrong answer. Killion turned and walked away.

"I was joking," Elliott said, her tone concerned, as they watched Killion weave through the people and disappear out the side doors. "That was an odd reaction." She looked at Lucy.

Lucy painted a bright smile on. "He's not a fan of Becks."

Understatement.

Elliott sighed, dropping her gaze to the ground. "No one is." And she was bothered by that—had been bothered by that.

"I am."

That earned her a smile. And like Pavlov's dog, she once again experienced giddiness. But her heart was walking out the back door, hurt.

Chapter Thirty-One

Killion

Lucy made her way to where he stood on the periphery, beyond the band and the dancers. She stopped a couple of times to bounce along to the music, grinning at her friends and fellow congregants. It wouldn't be like Lucy to ignore them. Nor a thankful hostess thing to do.

She headed to him, though, once she danced her way free. Her crystalline eyes silently begged him in apology and for understanding. As sincere as she looked, he was inclined to say fuck it and throw in the towel. Had it only been three hours since he was inside her? Less than three hours, then, to take him from giddy to devastated.

Of course, it had also been three hours ago that she'd compared being in his arms to being in Beckman's.

And he couldn't be fucking wounded or mad about that because he was the one who took his shot too late. He was the third wheel fighting for her affection.

Steps away, she pleaded with him. "Killion."

He took another drag of his cigarette. This had been the second smoke of the day. He knew she didn't like the habit—although it was one he shared with Beckman—so he was trying to quit. But he'd needed this one. The blow from Elliott had come unexpectedly, even if she didn't know she was landing a punch.

"It was just..."

"It's what she expects to happen."

Lucy rolled her eyes. "I have no idea where she got that from, considering Beckman's cold feet for a committed *relationship*. How did she leap to marriage?" She snorted.

"He's the legitimate partner, though."

She tilted her head, the apology back in her eyes.

"I feel like a dirty little secret. I know that's not intentional, and I crashed this party of yours and Beckman's, but it hurts and it's frustrating that I can't say you're mine."

"You didn't crash anything. It's not like you swooped in, knocked me over the head, and carried me off. You saw an opportunity and took it. And I took it, too." She stepped toward him. "We both wanted it. Probably since the beginning but circumstances..."

She knew his circumstances. He'd pointed out his shortcomings before, and he wasn't going to revisit them.

"I'm not sorry. I'm only sorry this is hurting you."

Killion nodded, accepting that she was sorry. He knew she meant it.

"What can I do?"

He needed to feel like this was real, that he wasn't a dangerous toy she was amusing herself with. He wanted *acknowledgment* of what they meant to one another—what he hoped he meant to her.

On the other hand, he knew she couldn't confide in any of her friends, especially Christy, considering she was Jonah's ex, and most of her other friends went to church with them. So no openness would occur there.

It would happen eventually, but not today. That was his hope, that one day soon he could take her hand in public, and this secret would be no more.

But there was one person…

“Can we tell my mom?”

Chapter Thirty-Two

Lucy

Lucy had met Rachel Murphy so many times that she'd lost count. But today was different. Before, she'd met Rachel as Killion's church sponsor and then as his boss. This time it would be as his girlfriend. And she was nervous. Did that make sense?

The horrible, intrusive thought she had while waiting outside the woman's door was that she was glad she only had to do this once because Beckman's parents were dead.

"I'm absolutely wretched," she mumbled to herself.

Her own parents didn't count. They'd always seen her the way they wanted to, and she obliged because it made them happy. She guessed. Why else expect so little of her and therefore praise her when she managed to accomplish... Well, anything. They loved her, she knew that, but sometimes parents unintentionally overlooked the potential of their children.

She struggled to bypass and mask her insecurities even as she morphed into the persona expected of her. And she was so good at it that few people saw beyond the act she'd perfected as a child. It led her to doubt herself—agree even—wondering if she was that naive, that helpless.

Despite being a successful single woman.

Most focused on the obvious: single.

To be fair, she did as well. But she wanted love. Her string of failed relationships was proof that although she wanted a crazy mad love affair, she wasn't willing to compromise or settle.

Still, she was afraid she wouldn't measure up. That Rachel would be disappointed that her son had fallen for someone like her.

Then there was the fact that she already had a secret. How was she going to explain that she had two boyfriends? Would it come up? Or would her guilty conscience—regardless of the assurances from both men—trip her up?

No, it wouldn't come up. This was for Killion. When he'd asked, it had surprised her, but it was a good surprise. She knew how much his mom meant to him, so introducing her as his girlfriend meant this was as real to him as it was to her. Even if she wasn't ready to go public yet with having two boyfriends.

Jesus. Two boyfriends. What the hell?

The memory slammed into her of that day with Jonah at the fountain. She'd asked for all the love. She'd thrown in a dime to double her luck. The universe was laughing its ass off at her because it definitely doubled her wish. There was no way she could have foreseen this outcome. And she wasn't complaining. She was reeling.

"Lucy."

She spun around, her yellow dress flaring slightly around her thighs as she did so. "Yes?"

Killion was in the doorway of Rachel's room. "You look like you were caught with your hand in the cookie jar."

He was smiling, his eagerness written all over his gorgeous face. Her heart tripped over itself seeing how pleased he was for this moment. This moment with *her*.

He jerked his head toward the room. "Come on in. She's dressed."

Another tumble of her heart. She loved and admired him for taking care of his mother. He never treated it like a burden, as some would. When Rachel needed him, he was there. She'd noted it before today, of course, and had commented on his devotion.

His response had been nonchalant. "But she's my mom."

Lucy approached him, taking his offered hand. His excitement was contagious, alleviating some of her anxiety.

Rachel sat in a small recliner by the window of her assisted living apartment. She wore a pink sweatsuit. Her brown hair was beginning to show signs of graying. She was only in her fifties, close to Beckman's age, Lucy realized with a shock. But the woman's age wasn't why she was in the facility. It was her health. Rachel had congestive heart failure and glaucoma. She needed the care to manage both.

"Lucy!" The woman held her hands out, her broad smile shifting the nasal cannula that delivered oxygen.

Moving forward to take her hands, Lucy returned the smile. She got close to the woman's face as Killion had taught her previously. "How are you doing today, Rachel?"

Upon Lucy's first introduction years before, she'd been instructed not to call the woman Mrs. Murphy.

"So much better hearing the news." The woman shot a proud glance in her son's direction.

Killion moved to sit on the windowsill. There were other options, but it was closest to his mom. He gave Lucy a bashful smile. "I sort of told her already."

Lucy settled on the oversized ottoman. "I hope you approve." And she hoped that approval would remain when his mom found out her secret.

Their secret.

"Oh, Lucy." Rachel squeezed her hands. "When you entered my son's life, good things started to happen for him. I'm happy for you both. Killion has had his eye on you for a while."

"Mom!"

Lucy laughed at Killion's shocked tone that his mother had called him out.

"You thought I didn't know? My eyesight might be shit, but my intuition is spot on. You talk about this woman constantly." Returning her attention to Lucy, she added, "I'm glad you two finally found your way to one another."

Lucy looked over at Killion. His smile remained in place, but now it seemed forced. Or maybe she was projecting, but she didn't think so. Because another man was in the room. One she wouldn't give up. Not that she would give up Killion, either.

So she answered Rachel. "Me, too."

For two weeks, she and Killion were the epitome of the cliché sneaking around. It bothered Killion—of course it did—but she wasn't ready to declare anything yet. What if something didn't work out? What if she got bored with one of them—not likely, but it was possible. What if Beckman cut her loose completely? So many what-ifs, so many things could happen.

Announcing to the world she was romantically involved with two men could only lead to drama she wasn't prepared to handle. Beckman and Killion knew her truth, their truth. For now, that was enough for her to manage. Did she feel like a bitch keeping Killion under wraps? Yeah, but this was a new relationship. While she was trying to balance her relationship with Beckman. This was not a situation she'd ever thought she'd be in. Where were the rules for this? She didn't know what to do, so she bided her time.

For what, she didn't know. She was looking for a sign, she supposed.

And Killion seemed better after they'd told his mom.

Because Rachel was the only person who knew about them, she and Killion were in Warrensburg whenever they had free time. He could be open with her there. Public displays of affection, kissing and holding hands, and she loved every second of his openness.

They'd taken the train from Union Station to Warrensburg on one trip. They cuddled in coach class, probably annoying the other travelers. She didn't care. She reveled in his attention. And she was certain she was the envy of all to be snuggling up against a beautiful bald, tattooed man. If she'd been on the outside watching them, she would have been envious.

On the way home, they'd tucked into a back corner, and he'd grinned devilishly as he played with her nipples until she came undone. She'd had to turn her face into his chest as she convulsed in pleasure against him, tensing with the tit-gasm. She'd bit his shirt—and probably some underlying flesh—but she'd been aware of his satisfied chuckle.

Of course she also kept her phone dates with Beckman. She'd orgasmed more times in the past few weeks than ever before. It wasn't a bad problem to have. Her only complaint was that Beckman wasn't delivering those orgasms in person. But these two men were the living embodiment of everything a woman could ask for.

Living.

Gage was still a frequent visitor in her fantasies. The added bonus was that she hadn't met him, so she could mold him into the most perfect human she could imagine.

The problems, self-doubt and guilt, crept in when she was alone. So she made sure she wasn't. That's when it was handy to have an imaginary boyfriend, too.

But it all came crashing down. It was bound to, of course.

Having worked at Easy Street Events for a year, she knew about the cameras on the property. So did Killion. But in their giddy, lustful bliss that night, they forgot.

Belatedly, she remembered something tugging at her memory as Killion carried her out of the kitchen. But the concern had dissipated.

She was wrong to have let it slip away from her.

Chapter Thirty-Three

Killion

Waking up with Lucy in her apartment wouldn't get old. It was a treat to be here with her, surrounded by her and surrounding her. He didn't mind her weighted blanket that turned him into a furnace. It was probably why she'd gotten into the habit of sleeping with her leg out from under the covers.

It didn't matter. Nothing mattered when he was in her orbit.

He'd been her chauffeur last night, picking her up from the mechanic. She'd rolled her eyes at him as she'd approached his truck. Opening the door, she forestalled his words.

"I'm not trading it in! It's not its fault." She slid onto the bench.

Lucy's yellow car was in the shop more than out, but she was loyal to it. He admired her determination to love the unlovable because he knew her love and devotion extended beyond vehicles. In this case, however, she needed to move on.

"What is it this time?" he asked.

"It was hit once. It hasn't responded well."

The insurance company should have totaled it out when she was rear-ended last year, but they didn't. Of course, knowing Lucy, she would have duct-taped the thing together and kept going.

Loyal.

Killion raised a brow expectantly.

She wrinkled her nose. "Fuel pump."

"How long?"

"A couple of days. Thank you for picking me up."

He shifted into gear. "You never need to thank me."

He'd driven her home. And stayed. He looked forward to staying the next couple nights as well. They could keep her car for weeks and he'd be happy. It gave him a chance to revel in domestication with Lucy. It fueled his imagination.

She'd insisted on cooking dinner for him as a thank-you. He'd obliged, although he'd insisted it wasn't necessary.

"I want to cook for you," she replied, smiling. "I like cooking and I like you."

"I like you," he responded. He'd wrapped his arms around her as she stood at the range, stirring cabbage and bacon. She'd said it was her version of a Polish dish. And she was a good cook, too.

They'd eaten dinner, then he cleaned up. They'd watched television with bowls of ice cream. When he'd gone down on her, she'd screamed out laughing, fighting to get away.

"Cold, cold!"

But he'd warmed her up quickly. Licking her like she was his favorite flavor. Because she was.

This morning, he made himself a cup of coffee and prepared Lucy's tea. She grinned as he handed it to her, although he'd prepped her tea many times. She was appreciative of the smallest things, the simplest of kindnesses. He loved that about her.

Once they arrived back on the property, the bliss was shattered, and everything changed.

Elliott was waiting for them in the office. Her presence wasn't unusual, of course. She owned the place, and she managed the accounting. But today, she wasn't there for the numbers.

Leaning back against the desk, arms folded over her chest, she swept her furious gaze from him to Lucy. And held.

Killion had seen Elliott mad only once, directed at Beckman, so to have her gray eyes spear Lucy so coldly and angrily was an unexpected shock. She'd barely sliced him; the steel daggers of her fury had one direction.

As he turned his head to gauge Lucy's reaction when her hand gripped the back of his shirt, he noticed the computer monitor. The security feed.

Fuck.

There was no way they'd be able to convince her it wasn't what it looked like because it was exactly what it looked like. Why the hell hadn't he remembered to delete it? He knew the cameras were always on.

"You're cheating on Beckman." It was an accusation, not a question.

"No," Lucy squeaked out behind him, sounding like she'd taken a hit of helium.

Without looking, he knew she was terrified in the face of Elliott's accusation.

"No?" the other woman demanded, sweeping her hand to the monitor.

"Beckman knows," Killion said, shifting to block Lucy from Elliott's gaze. "He's known."

Silver eyes flashed back to him, assessing and confused. Not trusting. That felt like a blow, her looking at him with disbelief.

"Boss—" he started, but she straightened off the desk.

Attention on Lucy again, she said tightly, "He deserves better than this, than you. He deserves someone who loves him." She shot a look at Killion.

"Only him."

"I'm sorry," Lucy whispered.

Killion's jaw clenched in anger, not because Lucy said she was sorry—meaning sorry about him—but that Elliott scared her enough to force something from her she didn't mean. Because he knew she wasn't sorry.

Prowling forward, Elliott looked like a panther ready to attack, and he wrapped his arm backward and shuffled himself and Lucy out of her way. Keeping Lucy behind him. Did he think Elliott would become violent? No, hell no. But if he was able to provide any comfort to Lucy in this moment, he would.

Without saying another word, judgment heavy in the air, Elliott left the office.

"Oh shit," Lucy whispered.

He turned, and she sagged against him.

"I need to call Beckman."

Chapter Thirty-Four

Beckman

"Becks!"

Lucy's tearful and terrified voice jarred him. He didn't know what was happening, but a crippling sensation of impotence overwhelmed him, knowing he couldn't be by her side to help her, save her, protect her.

"What's wrong?"

"Elliott knows. She's pissed."

"Knows...?"

"About Killion."

He grimaced. For Ellie to be pissed, she had to have seen or heard something more compromising than her employees out to dinner.

"How did she find out?"

Lucy's hesitation was a confession. Not that she needed to confess; he was the orchestrator of this fiasco.

"Pix, tell me. It's okay."

In a quiet voice, she answered, "It was in the office. We walked in and we'd forgotten or were stupid... And I hadn't thought to review the video feed. But she saw enough."

"I'm on my way."

"You don't—"

This time he was the one to hang up on her.

Fuck that if she thought he didn't need to rush to her side. He had plenty of PTO banked, and he'd constitute this an emergency. Thank god the District was behaving itself today—his desk, anyway—so he could bounce quickly.

Because Ellie's response wasn't about Killion and Lucy.

CHAPTER THIRTY-FIVE

Lucy

Pastor Vanessa oversaw the unloading of the items collected from the fundraising event. "Thank you for bringing the items in."

"We're pleased to do it," Killion said. "We're sorry it took so long."

Despite her levels of anxiety over Elliott's anger, Lucy grinned at his use of "we." The tingly feeling was a welcome reprieve from the constant stress since yesterday. Her eyes caressed him as he lightly descended the steps into the church basement carrying a wooden nightstand as though it weighed nothing. Her sigh bordered on a moan of appreciation.

Pastor Vanessa tilted her head, her smile all-knowing. "Miss Lucy. What is that I'm seeing in your eyes?"

Lucy met her dark eyes and gushed out, "Terror. Fear. Guilt."

"That wasn't the answer I was expecting, the way you were looking at that man. But okay, okay. It looks like we need to have a chat after this has been sorted." She indicated the truck that was half full.

Lucy's relief was instant. Why hadn't she thought to come to Pastor Vanessa earlier? With a nod, she responded thankfully, "Yes!"

Pastor Vanessa took a seat in the front row of the sanctuary. "All right, Miss Lucy. Out with it."

"I'm in love with two men." Her words echoed. She cringed at the rebound even though she and Pastor Vanessa were the only people occupying the space.

"Well, that is news. Now I understand the terror." Vanessa patted the cushion of the seat next to her. "Come sit down. Tell me about it."

Lucy plopped onto the red velveteen theater-style chair and babbled out her story, leaving nothing out: how the two relationships started, the rapid progression of feelings for both men, the sex.

Of course, Pastor Vanessa knew Killion, and she'd met Becks a few times. So it was easier to relay the journey from friendship to a romantic relationship with Killion, and as easy to recount how quickly and deeply she'd fallen for Beckman.

"Is it right, what I'm doing? Am I a sinner now?"

Vanessa patted her knee comfortingly. "You know how I feel about that word. There are no sinners if God is in their hearts. We're imperfect, but God understands that about us."

Lucy grimaced, her brain immediately jumping to Elliott. Holy shit, did Pastor Vanessa think Elliott, as an atheist, was a sinner? She gave herself a mental shake. The intrusive thought was a distraction from her current situation. No, Pastor Vanessa didn't think that; she adored Elliott, especially for Jonah. She wouldn't support them so much if she had any doubts about Elliott.

"So, am I imperfect? Does that mean I'm wrong for loving them both?"

"It's not an arrangement that would work for me. But I won't tell you what's right for you. If you genuinely love both men, and they love you back, and can love one another enough to give you what you need, it can work."

"They hate each other. And we aren't, you know, all together at the same time during..."

The mental image of the three of them in that situation both created anxiety and excited her. It would be awesome if that could be their dynamic, but it wasn't, nor would it be. They would be forcing themselves to do something for her they didn't want; she knew they weren't attracted to each other. And that was enough to dampen her desire for the fantasy. She would feel horrible making them do something for her they didn't want to do.

Vanessa chuckled. "Understood. Sleeping arrangements aside, I expect they might be able to find common ground."

Lucy snorted. "Not likely."

Pastor Vanessa nudged her with her shoulder. "It seems they found some already, Miss Lucy. *You* are their common ground."

"But what will people say? How can I show my face here with everyone knowing I'm having sex with two men? How do I deal with the judgment? Will it affect my job or the event space if people find out I'm in that type of relationship?"

Of course, if Elliott fired her after this, that would be a moot point.

"There's only one person judging you, and that's you."

Lucy grimaced, knowing that wasn't entirely true. People were lining up to point fingers.

"Anyone else judging from afar isn't something you can control. Nor should you waste your energy on their motivations."

"Elliott isn't 'afar'."

"Ah."

"She thinks I'm cheating on Beckman. She said he's deserving of a full partner who loves him and only him. And I see her point. What man only wants half of me?"

"Do they only get half of you?"

Lucy pushed her lips to the side as she considered it. "No. And they've never accused me of holding back affection, because I don't. I wouldn't know how. Their reassurance is constant, but how much is that for their own sakes? And how do I trust they'll keep that same energy as our relationships progress? It's easy now because Beckman is in DC."

Although, it wasn't easy for the same reason. She missed him horribly, and she knew it drove him mad to know she was here with Killion.

And to know that she was *with* Killion.

"Our hearts have an amazing capacity for love. It's endless. And you, my dear, have the biggest heart of anyone I've ever known. That's not a bad thing, Miss Lucy."

"I've pissed everyone off."

It was part of why she was here, hiding from the consequences while she waited for Beckman to arrive and rescue her. Or, at the very least, attempt to shield her a bit. Killion had tried, but they all knew Elliott's problem wasn't with Killion.

"Define 'everyone.' Because I'm not pissed off at you. Is Jonah upset?" Her tone was skeptical that her assistant pastor would be anything other than supportive.

Lucy shook her head. Honestly, she didn't know since she was ignoring his phone calls and texts because she was afraid of his response. But she knew Jonah wanted the best for her. She was sure of that. At the same time, he would be concerned about Elliott. She hated making him think he had to choose sides.

"I'm making the assumption that neither of your men are pissed at you?" Now she sounded amused.

"No."

"Then who is everyone?"

Lucy dropped her head, not answering.

Pastor Vanessa laid a hand on her knee. "Miss Elliott might feel some way about it, but that's her biscuit to butter. Stay true to yourself and she'll come around."

Lucy burst into tears, scared and hopeful. And thankful for the woman next to her.

Chapter Thirty-Six

Beckman

Beckman was about to knock on Lucy's apartment door when he heard banging, smashing, and yelling.

"Die, die!"

It was her voice.

Alarmed, he pounded on the door with one fist while trying the door knob with his other hand. "Lucy!" When the knob didn't turn, he reached for his gun… Only, he wasn't wearing his holster because he was on vacation. Fuck!

"Lucy!" he called again.

The commotion on the other side of the door ceased. Silence followed.

"Luce?" He was two seconds away from kicking in the door.

But it swung open, and she stood there, blond hair disheveled and cheeks rosy. She was wearing one of his button-downs—unbuttoned—he'd either left or she'd taken, and a bright red bra-and-panties set. Holding a broom.

"Hi!" She greeted him breathlessly.

Moving forward, his hand going to her waist as he guided her backward into the apartment, he asked, "What's going on? Is everything okay?" He scanned the open kitchen and living room, looking for a threat.

"Oh. Yeah. Sort of." She laughed and brandished the broom. "The smoke detector kept beeping. I sort of killed it." She pointed to the middle of the living room where the detector lay in several pieces, smashed.

He fought his grin. "You sure did."

"I'm too short to reach it, and they refused to change out the batteries until next week. Next week! So, I killed it." She looked down at it, grimacing. "I'll get in trouble for this. I'm probably breaking something in the rental agreement by destroying it."

"Understandable. I'd have killed it, too." Now he did grin, relief and amusement coursing through him.

She chuckled, turning to him. Then she gasped, eyes widening and beginning to water, her hands flying to her mouth. "Oh my god, you're here," she mumbled through her fingers.

"I told you—*oof!*" He caught her to him when she launched herself into his arms. "Hey, pix."

Arms and legs around him, she wildly kissed him all over his face and neck. In between pecks, she raved, "I. Missed. You. So. Much."

"I missed you, too."

Giggling—and holy fuck, what her giggles did to him and reminded him of—she released her legs from around him. He missed her legs instantly.

"You came."

Not yet, but that was definitely on the agenda. But he knew what she meant.

"I wasn't going to leave this to you to deal with alone."

The shine in her eyes dimmed as her anxiety crept up.

No, none of that. To distract her, he very obviously eyed her outfit. "Is that my shirt?"

Without breaking eye contact, mischief replacing anxiety, she fingered one of the buttons, toying with it. She batted her lashes. "It is. Do you want it back?"

"Fuck yeah, I want it back," he growled, kicking the door shut behind him. "Now."

"Come and get it." She taunted him.

He lunged forward, and she shrieked in surprised delight, jumping away from him. But he was faster. He grabbed her hand and tugged her to him, turning to press her against the wall by the door.

She gasped at the sudden movement and in anticipation of what he was going to do to her. Taking her other hand, he raised her arms, pinning her to the wall. The shirt she wore gaped open, exposing her lacy, racy bra and panties.

"Did you wear those for me?"

Her eyes widened. She hadn't known he was arriving today. He knew her attire was happenstance—lucky him—but she looked panicked at his question.

Leaning in to her, nuzzling her neck, he murmured, "Play along."

"Subconsciously, yes," she answered.

He grinned against her flesh before kissing her. "Good girl."

His words of praise relaxed her, and she became pliant beneath him. Ready and willing for him to do whatever he wanted with her. Shifting to hold both of her hands in one of his, he lowered his free hand to her breast.

Lifting his head, he grinned down at her as he lightly ran his fingers over her bra. Teasing her.

Lucy shivered. "Oh god."

Her big blue eyes glazed over; instant delirium. He loved that look on her face and the flush that reddened her pale skin. Barely a brush of her flesh and she was transported.

Her perky tits were straining against the material, so he freed them. Hoisted by the material, they were offerings for his hungry mouth to devour.

Lowering his head, he sucked in a hard nipple, laving and biting it. She squealed and squirmed against the wall, trying to tug her hands free. But he held her firmly in place, his hips pressed against hers. He sucked one stiff peak while pinching and rolling the other.

"Too much, too much," she panted. "Oh god, Becks."

He grinned against her flesh but didn't let up. He nipped at her, and she squeaked, dancing on her tippy toes and pressing against him as much as she could. Her skin erupted in gooseflesh, the flush of desire reddening her cheeks, neck, and chest.

No quarter was given despite her incoherent babbling and pleading. The tossing of her head from side to side, the gyrating of her body. She sucked in a lungful of air as she strained against him, back arched, and her entire body started to tremble.

"Jesus, Jesus, Jesus—*ah*!" Her muscles seized, and her cries halted as her orgasm overtook her.

Lifting his head, he watched her face, her eyes, as she stared sightlessly for a moment, pupils blown with pleasure. "That's my girl."

"Beck—"

He kissed her, mouth crashing into hers, their tongues sliding together. He released her hands. Freed, she wrapped her arms around his neck, pulling him closer and fitting her body more firmly against him. His cock was rock hard, and the friction she created was divine torture.

Kissing her neck, he murmured, "I'm not finished yet." He moved to kiss down her body.

"No, Beckman. Stop." She grabbed his hair, pulling him up. "I need you in me. Now! Please fuck me."

"Yes, ma'am." Her wish and all that.

He straightened, kissing her again as he—they—reached for his trousers. Their fingers raced each other, but she won when he unbuttoned and unzipped, slipping her hands in to grasp him.

"Fuck," he breathed out.

"That's the intention," came her cheeky reply as she slipped past his underwear to tug on him. Her hand was hot, her grip sure and firm.

"God, I've missed you."

"Same. Now get your dick inside me!"

"Needy," he crooned.

"Yes! Shut up!" She wriggled out of her red lacy panties, kicking them off.

Beckman didn't bother with divesting his pants. The sight of her pretty pink pussy short-circuited his brain. He was needier than she. Grasping her leg, he lifted it along his waist.

She grabbed his cock and lined him up with her; she was wet and hot.

Sinking into her elicited groans of satisfaction from them both. Her leg tightened around him, her foot on his ass pressing him closer. He wanted to savor this initial moment of being encased by her, her muscles squeezing and massaging. But she was already thrusting against him.

Lucy wasn't dominant, but she was demanding. She knew what she wanted, and she would have nothing less. He was lucky enough to be the man who gave it to her. In this moment with her, he was able to annex the intrusive thoughts that another man might be able to please her, too.

He withdrew and plunged into her again, their fucking becoming all need and satisfaction. She tore at his shirt, and it took flight. She rubbed her breasts against him, the sounds she made hardening his cock even more. Spurred on, he thrust into her.

"More, more," she begged.

So he gave her more. Mouths clashing, hands caressing and squeezing. There was nothing fragile about this woman satisfying her desire. And he wouldn't insult her by treating her like a delicate flower.

She used the wall as support—and his grip—to hoist herself up so she could better bounce against his dick. Her sweat-slicked hair was plastered across her forehead, neck, and chest. It clung to him as well; he loved it.

Squeezing her ass cheeks, he demanded, "Come, Luce. I need you to come."

"There. I'm *ah*—"

Her entire body clamped around him, his dick in a glorious vise.

In the throes of her orgasm.

He gritted his teeth as he rode hers out before he pulsed into her. Her arms tightened around him as she buried her face against his neck.

Smashed against the wall—she wasn't complaining—she remained wrapped around him as they caught their breaths, as their heartbeats returned to a calmer rate. As his body floated through the euphoria she'd provided him.

He placed a kiss against her moist temple before he said ruefully, "I fucked up with you."

"Excuse me?" she demanded, jerking her head up to look at him and furrowing her brows angrily.

But he saw the fear lurking behind the outrage.

"I made a mistake in not holding you closer, tighter." He didn't need to say more, that it was a mistake to let another man show her how he could love her, too.

Her eyes softened like it was something she'd needed to hear from him. But she teased him instead of giving in to the weight and apology of his words, shimmying her shoulders. "Is this post-coital babble? Are you saying that because I'm naked and hanging off you?"

He smiled. "No, pix. I'm saying that because I was wrong."

Her joy at hearing his words was genuine. As was the apology her eyes returned to him because she *wasn't* sorry that he'd given her that opportunity. But instead of addressing it, she laid her head on his chest and held him tighter.

A gentle roll of thunder drew his attention to the dormer-style window. He'd absentmindedly noted the rapidly darkening sky. With the thunder came the downpour, rain pinging against the glass.

Lucy was tucked against him, taking a catnap she'd earned. Once they found their way to her bed, he dragged her over his face, finally getting a direct taste of her. Her giggle, her moans, her panting, and her shrieks all settled something in his soul.

So afterward, yeah, he was content to lie there, soaking up her presence and the comfort being with her provided, cocooned by the weather. Every time he saw her, he fell more and more in love with her. That same depth of emotion, unfortunately, increased his fears. Fear of not being enough. It was a mantra: Four divorces. Ellie.

The fact she took his dumbass advice and was finding something in another man reinforced his fears. And they were now a rolling stone gathering momentum—he, Lucy, and Killion. Careening together, even if reluctantly, toward an outcome. What that would be was a mystery.

"Beckman!" she gasped, startling out of sleep.

Turning his attention from the rain-streaked window to her, he rubbed her back. "Hey, pix, I'm right here."

Her blinks were blank as she looked up at him before she woke up fully, relaxing against him. "Sorry. I dreamt you weren't here anymore."

"I wouldn't leave you that way."

She poked his chest. "Better never."

Fuck yeah, he loved her.

"What are your plans tomorrow?" he asked.

"You're here. You're my plans tomorrow. Tonight, tomorrow... When do you need to go back?"

"I took a week."

"Oh." She deflated.

"What? Not okay?"

"No, it's that the annual canoe trip is this weekend." Tilting her head back, she said gingerly, "Killion's going. It's been planned, even before..."

He gave her a reassuring jostle. "It's okay. I gave you little warning."

Or rather, Ellie gave them little warning.

She sat up, her expression grave. "I don't suppose you've spoken to Elliott yet?"

Beckman also sat up, shaking his head. "No. They don't know I'm in town. I thought we could arrange a time tomorrow."

Lucy wrinkled her nose, expression apologetic. "I'm sorry I made a mess."

Pulling her into his embrace, he assured her, "You didn't. This is on me."

More than she realized. Kissing the top of her head, he asked against her adorably disheveled hair, "How about if I run out and pick up some pho? The weather demands it and I have a craving for that little place downtown near Columbus Park."

She nodded. "I love that place, too. Bring back some shrimp and sweet potato fries?"

"You got it."

They moved then, leaving the bed and wandering through the apartment, collecting clothes. He picked up his shirt she'd been wearing earlier. "This and nothing else."

Grinning, she slipped it on.

Dressed, keys in hand, he dropped a kiss on her lips before leaving the apartment. The few hours spent in her arms eased the knot in his stomach, making way for sustenance.

He ducked his head as he walked through the parking lot, although the rain was unavoidable. He glanced upward, and his heart tripped over a double beat. Lucy was standing on her balcony, wrapped in his shirt. Looking like a goddess. He waved with one hand and reached for the rental car's door handle, blinking away the rain so he could focus on her.

"I love you!" she shouted from her balcony, her voice carrying over the rain as it pummeled down on him.

He smiled, not minding the drenching because Lucy's love was a warm blanket.

"And I love him." Her tone was both apologetic and determined.

The apology in her voice wasn't because she was sorry she loved Killion, but it was because she was sorry it hurt him to hear it. The determination was because she was sure.

Beckman regarded her silently, giving away nothing of his thoughts. Her words didn't diminish or dispel the feeling of warmth her declaration for him had given him, even if another man was included.

Interesting.

And he knew she was sincere, about them both. Lucy loved quickly and deeply, but she didn't love cheaply. If she said it, she meant it.

Chapter Thirty-Seven

Lucy

Elliott had intimidated her from the first time they'd met. She hadn't done anything to Lucy to make her afraid, but she was a strong woman, both literally and figuratively. Although Elliott was younger, she carried herself with such authority that Lucy sometimes forgot *she* was the older one. Honestly, Lucy was envious of her.

Right now, she was terrified. Elliott's silver glare was cutting. If it'd been a knife, Lucy would be bleeding. She was relieved when those silver daggers flicked to Beckman, and her piercing look crumbled.

"You don't deserve this. You don't deserve anything less than everything."

They were in Parkville, standing on the path that led to the Truss bridge. Jonah had suggested the park as neutral ground. That he felt they needed the neutral space scared Lucy even more.

"Kid—"

"No, it isn't fair. It's so unfair to you. You shouldn't have to be anyone's second choice, to share." Elliott rounded on Lucy. "You're so fucking selfish. Why isn't he good enough?"

A chorus of "Heys!" came from Jonah and Beckman, jumping to Lucy's defense.

Lucy shook her head. "I-it's not like that."

"Every relationship dynamic is valid," Jonah said quietly, reaching for Elliott, but she slapped his hand away with a warning glare.

"I'm not your congregation. Don't preach to me."

Jonah remained quiet, but his eyes promised punishment for her outburst. Not that Jonah would hurt her, of course not; *their* dynamic wasn't the norm, either. Jonah would work out Elliott's issues on their private rope course. She kind of wished he'd worked away some of her issues before they'd arrived here.

Lucy forced the mental image away, not wanting to imagine her friend's sexual activities. Although they were getting up in her business about hers.

"Kid."

Elliott's attention swung back to Beckman. Her angry countenance again morphed the longer they stared at each other. Fury dissolved into sorrow, guilt. That expression on Elliott's face broke Lucy's heart despite her fear. All could read the judgment Elliott was passing on herself: *This is my fault.*

Lucy expected Jonah to intervene, to insert some less preachy wisdom, but he was too busy glaring at Beckman to provide guidance. Her best friend was pissed that his woman was hurting, and she knew Jonah laid all the blame at Becks's feet.

Now that she knew, it was obvious.

Jonah was usually the balance in these situations, but his equilibrium got yeeted out the window when Beckman was involved. He used to defend Lucy the same way, and she was saddened, jealous, and resentful that his priorities had shifted. Although, how many men did she need? She had both Killion and Beckman. It wouldn't be fair to demand Jonah, too. So, even if she wouldn't admit it, the selfish statement rang true.

Not knowing if she was throwing gasoline on a fire, Lucy said quietly, "He doesn't only get half of me."

Pastor Vanessa's words gave her strength. And Lucy knew her own heart. But she may as well have held her peace. Jonah cast her a brief look to acknowledge she'd spoken, but she wasn't sure he'd heard the words.

The standoff was tense, everyone in their own feelings. She was grateful Killion wasn't present to experience this because he was already unsure about the future of their relationship. And this wasn't about him. It wasn't even about herself. This was about Beckman and Elliott. Lucy was certain that if their past, their relationship, had been normal, Elliott wouldn't give two flips who Beckman was with, or how. She'd want him to be happy. And he was. Lucy knew she made him happy, as happy as he made her.

Another piece of evidence was that Elliott wasn't defending Killion as vehemently as she was Beckman—or at all. Because if the dynamic bothered Elliott, then she should be outraged on Killion's behalf as well. And she wasn't.

There was only one biscuit Elliott needed to butter.

Chapter Thirty-Eight

Beckman

The sensation of being ripped apart, forced to choose, sickened him. There was no choosing. Ellie was his family. Lucy was the woman he loved.

Tapping at the back of his brain was the realization that Lucy must experience the same sensation with him and Killion. But he shoved that epiphany aside because these women were his priority right now.

His instinct was to go to Lucy and hold her to provide her with comfort and support. But he also wanted to bear-hug Ellie like he'd done when she was a child, reassuring her. Her guilt was misplaced. She wasn't angry because of his relationship with Lucy. She was angry at herself.

And Luce, his bright pixie, was distraught with the belief that she was the cause of this rift, this tension. He hated her distress, her fear that this would be irreparable. One, Lucy wasn't the cause; two, if his and Ellie's past had taught anyone anything, it was that they were capable of forgiving.

He assumed Jonah was experiencing the same tear, which was why he was standing between the women, his hands shoved into his pockets. Beckman had no doubt that Jonah wanted to support Lucy despite the fact he wasn't wholly supportive of him. At the same time, he was pissed that Ellie was hurting and he couldn't do anything about it. Beckman had no illusions that Jonah believed he was responsible for the distress of the women.

Deservedly so. He could see it from Jonah's perspective, which was perhaps the correct way to view the situation. First, Beckman had pursued Lucy after Jonah had warned him off. Then, months into the relationship, when Lucy was all in, Becks had slammed on the brakes and encouraged her attention elsewhere.

How the fuck did he imagine this wouldn't blow up in his face?

Lucy, however, was blameless. He was prepared to declare as much when a tear slipped down Ellie's cheek.

All bets were off then. This couldn't go on any longer, the tiptoeing around their past and pretending it didn't affect them. Now wouldn't have been his choice for having this discussion, in public, in front of Lucy and Jonah, but it needed to be now because the anger here was his fault, the culmination of his and Ellie's past actions. Another crescendo of pain.

The fallout would keep coming until they addressed it.

Beckman closed the distance separating them, grabbed Ellie's arm, and pulled her after him.

Noticing Jonah's shift to interfere or follow, Beckman pointed at him. "Stay!"

He didn't know who was more surprised that Jonah obeyed.

Beckman led Ellie onto the bridge, walking her halfway down the planks so they were centered. The park was sparsely populated, and Beckman imagined the force of emotions blasting from all of them deterred folks from wandering into their path.

Ellie ripped her arm from his grasp and walked to the railing, looking out at the river. While she contemplated the water, Beckman tossed a glance to

Lucy. She was tucked under Jonah's arm. Her expression was distraught as she watched him. Jonah looked more hostile, but at least he was offering Luce some comfort.

Returning his attention to Ellie, he studied her profile, leaning his hip against the rail. "This has nothing to do with you. With us."

She flinched at the last words, and another tear tracked down her cheek.

"I've told you before, you need to let this go."

She maintained her silence, staring out at nothing—or into the past—while the wind toyed with the ends of her dark tresses.

"Kid—"

"It isn't only about that, about us. It's about *us.*"

He understood her inflection to encompass Gage. He waited for her to go on, not missing how his heart added an extra painful beat.

"He held a gun to your head."

One would think he'd have a clear image of that moment, but it was blurry. Considering his training, he should have been tuned in, but he'd dissociated. There'd been too much going on, too many feelings to sort through. "He held it to yours, too."

"Because of me. If not for me, the last time we were all together, a man who was family to you wouldn't have held a gun to your head. He threatened to kill you. He probably would have, if..."

Beckman dropped his gaze.

If.

If she hadn't been honest with Gage, there was a good chance Gage would have shot him. So, she'd saved him but condemned her brother.

The shock from that day had the power to freeze his body despite the day's heat. He purposefully hadn't stopped to process what happened on the level Ellie clearly had. He shoved it away, perhaps the first thing he didn't want to closely examine. There was fuck all he could do about Gage, but he liked to think he'd had a hand in Ellie finding her way again.

What they'd done together? He was simply relieved it was over. He hadn't wanted to look harder at it. Not until she forced it on him. He'd been content to tear apart and obsess over the periphery: Gage's mental state, Ellie's distress, then Gage's suicide. After that came the business of an investigation to keep his mind busy, a funeral, and keeping Ellie alive even if she hated him. Giving her another outlet: kickboxing.

These were things he could do, could control. Replaying that day in his head wouldn't serve a purpose. It wasn't his proudest moment, but none of what he and Ellie had done was anything to be proud of.

"This is history, Els." He needed it to be history and for it to remain in the past.

She didn't miss a beat, as though she'd been primed for this conversation to happen at any moment for the past year. Maybe she had been.

"It will never be *just* history. Not when you still haven't blamed me, Becks. I know you do, so yell at me, curse me." She turned toward him, desperation written on her face.

"I won't do that."

"I need you to. I need to know what I did to you. Otherwise, I'm creating my own narrative, but I don't think it's as harsh as it should be." She paused. "I need to know if it's possible to forgive me."

"I already forgave you."

Her steel eyes became steelier, stubborn. That's when it belatedly hit him that she was talking about herself, not him.

Needing a second to avoid her tortured gaze, because the last thing he wanted for her was her continued self-flagellation, he turned and glanced back at their audience. Jonah and Lucy were now talking, but Jonah's attention was transfixed on them, looking like a sprinter waiting for the signal.

Returning his attention to her, he said adamantly, “I’m not punishing you for something I participated in.”

Her eyes shimmered with fresh tears. “But would you have ever fucked me if I hadn’t done what I did?”

“No.” The answer was instant, because it was true.

Relief and regret reflected back at him. He understood the relief was from breaking through and having a moment of absolute truth between them, finally. The regret was for the obvious.

“I shouldn’t have done it then, either. I never should have. But Ellie, I keep telling you, I made a decision. It was the wrong one, but I made it. I kept making the wrong decision.”

“You could have had a normal life. Instead, you're healing from scars I inflicted, something you never asked for, and it looks like you're allowing yourself to accept less because of it.”

“Lucy is not less,” he growled. “And if you're going to be outraged for me, where is your outrage on Killion’s behalf? Or Lucy’s for not being able to get a whole man with either one of us, so she has to piece us together?”

She blinked as though he’d slapped her, and he knew it was because neither Lucy nor Killion had been a concern for her. But he didn’t pause to give her time to absorb or respond to his questions.

“And four divorces is not normal. That was *before* you, Ellie, those failed relationships, not *because* of you.”

“Before me.”

His slip up was a sword she drove into herself, like there had to be that distinction in his world: Before the catastrophe that had been her, and after.

“Stop.”

She stepped closer, her demeanor steely. “Tell me what I did to you.”

He maintained his silence, swallowing hard. He stared, not wanting to provide her more ammunition with which to torture herself. At the same time, if he wanted this to end, for both their sakes, he needed to be honest. A year ago, though, this wasn't a conversation they were ready to have. Much less, three years ago. Cocking his head, he studied her face, gauging how prepared she was.

"I can hear it now," she said quietly, giving a small nod in acknowledgment of his concern. "I need to. I don't want to hurt you anymore, but I need this from you."

His chuckle was derisive, cutting. Of all the things she'd needed and taken from him, handing her the tools with which to blame herself was the hardest. Tears pricked his eyes. They both needed this, but he was hesitant about picking at the wounds—his and hers.

But her sorrowful expression was also determined. Her eyes were clear and pleading, willing his words that she knew would cut her. He wasn't going to be able to walk off this bridge without telling her.

But wasn't that why he'd dragged her here to begin with?

"You really want to hear this?"

She shifted her gaze behind him, a calmness enveloping her in that short glance, as though seeing Jonah grounded her or gave her courage. Maybe he did, because she knew no matter how ugly she might feel over what she'd done, the man behind him would love her regardless. And that's why he respected Jonah even if the feelings weren't mutual.

"Yes." Her voice was strong, sure.

He remained silent for the span of a few more heartbeats before laying out the weapons for her to choose. "There were nights I drank myself into a stupor to numb the self-hatred, the disgust I felt for giving in to you. I drank to black out the pain of lying to your parents. Drinking and smoking to excess, I almost lost my job. The photos? Making me re-enact the nightmares I was faced with every day while fucking you? Blaming myself for introducing you to them? That was my punishment for touching you in the first place, so I convinced myself I deserved it."

She shook her head to deny his belief, to silently and vehemently assure him he was wrong to blame himself. But she maintained eye contact, riveted.

"The worst, though? I was your family until you took that away from me." His voice cracked.

She sucked in a breath, as if this wasn't a toll she'd expected had been taken.

"You removed me so easily because you didn't see *me* as family—you never would have chosen me if I had been."

He stopped to take in a steadying breath. He imagined the tears slipping down his cheeks were as numerous as those gliding along hers. "You took *my family*, Els. But I couldn't be mad at you because I let you do it."

She swallowed hard, but she didn't look away, as though her stare could siphon his pain and make it hers. "I trusted you. I *trust* you. And your loyalty was rewarded with the worst part of me."

"Els—"

"I am so sorry for betraying you, Becks. You have always been my family, and I don't care how fucked up that might sound. I'll never be able to give any of that back to you, or replace those years for you, or give Gage his life back. No matter how much I wish I could. All I can be is sorry, and it's not enough; it will never be enough. You deserve so much better."

Beckman nodded in acknowledgment of her words, accepting—knowing—she was sincere, and had been sorry for a long time.

He reached up and gently brushed away a few of her tears. "Let me have this, no matter how it looks. You keep telling me what I deserve. I *deserve* to be happy. I want her, I love her."

Her expression morphed from apologetic to defensive. "How?"

Wiping at his own cheeks, he chuckled. "How? How do you love Jonah?"

The gleam returned to her eyes as she once again glanced behind them.

He pointed at her to emphasize his words. "*That's* how; I just fucking do."

Her attention on Jonah, she smiled, the action involuntary. "Yeah. I just fucking do."

He watched her beaming face streaked with tears, seriously fucking happy that she had the sparkles back in her eyes when she looked at Jonah.

"I want a family."

Her eyes returned to him sharply, rebuking, so he smiled. "You have your family with Jonah."

"And you."

He nodded. "Yeah, but I want what you and Jonah have. And I want to try that with Luce as soon as I get out of my own way about my hang-ups."

Ellie snorted, tossing out her hand. "But she wants a family with twenty other men."

"Els." He rebuked her.

She huffed out a sigh, shaking her head. Stubborn kid.

He let the flash of attitude breathe before he asked, "Is this what you wanted? Promise me you won't internalize this shit any more than you've already done. It happened, we both fucked up, but let's get beyond it."

She wiped her cheeks, sniffling. "I'm afraid it's not going to be that simple."

"Do you forgive me?"

Her entire body jolted. "For what?"

"For enabling you. For not understanding on a deeper level and helping you instead of fucking you."

She was stunned. He swore he could see the machinations working in her brain.

Finally she shook her head. "You were my lifeline more than you know. My friend, my family." She smiled through her tears. "My Becky."

He narrowed his eyes in playful reprimand at the nickname.

"Looking back now, knowing what I know—what everyone kept from me—I see how destructive my behavior was and how bad it could have gotten if I hadn't had you." Her brief smile was self-effacing. "I was so dumb, thinking I could behave in that manner. That it wouldn't come back to bite me in the ass. I wanted to keep going until something gave. Whether that was pushing you too far, or finding the wrong man..." She shrugged. "I never foresaw that it would be Gage."

Silence hung between them, both acknowledging the truth of her words, the wound she would continuously pick at. Maybe she needed the pain, like she needed the rope, its embrace comforting because blaming Gage for his own actions was something she wasn't capable of; it would force her to look the truth in the face, that she hadn't been enough for her brother. That her love for him was stronger than his for her, and he'd left her.

He took a step back, once again allowing the emotion between them some air. But she wasn't going to give him a reprieve.

"Tell me about the zoo."

He didn't understand her request at first. Then it hit him full force. "Jonah told you."

She nodded. "He'd told me to ask you, but... I suppose... No, I didn't want to know more than he'd said because I didn't want it to matter. I don't remember it, and I didn't think I wanted to. But I want to know."

Beckman regarded her steady gaze. She was resolute. Taking a deep breath, then blowing it out, he said quietly, "I wasn't there when it happened, when you were taken. From what I know, your mom looked away for one second. You'd been feeding goats, she'd said. She'd looked to see where Gage was. When she looked back, you were gone."

Ellie nodded, her eyes silently urging him to go on.

"My first thought was that my ex-wife, Diane, might have taken you. She'd been obsessed with you, treating you like her own child; she was baby hungry." He shook his head. "But it wasn't her. She was alibied."

"Who was it?"

"We don't know. He wasn't caught."

"Why are you sure it was a man?"

His stomach pitched. He hesitated, avoiding her searching gaze. "If you don't remember, that's a blessing, Els."

"I was found in a storm in a lake. Naked. Clinging to rope."

He nodded. He hadn't been the one to find her, either. It had been her father. Vince had been determined to burn down the world for his daughter. Despite the weather, he'd kept going. If she hadn't been found when she was, or alive, he didn't know that Vince himself would have survived.

"By Dad."

Again, he nodded.

"How did he know where to look?"

An involuntary single laugh escaped him. "He didn't. It was dumb fucking luck. The petting zoo was at the lake. I suppose he started with a perimeter closest to where you'd last been and kept going."

Looking at her, he said sincerely, "He'd almost lost you once. He was not going to lose you this time."

Her chin trembled, and tears filled her eyes once again.

"You were their world: Vince, Char, and Gage." He'd hoped his words would give her comfort, because they were true.

Now the tears fell as she brokenly reminded him, "But they all left me."

He almost started crying again with her, seeing her pain. He shook his head. "Not by choice."

She huffed out a watery laugh. "Gage was by choice!"

He reached for her, but stopped himself. Instead, he balled his fists and shoved them into his pockets, keenly aware they were being watched.

"Gage did not choose in the way you think."

She must have noticed his restraint in pulling her into his embrace. She once again turned mournful eyes to him. "You won't hug me anymore. It's like you're afraid I'll... or you'll... I don't know. Want it? Like it?"

He treaded lightly into the question. A year ago, it had been habitual for her to start to disrobe in front of him; muscle memory, even though neither of them wanted it.

"Do you?" He couldn't imagine she did, but Ellie did a lot of things he couldn't imagine.

"Not how you think, but I miss it. The ease, how safe I'd felt." More tears spilled. "And I ruined all of it, and now everything is weird because of me." She indicated with a wave of her hand to the pair behind him. "I should have been able to introduce you to one another, like normal people do. Jonah's a good man, and so are you, but I am a disruption between you both."

"I'm trying to respect his boundaries."

"What about me? Because I should be able to hug my family. Especially when you're my only family left." Her sob ended with a hiccup.

"Goddammit, Ellie."

Fuck Jonah, fuck being respectful of how that man would feel, seeing his arms around her. Between the two of them, Els should have always come first, and she was right to call him on it.

Reaching out, he pulled her into his embrace. "This fucking ends. This ends right here."

Chapter Thirty-Nine

Lucy

"Stay!"

Lucy's eyes widened when Beckman issued the command to Jonah. It would have been comical if her stomach wasn't in knots, and if her best friend wasn't looking murderous. Okay, not murderous; Jonah wasn't capable of it. But he didn't look happy.

In an effort to relieve him of some tension, and to comfort herself, she slipped under his arm. The action made her realize that this was a pose they didn't take anymore. Under his arm is where Elliott resided, not that she minded, but she missed their closeness, the easy camaraderie they'd had since childhood. So many things had shifted, including their Sunday morning coffee routine before church, or Jonah randomly showing up at her place, where they'd chat on her balcony, regardless of the weather.

It hadn't been a conscious thought until now, how their relationships with other people took them away from one another. At least he automatically completed the gesture by tucking her in at his side, even if his attention didn't falter from the two walking up the slight incline to the bridge.

The need for such scrutiny, in her opinion, was unnecessary. Either he actually thought Beckman might hurt Elliott—or vice versa—or he was using them as an excuse to avoid her, which would also be out of character for him. Jonah loved to dispense advice, and he was good at it.

"When did you stop caring?" she asked.

His brief glance was confused. "About what?"

"Me."

"What are you talking about? We're here because of you—" He corrected himself quickly. "For you."

"I'm sorry to have disrupted your day. Or rather, sorry to have pissed off your girlfriend."

Jonah tossed her an exasperated look. "She's not pissed, she's hurt and confused."

Her own biscuit to butter, Lucy mentally recalled. But Jonah had some biscuit buttering to do as well. "I fondly recall a time when judging wasn't something we did. Wow, it seems so long ago."

He ignored her baiting.

Looking up, she asked, "Do you remember when you and Elliott went on your first date, and you came by my apartment afterward? How excited I was for you?"

He smiled, his features softening. "Yeah."

Turning toward him, she asked earnestly, "Can't you do that for me now? Pretend to be my friend who is excited for me?"

Finally, his full attention was caught, and his arm dropped away. "Lucy. I am your friend."

" 'All relationships are valid'—you just said that—so why isn't it valid when it's me? You know how long I've been looking for someone to love. How was I supposed to know it would come in multiples?"

Jonah shifted, casting another glance to the pair on the bridge. "It's hard for me to be excited about Beckman."

"No kidding. I hadn't noticed. But what happened to when you said if I'm happy, you'd never try to take that away?"

"Because I don't think you *are* happy."

She narrowed her eyes in warning, daring him to say the unspoken words: He thought she was desperate to be happy. "Why not?"

Instead of answering, he asked, "Why Beckman? Especially now that he won't commit."

"Why is this the first time you've asked me that?"

He hesitated before answering. "Like I haven't been texting."

Oops.

But he continued, "Because you move through relationships quickly. I thought this would be no different. After DC, I was expecting to hear you'd broken up."

"Wishing, more like," she mumbled.

"What makes you so sure about him? About how you feel about him? Why are you putting up with his caginess?"

"Because I do love him. I've never felt this way. I know—and you knew—that I was more hopeful I could find something tolerable about the others than optimistic that I would. It was forced. Being with Beckman is easy."

Jonah studied her face, looking for the lie. He wouldn't find it.

"Also, because of Killion."

"We've known each other for a while, we're friends. We like each other."

"And in that time, you never once hinted at romantic feelings toward him. And you would have said something."

She wrinkled her nose, looking away.

"Am I right?"

Of course he was right. "Things changed."

"What changed? When? How?" He shifted into her line of sight.

She tossed out a hand in exasperation. "I don't know, Jonah, they just did. We've always had a playful relationship and flirty banter. We've always liked one another, ever since he came into the church for the parolee program. Did I jump his bones? No. But our friendship was instant, you know that."

It was never at the level of her and Jonah, the friendship, but nothing would be. They'd known each other since birth. "Say what you obviously want to say."

"Are you with Killion because you're afraid Beckman won't step up, that he won't commit? Are you using him to hedge your bets?"

Her jaw dropped. She was stunned. "Is that what you think of me?" She lightly shoved him. "You think I would do that to Killion? To Beckman? This hasn't been easy, FYI, not that you would know because I haven't had a real conversation with you since I called from DC weeks ago."

Intentionally.

He looked away again, his brilliant green eyes narrowing as he assessed the obviously emotional conversation occurring yards away. But one thing Lucy knew was that Elliott could hold her own—and so could Beckman.

"And he's my employee." She added wryly, "I'm breaking all the rules. But seriously, do you think Killion would allow himself to be used?"

"If he thinks you're genuine in your feelings toward him, yeah."

"They are." She looked at Beckman and Elliott. "I am crazy about both of them. It's not what I expected, and I've berated myself more than Elliott ever could. I feel guilty. Don't you think I feel guilty? I even told Pastor Vanessa, looking for... something. Comfort? Absolution? A friendly ear?"

She turned away from the scene and surveyed the main street of Parkville.

"You spoke to Vanessa?"

He had the nerve to sound wounded.

"You haven't been around."

"Luce. I've been around."

His tone rebuked her, and she deserved it. He had been around, and she knew it—had the many unanswered texts to prove it—because she was the one busy avoiding him.

"If it was anyone other than Beckman?" Her gaze drilled into him, and he knew what she was really asking because Becks and Elliott were playing out their own coming-to-Jesus moment not far from them. "And how can you be sure your unease with him isn't plain old male ego? Or jealousy?"

Jonah shook his head, his expression one of irritation. "We need a bigger conversation than this if—"

His words halted when he turned from her again. He tensed. Lucy followed his line of sight to the bridge. Beckman and Elliott were hugging—a real hug, not a quick one-armed hug. No, this was an embrace that sought and gave comfort. Lucy's heart melted, knowing how much Beckman needed that from Elliott.

Jonah took a step forward, but Lucy grabbed his arm. "No. Let them heal."

"She's crying. I hate seeing her cry."

"She's been crying. And he's there for her."

Just as he'd always been there for her. And then simply, none of their past mattered anymore because Lucy finally understood.

Chapter Forty

Killion

That motherfucker. Yeah, he'd known Becks was in town. Lucy called to inform him that Beckman had flown in for an intervention with Elliott—on Lucy's behalf—so Killion couldn't be mad about that. In the end, it benefited him as well, Beckman confirming that he'd known about Lucy and Killion and was okay with it.

Well, maybe not okay, but as okay as Killion. He assumed. He could guess that in the back of Beckman's mind, he was waiting for the moment she would choose. Because *he* was sure hoping there would be a decision.

Did he know there would be a comeuppance? Yeah, he did. Not that it had been his idea to sneak around. He knew carrying on as they had hadn't been a good idea. Secrets never were, especially one this big and unexpected. So he deserved Elliott's temper, too. Not for the relationship, but for the dishonesty.

He hadn't expected, however, for the majority of that anger to be directed at Lucy. He'd tried to shield her as well as he could and take his equal share of the blame. But Elliott seemed to have only one target. Was it because she thought Lucy was cheating? She didn't appear to have heard that Becks was aware of the circumstances.

When Elliott had walked away, Lucy had called Beckman, giving him a heads-up. Afterward, she'd stared down at her phone. "I should leave."

He'd wanted to leave, too, to escape any further wrath from Elliott—or Jonah, for that matter. But he hadn't pressed her. Instead, he'd told her he would pick her up to help deliver the donations to the church. She smiled and nodded.

The church was the last time he saw her. Because after that, Beckman had arrived. The worst part—besides driving himself insane imagining them together—was that he was supposed to stay with Lucy until they left for the river. That wasn't going to happen now. Lucy suggested she'd meet him at Easy Street on Friday, and they'd drive down together.

He'd offered to pick her up instead. When she agreed, it felt like a win, although he only saw himself as losing in that moment.

Chapter Forty-One

Lucy

For years, it had been her and Jonah's tradition to meet at the coffee shop on the Plaza. It was the perfect time and location for Sunday mornings because it was close to the church they attended. After satisfying their caffeine addictions—Jonah with coffee, she with tea—they walked together to service.

They maintained the tradition after Jonah got together with Elliott. And regardless of who she was dating, no one would keep her from her caffeine and catch-up dates. It didn't matter that she and Jonah saw each other often. This time was special especially since his random drop-ins at her apartment had petered away.

At least she'd honored the tradition until recently. And today wasn't Sunday.

She'd been avoiding Jonah. Or rather, the mirror she was afraid he'd hold up to her. He'd done some of that the other day, but he'd also been distracted. Despite the many opportunities for their paths to cross, she'd successfully dodged him. He made it easy, not forcing a conversation. Until now.

She blew on her steaming cup of London fog tea, watching him over the rim of her porcelain cup as Jonah settled in the seat opposite her. He didn't pretend interest in his steaming brew as he regarded her patiently. She felt like a disobedient child whose parent knew she was in the wrong and was waiting for her to confess.

Setting down the cup, she defended herself. "I'm not doing anything wrong. And I don't know why you think you have a right to say anything about who I'm fucking."

A few heads turned their way at her declaration. She stared back until they looked away, then returned her attention to Jonah. His eyebrows were raised, but he wasn't shocked. She was no longer capable of shocking him. At least she didn't think so.

"Is that how you're going to break this to your folks? Telling them you're *fucking* two men?"

Cheeks heating, she dropped her gaze to her tea. "I love both of them," she offered sheepishly, referring to those two men. About her parents, she added, "And I imagine they'd expect it of me, their silly goose."

"They love you. They'll be concerned more than anything."

"Because they think I'm helpless." She shrugged. "Hell, what did they expect from someone they named Lucy? It's like they branded me. And growing up with that song..."

"That song is about LSD."

She pulled a face, widening her eyes to convey her annoyance. "Right. Loopy Lucy."

Jonah reached out and took her hand. "You're not loopy. Being a dreamer is not a negative. I love your optimism. I love that you reach for stars no one else sees. I love it even more when you prove us all wrong." He squeezed her hand. "Because you're more than what others expect of you."

"That's because no one expects anything from me. I'm a caricature."

That she had almost the same conversation with Killion didn't escape her.

"That's their problem. Because I expect a lot from you. I know the depth of your empathy, your ability to love. How smart you are. I'm probably the only person to know how easily school came to you, that obtaining your master's degree was a walk in the park for you."

"I liked the subjects," she mumbled dismissively. "I failed Greek."

"It was ancient Greek during undergrad." He reminded her. "Unless you plan to time travel, I think you can let that one go."

She smiled.

He continued, "Every project you take on at the church is because you're passionate about it, not because you feel obligated. You make a difference. Take a moment to reflect on all the ways you've touched people's lives; that's a gift. And you've made Easy Street Events a success again."

The latter was a team effort.

"Why do I feel like there's a huge 'but' coming?"

He sat back and took up his coffee. His pretty green eyes remained steady on her, and she felt like a bug under a microscope. He could read her like a book. He sipped, then returned the mug to the table.

In Jonah fashion, he volleyed back. "Why do you think there's a 'but' coming?"

Dropping her head back with a groan, she stared at the ceiling. "Don't make me be introspective. Tell me the answer because, as much as I like your words, I feel like you're patronizing me."

"You're aptly named."

Righting her head, she braced herself for the heartache her best friend was about to deliver. It wouldn't be anything she didn't already know, but hearing it laid out was going to smart.

"You spiral fast."

That wasn't news to either of them, but it still stung. That's how she was made, she couldn't help it even if she didn't like it. Her feelings were sometimes overwhelming.

"That leads you two ways: into self-doubt and self-pity, or grabbing onto things you can't possibly obtain."

She wanted to tell him to go fuck himself, but he was right. And it wasn't like they'd never had this conversation before, but it wasn't common, either. He knew it hurt her, and she knew he hated hurting her. The truth hurts, after all.

"Like Gage."

One name and her heart leaped forward thunderously, guiltily. Jonah was perceptive, but she hadn't known the depths into which he saw. Or maybe he was guessing. Downplaying, ignoring her internal reaction, she asked, "What about Gage? What do you mean?"

He canted his head expectantly. Knowingly.

Nope, she wasn't going to fall into his trap again. "Seriously, what? You need to lead me down this path because I don't know what you're trying to infer."

Hiding behind her tea, she drank it while racing through her memory to pinpoint the tell that he'd picked up on. Yes, she carried the man's laptop around like a talisman. And Jonah had caught her, more than once, watching the videos of Gage and his guitar. He also knew she'd found his suicide letter. That had been one of their arguments last year: his assumption she'd been snooping around and found it. Her defense of Gage at that time might have given him a deeper insight.

"Keep your head in the game that matters" was what he'd told her then, and she'd been careful ever since. Right? Of course, only a few short months later, Beckman had appeared. And *he'd* become her conduit to Gage.

"How's that obsession going?"

She imagined her red face extended into her scalp line, but she didn't back down. "Define obsession. If it's being aware of the man who created the space where I work, I told you last year, I can't get away from it. I am literally surrounded by Gage and Elliott Rork. They're everywhere."

Now she was paranoid. Did she sound obsessed? It was a *fact* that Gage built Easy Street Events. His picture was on the wall in the office. And on the website, because she'd added it with the backstory of the event center being constructed. But that wasn't an indicator of an obsession; it was good marketing.

What Jonah didn't need to know was that she talked to the picture—he'd caught her last year doing it but hadn't figured it out—and sometimes she masturbated to it. Was it professional, getting herself off at work? No. But it also wasn't an obsession, no more than picking up a picture of a hot dude and doing the same thing was.

Right?

"I'm not obsessed. I can appreciate the man and what his vision had been. I love working at Easy Street. But beyond that, I don't have time to think about him. I have real world issues."

Deflection at its finest.

"Issues. You're referring to Killion and Beckman as issues."

"The complexity of the relationships, yes. Not with them individually, but—" She waved her hand between the two of them. "Conversations like this. Doubts and judgments of others."

"I'm not judging."

She wrinkled her nose, not buying it. "Okay, president of Elliott Beckman's fan club."

He let the sarcastic comment go with an irritated look, not taking the bait.

"Despite all the things you've said, you don't trust me. Too pie-in-the-sky."

He shook his head. "You say that as if it's bad. It isn't. Like I said, I love that you reach for the impossible. But I'm afraid this is a reach too far with Beckman and Killion."

Trying to channel her inner Pastor Vanessa, she lifted her chin defiantly. "That crumb has nothing to do with my cookie."

Wait. That didn't sound right.

Jonah bit his lips, fighting the laugh, his eyes sparkling with amusement. She grinned at her faux pas, which gave him permission to laugh out loud.

"That sounded better in my head." She added, "Pastor Vanessa has the best lines, but I'm no Pastor Vanessa."

"Which line?"

"That's your biscuit to butter." She smirked. It was a good line. "My relationship with Beckman and Killion is ours to figure out. And I think you don't like Beckman because you're jealous. I've said it before."

Jonah shook his head.

"Oh no, you've ripped me the duration of this conversation, it's your turn to take it, bestie." Leaning forward, she added meanly, "If he was only her uncle, you wouldn't have an issue with him being in her life, or mine. But because he's literally been inside her—"

"Stop. Some words you can't come back from, Lucy."

She narrowed her eyes. "You're jealous."

"He groomed her."

"He didn't. You want that to be the truth because it absolves Elliott from all responsibility, but it's not the truth. Deal with that biscuit or cookie or whatever it is." She flung her hand out in the direction of the church. "Maybe you need to start listening to your own sermons."

"What are you afraid of that you think you need them both?"

"Fuck you." Her voice was small, no bite behind the words. But of all he'd said, that question hurt the most.

What was she afraid of? Being alone and unloved for another minute, day, month, or year. She was afraid she'd never get another chance, that no one else would want her. But that wasn't why she wanted both Killion and Beckman. She loved them, and as each day progressed, she was unable to see a future with only one or the other.

So her fear was that she'd end up with neither.

Chapter Forty-Two

Killion

Once again, this motherfucker had some nerve.

But this development was out of left field, Beckman showing up at the launch site for the canoe trip. Maybe it wasn't unexpected for Lucy, considering the man had stayed at her apartment and she wasn't upset. In Lucy fashion, she sprang into action to accommodate the latecomer.

The interloper.

The intruder.

The uninvited guest.

No matter how good Lucy was at making order out of chaos, the head-count was what it was. Because this had been a planned adventure, there wasn't another solo canoer. So Lucy determined she, Killion, and Beckman would share a canoe. If he hadn't been looking forward to this trip with Lucy—and yes, feeling like he was included now as an official part of the family, so to speak, because of it—he'd have offered to ride alone. Two things there: He'd been asked first, and he didn't want Beckman to be able to dominate her attention.

"It'll be fun. I get to ride in the middle like a queen."

"Fitting." Beckman winked at her.

Killion wanted to deck him. Of course, that would end with Killion back in jail, hitting a cop—or anyone—even if the bastard deserved it. But damn, this was supposed to have been their time, his and Lucy's, a couple of fun days. And Becks didn't look the least bit embarrassed by crashing the party. In fact, he shot Killion a smug look.

Fucker.

Jonah and Elliott were nearby, Elliott's watchful and assessing attention on Jonah, ready to jump to Beckman's defense.

But Jonah shook his head, trying to sound amused. "You constantly amaze me, Lucy, in how you manage to get out of hard labor."

"Not last year," she groused back.

Only, Lucy was amused.

And bless her generously loving heart, she saw only the beauty in having her two men with her, even if everyone else tensed up, albeit for different reasons.

Okay, maybe only he and Jonah had tensed up. Elliott wasn't tense; she was cautious. Killion had an idea of how much it bothered her that the man she loved wasn't a fan of the man she'd grown up with. Killion had been at the bag with her as she pummeled and kicked out her frustrations.

Lucy wasn't tense, nor was Beckman.

So yeah, he and Jonah.

No point in throwing a fit. He wasn't going to toss his hands up in defeat and walk away, not from Lucy. He would sit his ass in the canoe simply because it made Lucy happy. Fuck Beckman.

"Hey, third wheel," he called out, catching Beckman's attention. He tossed an oar at him. "Keep us from capsizing."

"He's not a third wheel." Lucy chided him. "All are welcome."

She headed toward the canoe. Jonah had already cast off with Elliott, and both were eyeing the trio from the water as Jonah dragged the oar to turn into the current.

Lucy approached their canoe, and he and Beckman leaped forward to help her into the contraption, causing her to grin even wider.

"I'm going to love the attention. I think this is the first time all three of us have been together at the same time. Since, you know."

He knew; since she'd started dating both of them. He exchanged a glance with Beckman. Challenge quickly morphed to resignation. To make her happy, they would have to put their dicks away.

And they wanted her happy.

The remainder of the launch went smoothly. After they were gliding in the waters after Jonah, Elliott, and the others, he relaxed. Beckman seemed to be competent enough to steer. Lucy remarked happily about the gorgeous weather.

Eight hours. That was all he had to last with the motherfucker. It felt like more of a sentence than actual prison time. All he needed to do was keep his head down, not let the man get to him, and focus on Lucy.

So that's what he did. His conversation was directed toward her. They had a small water fight that rocked the canoe so much that they took on water. Lucy squealed in delight, subsiding into giggles, which of course reminded him of the giggles she emitted when he licked her clit.

Unable to stop himself, he'd looked over his shoulder at Beckman. The other man had a private smile, his eyes on Lucy. Fucker knew that about her, too. To be fair, Beckman had been there first. But nothing about this seemed fair. And seeing her look at him, the ease they had with one another, well, it was looking more and more like there wouldn't be a choice. Or at least, she wasn't making one.

Elliott waved them in from the sandbar. Lunchtime.

Killion leaped out to assist with beaching the canoe. That left Beckman to watch as Killion leaned over and assisted Lucy out of the boat. Becks exited last. Lucy leaned back in, grabbing a cooler.

"Need help there, pix?"

"Nope, I'm good."

And she was. So very fucking good, her cheeks flushed from wind and sun despite the large red floppy hat. She headed toward the pit where Jonah had started a small fire, presumably to heat up their lunch.

Elliott was standing to the side, her expression impassive as she looked between him and Beckman. Becks smiled for her, and she visibly relaxed. The expression she shot him was along the lines of a warning to behave himself. Then she turned and headed toward the campfire, passing Jonah. He reached out, their fingers tangling briefly, taking any excuse to touch.

"Do we need anything else?" Beckman asked, looking at the items in the canoe.

"Heat stroke for the old guy," Killion muttered to himself, but the wind caught his words, or Becks had supersonic hearing, because the older man smirked.

Great. Nothing like providing evidence of his displeasure—although it should be assumed—like being heard. He was also sure that the other man was chalking it up to insecurity.

"Older means more experienced."

"Older also means she'll be feeding you porridge in two years," he shot back. "No wonder you need me so I can keep up with her while you're napping all day."

So much for putting away their dicks.

Killion answered the original question, though. "No, everything we need for lunch is in the cooler. Except, do you have a meal? It didn't look like you packed much."

That was true, considering the man had appeared out of nowhere this morning.

"We have enough to share," Jonah said quietly.

"Thank you," Beckman replied.

"He should have to hunt down his own food. I, for one, am eating my entire meal. I'm not feeling generous enough to share today."

"Is that right?" Beckman asked, dark humor in his tone.

Killion understood immediately that they were no longer talking about food.

"Speaking of hunting," Beckman started casually enough, but his calculating attention was locked on Killion. "Does Ellie still have that gun in her nightstand, Jonah?"

Killion tensed. His anxiety spiked high so quickly that he almost passed out. He swung his head toward Jonah for the answer, blaming his sudden outbreak of sweat on the day's heat. Jesus Christ, there was a weapon on the property? Yeah, Beckman was trying to make him uncomfortable, but this was a threat. That he hadn't known about the gun didn't matter. He was on parole and living on the property. It was a one-way ticket back to jail.

Jonah narrowed his eyes.

Killion could tell he didn't like the question, either, also understanding the implication.

"No." The response was adamant.

Beckman didn't look convinced. "Are you sure? That was her daddy's gun."

"It's at the shop in my safe. She moved it there from her safe deposit box." He glanced at Killion. "She knew the risk of having it on-site with you there."

The unspoken words were that Elliott had his back.

Killion's stomach flipped in relief. He glared at Beckman, who looked amused at being able to so easily unnerve him. It bordered on bullying, and it sure as shit would ensure Killion and Lucy wouldn't end up together.

"Bastard. I'd hit you if that wouldn't end me in jail, too, but I can't."

There was a beat where all they heard was the tripping of the river and birds calling. Into the sounds of nature came two words, spoken so calmly they might have been the wind: "I can."

Killion barely registered the words before Jonah threw a perfect punch, landing squarely on Beckman's jaw.

Beckman stumbled, the force of the blow having knocked him sideways. But he caught himself, cradling his cheek as he glanced back at Jonah, a mixture of shock and admiration on his face.

Killion gaped in disbelief. The shock, Killion understood, because he was also taken aback. They all were. The admiration, though? Killion wasn't certain where to begin with that one. That Jonah finally gave in to the desire he'd had all along to deck Beckman? Or that he appreciated the man for sticking up for his friend? Maybe both, but Killion was inclined toward the first.

Jonah looked as satisfied as Killion felt, a grin breaking out, despite the startled yells from Elliott and Lucy.

CHAPTER FORTY-THREE

Beckman

The morning had gone as well as could be expected, considering he'd ambushed the group. Had he planned on a canoe trip? No, but he couldn't help himself. He was on vacation, and he wasn't going to sit by himself in Lucy's apartment, letting his imagination get the best of him.

Lucy hadn't missed a beat, didn't even question him over his appearance. He'd expected Killion's reaction and was impressed that the younger man hadn't taken more umbrage at his presence. Jonah's watchfulness was also expected. The right hook had been expected, but not today. Someday, he knew it would happen. Although not a violent man, Jonah had a score to settle.

And holy shit, Ellie had taught her preacher well. His face felt like it was on fire, but he couldn't stop laughing. This punch had been a long time coming, and it didn't have anything to do with defending Killion.

Straightening, testing his jaw, the look on Jonah's face told him there would be no hugging it out now that the younger man had done what he'd been wanting to do for almost a year. He glanced over to gauge Ellie's reaction.

Her stricken expression gutted him. He didn't want her to feel the need to defend him, especially against Jonah. He could handle himself just fine, and it hurt knowing she was torn when she shouldn't be.

Whipping Killion into a frenzy was one thing. It was an empty and mean-spirited threat. After all, he himself had told Ellie when she'd hired Killion to get any weapons off the property, and he knew she'd done it.

Seeing the pain on Ellie's face over his foolish prank humbled him. Despite their come-to-Jesus moment, guilt was reflected back at him, knowing as certainly as everyone here that Jonah's actions were because of her. Or at least, in defense of her, and she didn't think she deserved it.

Becks nodded toward her, saying to Jonah, "Better go take care of her. She's fit to be tied."

Jonah's expression turned thunderous, and he stepped forward threateningly. "Are you asking for another one?"

Realizing what he'd said, Beckman held his hands up in surrender. "It's a turn of phrase, but I'll find a new one."

"See that you do." With a parting warning glare, Jonah turned and headed toward the women.

Lucy, however, was making her way to him and Killion. Her expression was as thunderous as her friend's. When Lucy passed Jonah, she purposely shoulder-checked him, her eyes blazing.

When she shifted her attention to him, those beautiful blues were full of distress. Damn it, that was not something he wanted for her.

"It was all me." He confessed, holding his arms open.

She slipped into his hold and hugged him, angling her head back so she could survey the damage done.

"I asked for this."

She looked stricken, her gaze roving over his face. "Jonah has never hit anyone, ever."

Beckman grinned, wincing slightly from the movement. "It needed to be done."

Sadness slipped into her expression.

He jostled her briefly. "It's all good, pix. He and I will be singing by the campfire tonight; it's okay." He looked over her head where Jonah was having his own moment with Ellie, shuffling her backward toward the trees, away from their little campsite.

Dropping his gaze back to Lucy, he leaned forward and kissed her nose. "Men work out their shit differently. I promise you, we're fine."

"What does he need to work out that ended with his fist in your face?"

"It was something I said."

"About Elliott?"

He caressed her cheek with a finger and smiled despite his painful jaw, preparing himself for a repeated gesture. "It was what I'd said to Killion."

Chapter Forty-Four

Killion

The fuck?

He'd personally hoped Beckman's shitty behavior would signal the end of Becks, but no, she was looking at him as though *he'd* been the wronged party. Meanwhile, here he stood, the third wheel since Jonah and Elliott had disappeared into the woods, and he had to witness Lucy babying Becks. He'd have a bruise—earned it—and Killion couldn't help wishing Jonah had hit hard enough to knock the man out. Jonah hadn't pulled his punch, though, proving that Becks had a hard head. And Killion was grateful his friend would defend him like that.

"Wait. You said *what*?"

Killion refocused. Lucy stepped back, her expression scandalized. He couldn't stop the smirk as he watched. Finally! He couldn't hear Beckman's response, but Lucy's reaction informed him that Becks was honest.

She tossed a concerned look to him. "Are you okay?"

He jerked his chin at her. "I'm fine."

Turning back to Beckman, she stuck a finger in his face. "That is not okay! I am not okay with that!" She then swung her pointer finger toward him. "Apologize!"

Killion shook his head, although she wasn't looking at him. "It's okay, it doesn't matter."

"It matters to me!" She tossed him another look. "Because you matter to me."

Well hell, if that didn't make it all better, he didn't know what would.

"It was a dick thing to say. I am sorry." He even managed to look sincere as he said it.

"Don't apologize to *me*, apologize to Killion!"

Beckman looked over her head at him. "I'm sorry, man. It was fucked up to infer something as serious as sending you back to prison."

Killion shrugged as though it hadn't bothered him, but it had been the lowest of blows. Despite their love for the same woman—or maybe because of it—he hadn't thought Beckman would stoop that low.

"Is being returned to prison a threat you're going to make more than once?"

"No. That had been uncalled-for."

Killion jerked his head once in a nod of acknowledgment.

"And I'm not that insecure when it comes to you."

Oof. That one hurt. Of course Beckman wouldn't know what it was like to be that insecure. He was the guy tossing guys like himself into jail. Lucy had the judicial opposites of men. A cop and a parolee.

Chapter Forty-Five

Lucy

Men! Her men, specifically. All of them, including Jonah. *Especially* Jonah, right now. She'd almost peed herself when she'd seen Jonah punch Beckman. It was so out of the blue. One minute, the three men were chatting by the canoes, and then the next: Bam! She'd never seen Jonah strike anyone in her life.

And he'd chosen his one time to throw a punch to be at *her* boyfriend.

Of course, after the initial shock of seeing her best friend and a pastor hit another human being, the resulting expression of immense gratification on Jonah's face told them all the same thing: This had been a comeuppance. She didn't need to know the context to have figured that out.

Back at the campsite, she led Killion and Beckman to their tent. Irritated, she tossed open the flap and stepped inside. She turned, leveling them both with an intolerant stare as they entered.

They looked around the space, then at her. She could see the thought bubbles over their heads as they realized two things: She expected them to sleep together in these tiny confines *and* there were only two sleeping bags.

Of course there were only two. Beckman had been a surprise guest. She didn't miss Killion's baleful glance sent the other man's way.

Jealous jerks.

Rubbing the back of his neck, Beckman added fuel to the already-tense fire. "I'm calling dibs on sharing one of those with Luce."

"The fuck you are," Killion growled back. "I was here first!"

"Technically," Beckman started, a goading grin breaking out on his bruised face.

He was seriously inviting another bruise, only this time from her.

"Knock it off! Neither of you is sharing with me." Lucy interjected.

The two men exchanged startled glances at the suggestion of her words.

"I'd rather sleep in one of the canoes instead of with him. Mosquitos would be friendlier bunkmates," Killion declared.

Beckman indicated the tent flap. "Sleep well."

Standing straighter, Killion narrowed his eyes. "Never mind. I'll happily sleep between the two of you."

"Lord have mercy," she mumbled. Lucy put her finger in Killion's face. "Let's get something straight. I'm not choosing you." As his expression began to fall, she swerved to place the same finger in Beckman's face. "I'm not choosing you, either."

"Pix." That one word demanded more of an explanation from her.

Stomping her foot to add emphasis to her words, she said insistently, "I am not choosing! I will not do it, and you can't make me." She sounded like a toddler, but she didn't care. "So you two are sleeping in here tonight, together. Work your shit out. But if he"—she indicated Killion—"hits you, Becks, you can't hold it against him. At the rate you're going, you're deserving of all the sore jaws you've earned."

Beckman stared back at her without comment, but his cockiness receded.

Good enough.

"Where will you be?" His question was laced with concern. She tried not to melt from his tone, the one that made her feel safe.

"I'll be with Shari and Justine." She glanced between the two of them. "I know this isn't ideal for either of you. But I need you both. I want you both. I love you both! I'm not asking for you to become best friends, but can you start by not being enemies? For me? Can you try? I know it's a lot to ask, and egos—"

"We'll try." Beckman assured her, and tossed a prompting look to Killion.

Killion nodded. "Of course, sunflower."

"She hates sunflowers," Beckman pointed out. "Maybe stop calling her that?"

"No, don't stop." She smiled at Killion, who looked momentarily chagrined before she continued, confessing, "I like it when you call me that. Because *you're* the one calling me that. I like it from you."

For the first time since Beckman had surprised them this morning, Killion looked relieved and at peace. That expression of his made the stress of the day worth it.

Chapter Forty-Six

Beckman

Ellie skipped out on the after-dinner chat. As the younger woman walked past him, she crossed her eyes to express she'd rather eat dirt than stay and listen. He was confused by her exit because it appeared Jonah was leading the discussion. He'd restoked the campfire and taken a seat on a tabletop.

Or maybe that was why. They'd been in the woods longer than a lecture called for, but he wasn't going to let his mind wander. He, Luce, and Killion prepared the easy lunches, talking about nothing. She'd handed him a bag of melting ice for his jaw, but the topic itself was left alone. Their nonsensical chatter filled the air and attempted to ease the earlier tension.

When the two returned, Ellie had given him another mournful look.

"I'm okay, Els."

Jonah had taken a seat next to her. And despite whatever had happened in the woods, Ellie shot him a look that said he was going to catch hell later. Becks had snickered into his sandwich. *That's his girl.*

That evening, though, he remained at the picnic table with Lucy. Of course he did. And Killion. But if he'd been put under oath, he couldn't have recalled a single thing anyone said. He was too wrapped up in the fact that his rash decision months ago had led them to this moment, and now he, Lucy, and Killion were reeling in the consequences of his inability to commit.

Lucy loved him. She loved Killion. It hadn't been the first time he'd heard that sentiment from her about the other man. But he wondered if it was the first time Killion had heard it. A tiny part of him was sad, if so. Lucy's love was special, and Killion deserved to be able to bask in it alone with her.

Yeah, he knew how fucked up that sounded. Especially when all he wanted to do now was go back in time and change his answer.

Before long—he didn't think much time had passed, though it was a couple hours later—everyone slowly dispersed, saying their good nights. Lucy gave both him and Killion pecks on the lips and walked away with two women.

This evening hadn't been what he'd expected, and as stories were swapped, he understood why Ellie opted out. She was an atheist, had been raised an atheist. This sort of thing—*testimony*—wasn't her jam at all. It definitely served her some karma, though, to have fallen in love with a pastor. Not because of her beliefs, or lack thereof—hell no—but because of the she-devil she'd been before Gage had died.

This was something he'd believed in once, a long time ago. He leaned more toward the jaded side of life now. But there was something to be said about the power of community and confession.

Maybe that's why he remained at the table after Lucy disappeared and Killion wandered away. He assumed Killion sensed Beckman wasn't going to hash it out with him here. Or maybe he had to take a piss. Who knew?

He watched Jonah clean up abandoned paper plates and other odds and ends. Eventually, it was only the two of them, the only sound between them the crackling of the fire. Jonah was aware of him, but didn't speak. There was no animosity in the air, just curiosity and patience.

Eventually, Jonah took the seat opposite him and rested his elbows on the tabletop. He assessed the bruise on Beckman's face, but he didn't look proud or ashamed. Of course, there was no reason to be ashamed. Becks once again acknowledged it had been a long time coming. All the times they'd been in a room together, their conversations had been surface level. Weather. Sports. Neither had been interested in more.

Nah, that was wrong. Beckman would have preferred they'd gotten along better. He liked Jonah. He liked and respected that Jonah would set aside his personal beliefs and punch him in defense of Ellie. Not that she needed defending.

"Have something to confess?" Jonah asked quietly.

Beckman smirked. "I thought you weren't a priest."

Jonah laughed softly, clearly remembering their last conversation of any substance. He shook his head. "No, I'm not. But I do counsel."

Almost what he'd said then. Beckman pointed to his own face. "I wish you'd done this months ago."

Jonah smiled. "Me, too." He sobered almost as quickly. "Don't make me do it again."

Beckman understood that this time it wasn't about Ellie. This time, it was about Lucy. On the second day they'd met, Jonah had warned him to stay away from her. Obviously he hadn't.

"Believe it or not, being on your bad side is not a place I want to be. I've told you before, I like you. Especially for Els. I hate that our not getting along hurts her."

A flash of concern and regret flitted across the other man's face. Yeah, he hated that, too. Of course he did. The emotion was quickly schooled into an expression Becks was familiar with, and one Ellie referred to as his pastor face: calm and receptive.

It didn't escape his notice, however, that Jonah didn't correct him about being on his bad side. There was nothing to correct. And it was a familiar feeling. Perhaps that was the best place to start.

"The Rorks were family to me. At the same time, they weren't. I experienced anxiety from the start of the friendship. It'd been an unusual and unique introduction into their worlds, and I hadn't had the maturity to deal with that specific circumstance."

Jonah knew the story, so Becks didn't belabor it.

"I remember being afraid that they felt obligated to befriend me. As time went on, I couldn't shake the feeling that one day, a wrong move on my part would take them from me."

Jonah quirked an eyebrow at the last part, silently pointing out that he'd taken one hell of a wrong move once.

Beckman ignored the expression. "They'd never said or done anything to make me think that. They were warm, welcoming, and genuine. But I feared that the family I'd been accepted into could disappear from my life as quickly as they came. I wanted to be grounded, to feel cemented, and I never accepted that they'd provided that for me."

He paused, loss and sadness washing over him. "Well, they have disappeared. Slowly is almost as bad, losing them over time. Except Els. *Almost* Els."

Jonah held his peace regardless of how he felt. A log fell on the fire, shooting sparks into the air. Becks glanced at it, reminded of a wintry night and a devastated woman burning rope. He looked away quickly. She'd come a long way since that night. He'd like to think he had, too.

"I tried more than once to capture that feeling of family, but those relationships failed." Glancing up, he said meaningfully, "Then, *Ellie.*"

Jonah's nostrils flared, and his jaw tensed like he wanted to hit him again.

Yeah, he knew what Becks was referring to.

"This all sounds like I'm trying to justify something."

"Are you?"

Beckman flipped the question. "Should I be?"

Jonah held his peace, patiently waiting him out.

"I don't know. Maybe I'm so desperate to cling to something that I'll let another man into the bed"—he noted Jonah's glower and corrected himself—"*affections* of the woman I love."

Something shifted the other man's gaze before he quickly looked down, appearing to have dropped into deep thought. Or praying.

"I know I fucked up. She knows I fucked up. It doesn't change how she feels for Killion."

"Nor does it change how she feels about you," Jonah added, looking up. He sighed heavily, casting his gaze around the darkened campsite before asking, "Why did you do it? Push her away? As her friend, that infuriates me. As a pastor..." He pulled an ironic expression. "I'm still infuriated."

"Because you'd warned me off?"

Jonah shook his head. "Because you hurt her."

His words delivered another deserved punch, this time to the gut. It was true, and he knew it. "It was me being selfish and scared."

"Tell me why?"

Beckman sat back and reached for his cigarettes. Holding up the pack, he raised a brow, questioning. His habit wasn't a secret, and normally, he wouldn't seek permission to smoke. But Jonah was an environmental and health enthusiast—his pizza addiction notwithstanding. If the man didn't want cigarette smoke in his face, Becks didn't want to repel him.

He'd remained at the table for a reason.

Jonah looked at the pack before nodding. To his credit, his expression remained neutral.

"I panicked." Becks lit the cigarette, drawing in a lungful before turning his head to dispel it. "Her leap from hearing about me and Ellie to a committed relationship threw me. I'm not proud of my response."

Regret it immensely.

"But that was my knee-jerk reaction. Why?" Beckman shrugged. "Deeper issues at play, in hindsight. And a shit ton of arrogance, thinking I could send her out into the world and she wouldn't be interested in anyone else. Arrogance, conceit. But..."

"But?"

Beckman scratched the back of his neck, looking down at the table. "I wanted to know how Killion was going to fit into our lives. I knew they were close. Was I having those thoughts consciously at the time she'd asked? No."

"There's more." It was a tone of certainty, not a question.

He nodded. "Timing. It's a cop-out but true. Those questions, that uncertainty, lingered. I was also—still am—afraid of failing her like I'd failed my other relationships. I'm including Ellie in that. But as valid as those reasons are, it wouldn't have been fair to Lucy if I jumped into a commitment when Ellie and I hadn't resolved things."

Jonah scratched his chin, turning away. He surveyed the state of the dying fire and cast his gaze again over the campsite before focusing on Beckman again.

"These things are my fault, I know. I didn't mean to lead her on. I should have been honest with her from the beginning, but..." He took another drag of his cigarette. "But I hadn't expected *her*.

"I wasn't self-aware then, not that I'm a champion of introspection now. Being with her, around her, has forced the confrontation with myself. I want to be better for her. I took the fucked-up route to get there and shoved her into Killion's arms."

"I was surprised by that development, although I shouldn't have been," Jonah admitted. "I hadn't been paying attention, either."

Not an excuse, but a fact.

Jonah shifted on the bench. "I'm struggling to maintain the neutrality of a pastor, but I'm failing. So I'm speaking to you as her friend."

"I don't want neutrality."

"The longer you give her hope, the harder it will be for her when you decide to bounce. So get out now if you can't give her what she wants. And who she wants."

The suggestion brought out a feral, possessive side of him. "I'm not going anywhere. You need to have this conversation with Killion."

Jonah considered him for a few minutes before stating evenly, "Polyamorous relationships require a solid foundation of trust. And communication."

Beckman wanted to point out that Jonah wouldn't know the first thing about it before it registered that the label didn't chafe. He'd teased Lucy about it once, but realization smacked him in the back of his head. Unless he walked away, this was going to be his life.

Him, Lucy, and Killion.

He'd known that for a while, although he held out hope it wouldn't last—that Killion wouldn't last.

"Make sure it's what you want."

Beckman acknowledged his words with a single nod. "I'll do anything to make her happy. Because her happiness makes me happy."

Jonah gave him a genuine smile. "Good to hear. Good luck."

It felt like acceptance.

Beckman chuckled. "I told Lucy we'd end up together by the campfire."

Chapter Forty-Seven

Beckman

A light shone from inside the tent as he approached. He hoped to hell it was because Killion was being considerate and left the light on for him. After the conversation with Jonah, he was drained. It was a good tired, but at his age, tired was still fucking tired.

And his face fucking hurt.

When he ducked in, though, Killion was awake, sitting on his sleeping bag, attention on his phone. Upon his entrance, the other man looked up. The sullen expression on his face undoubtedly mirrored his own.

He had to give the kid credit, waiting up for him instead of taking the easy out of hitting the hay. They exchanged looks of resignation. It'd been a long day, but they had an assignment to work their shit out.

As if it was that easy, despite his conversation and the optimistic outlook he'd had while sitting in the open night air with the soothing fire crackling beside them as they'd chatted.

They didn't talk as Beckman prepared his sleeping bag for the night. When their gazes clashed, they looked away as quickly. The silence between them was uneasy yet anticipatory.

He stripped down to his briefs before collapsing onto his flat bed, staring at the fabric above him. It was a small fucking tent. No matter where he looked, Killion was in his peripheral vision.

"I, uh..." Killion hesitated. He stood up.

Beckman shifted his gaze and frowned in question. Was he about to give a speech?

Killion indicated his jeans. "Commando."

Beckman stared back. For fuck's sake. "I'm not interested in seeing your junk, man. Keep your pants on."

"It wasn't permission but a warning." Raising a cocky brow, he unbuttoned his fly. "I didn't want you to be intimidated."

"Jesus Christ." He rolled onto his side. "Just get in your bag and go the fuck to sleep."

Because yeah, despite Lucy's order, he was not in the mood to talk to this kid. He was in pain, and he was wiped out.

"Sure thing, Dad."

Before Becks snapped back that he wasn't old enough to be referred to that way by a grown man, he did the quick math. Yeah, he could be his father.

"Get the light," he ordered instead. Call him a dad, he'll bark out orders like one.

He heard Killion moving around, the slide of the sleeping bag, then the lamp was shut off.

Sounds of movement in the camp, passersby, the river, and night creatures invaded the space. Light occasionally illuminated the tent as people walked by with flashlights. Beckman shifted on the hard ground and waited for sleep to overtake him. He was too old for this shit. Despite his exhaustion, sleep was elusive. Killion's breaths were even, but he knew it wasn't the breath of someone who had fallen asleep.

The air became heavy with expectation. Beckman lay unmoving, waiting. Thankfully, he didn't have long to wait.

"How the fuck did you and Elliott happen?"

He'd had this conversation with Jonah months ago. It'd been a valid concern and question from Jonah, but not from this punk. Ellie was his boss, and her business wasn't his.

"We were both adults. But I'm not discussing her with you."

He didn't know what Killion knew beyond that there'd been a sexual component to their relationship. And he certainly wasn't going to enlighten him to the fact that it was Ellie who'd initiated it. That was hers to share alone, not that she was required to do so, and he was at least man enough to take the hits for her. Too bad he hadn't been man enough then, not only sending her home to her parents, but also telling them the stunt she'd pulled.

Her dad would have locked her up. Since she had gone missing as a toddler, Becks was certain Vince looked for any excuse to do just that, to keep her safe. Or—and most likely—Becks would have been banished from the family.

Fear of losing them had guided his horrified reaction to her then.

Fear was also what dictated his rollercoaster relationship with Lucy.

Beckman sensed the other man's irritation at the answer. He rolled onto his back, trying to get comfortable, but the position was as uncomfortable as lying on his side.

Him and his bright ideas, following them down here.

"Why Lucy?"

"Why am I the one being interrogated? What about you, going after her when you knew she was with someone?"

"Was she, though?" he shot back. "Kinda recall her being cut loose."

Beckman growled, "I didn't cut her loose." He shifted, rolling onto his other side so he could prop himself up on his elbow. Eyes acclimated to the dark, he sought out the younger man's shadowy profile. "If I had, I wouldn't be here."

"If you hadn't, *I* wouldn't be here."

He clenched his teeth. Fair point.

"Thank you, by the way, for being dickless or scared or whatever the fuck because it did give me a second chance." He raised his hand, rubbing his bald head. "I suppose it's my first chance but a second opportunity."

"I didn't do it for you."

"Yeah, I know."

"Why second?"

A resigned sigh escaped the younger man. "Okay, then." He sat up, reaching over to flick the lantern back on. "Let's do this."

Beckman frowned. He thought they already were, but he didn't press the issue. Instead, he matched the other man in sitting up, trying to appear as fluid in movement even though his bones and muscles ached.

Killion's side-eyed assessment of him told him he hadn't been as smooth as he'd hoped.

But he continued, "Second, because she'd been with Greg this time last year. And I'd just gotten my job at Easy Street; I was in no position to offer her anything."

Beckman's silent regard of the younger man spoke for itself. When Killion looked away, doubt in his conviction screamed louder than a voice. Seeing the uncertainty in the cocksure kid didn't make him feel any better. There was no gloating here. Oddly.

"Why'd you wait?" Becks asked quietly.

"I wanted to have a little bit of success first instead of being a fucked-up charity case. Maybe have moved off the property. I thought I had time. And why Lucy?" He smiled, more like a bashful boyish grin. "When I joined the church program, she was just... Lucy. She wasn't condescending or judgmental. Her support and enthusiasm for every stupid milestone I made were unfailing. I looked forward to spending any amount of time with her. I looked forward to *her.*"

Beckman understood the power of her positivity. He was lucky to have been able to bask in her love as long as he had. He admitted, "My first night with her, I was able to share memories with her I'd bottled up for years. And she was—and is—my safe space. I hope I'm that for her, too."

Killion watched him for several beats. "Then why not man up and give her what she needs? Why give someone like me the opportunity to take her from you?"

"You aren't taking her from me. I'm not going anywhere. And neither is she."

The younger man shot him a dubious look. "So you're, what? Gonna share her? How considerate of you. Is that fair to any of us? To her?"

"She knows what she's asking for. The question is whether we can give her what she wants." He paused, watching the younger man deal with his frustration.

Killion wanted a different outcome. So did he. But this was where they found themselves, on the brink of a relationship between the three of them.

Killion didn't respond. His hand went to his bare chest. Beckman recognized the movement as looking for his smokes. The gesture was habitual, maybe even self-soothing.

"Are you capable of walking away from her because she loves me?"

Killion shook his head. "No. But how is this supposed to work? I'm not sleeping with you or fucking you. This won't be a threesome."

"Definitely not."

"She wants a commitment. I can do that for her." Killion's gaze challenged.

Beckman nodded slowly. Odd as it may be, or as fucked up as he was, there was less pressure knowing he wasn't the only one responsible for her happiness; it was a daunting prospect, being someone's whole focus. Maybe that's why his marriages had failed: not their expectations of him, but his demands on himself that he'd projected onto his wives. Ellie had been the excuse not to put himself in that position again; he saw that now, and it'd been wrong on so many levels.

"She isn't a slice of cake. She's a whole person who has an infinite ability to love. She's remarkable that way. I can't take my love away from her any more than you can. I'm not willing to give up receiving that from her, either."

Killion shook his head in acknowledgment.

"We aren't going to work this out in one night."

The expression on Killion's face suggested it wouldn't be in the near future, either. "So what do we do? We had an assignment." He smirked as he said the latter.

"Agree to figure out how to give her what she wants and needs."

Again, Killion nodded. "I can do that. She's worth it." He eyed him critically, the cockiness returning. "The only flaw she has is what she sees in you."

Beckman chuckled. "I was thinking the same thing."

It wasn't the common ground Lucy hoped for, but it was a start.

Chapter Forty-Eight

Lucy

Watching Beckman and Killion exit the tent the next morning was a treat. She'd been sitting at a picnic table advantageously situated so she could drink her morning tea and stalk. The only thing that averted her attention away from the zipped flap was the intermediate weather notices that informed her of a storm and possible tornadic activity in Kansas City.

After a while, she ignored the texts from the news station. It was summer. It was the Midwest. Tornado watches and warnings were a way of life.

Last year, a similar storm system had knocked power out at Easy Street Events and wreaked havoc on the trees. It was memorable because that's the first time she knew Jonah had stayed the night with Elliott. As if that hadn't been monumental enough, the damage to the trees had given Lucy an uncomfortable front-row seat to Elliott's aversion to ropes. Then, at least. Experiencing the woman lose her shit over it—Lucy had been in the direct line of fire—had been frightening.

So KC could ride this one out without them.

Besides, the flap was being unzipped. A pack of wild boars racing through the campsite wouldn't have been able to tear her eyes away.

Beckman pushed out first, looking like the sexy silver fox he was, graying hair disheveled and blinking at the light. His bruise was darker in color, but it made him look more appealing. Rakish and dangerous. Lucy grabbed onto the table to keep from propelling herself into his arms, wanting to drown in his quiet strength that soothed her soul.

He moved aside, holding the material back as Killion emerged. Shirtless. Holy hot damn. Gorgeous body and tattoos on full display. Yeah, she'd seen him yesterday and many times before fully nude, but he was so striking and toned, it was like she forgot how beautiful he was until she saw him again. And the two together, not having noticed her yet, looked companionable. To a casual observer, they would look like friends.

Beckman handed something over wordlessly. Killion accepted it silently, nodding acknowledgment. As though they'd rehearsed it, they both placed their cigarettes between their lips in tandem. Becks produced a lighter.

Even though it was a cigarette they were bonding over, Lucy saw it as a step forward. She knew Killion was trying to quit, so his acceptance of the offering she decided to interpret as a truce between them.

"Good morning," she called out.

Two sets of eyes swung her way, seeking her out. When they spotted her, Beckman grinned, his blue eyes smoldering. Killion's hazel sparkled, like seeing her lit the morning up instead of the sun.

"Pix."

"Sunflower."

She'd died and gone to heaven.

"Did you sleep well?" she asked, gawking at will because some gifts weren't to be taken for granted.

They exchanged a glance before both shrugging. She bit her lips to keep from laughing out loud because it looked to her like they had come to some sort of truce, but neither wanted to admit it. Fine.

"I'm glad to see the tent still standing." Okay, one joke, but it returned their smiles.

Dropping his barely smoked cigarette and crushing it out, Killion started toward her.

"You are not leaving that on the ground, Killion Murphy!" Elliott's voice rang from across the campsite.

"No, ma'am." He assured her, casting his glance around to find where she was located. Not succeeding, based on his confused frown, he retraced his few steps and picked it up. In an over-exaggerated show, he walked over to a dented trash can, tested the butt for heat, and dropped it in.

Beside the tent, enjoying his smoke, Beckman was chuckling.

Wiping his hands on his jeans, Killion started toward her again.

"Coffee is—" Lucy started before her phone vibrated with an incoming call.

Looking at the screen, she saw it was the alarm company from Easy Street Events. Frowning, she picked up her phone, wondering if the storms had messed with the system.

"Hello?"

She listened to the voice on the other end, and her body went cold, a ringing echoing in her ears. Through the fog, her head spinning, she saw both Beckman and Killion hurry toward her, twin expressions of concern.

"Pix?" Beckman asked, bringing her attention to him. "What's wrong?"

He and Killion had reached the picnic table. Becks braced opposite her, his hands on the tabletop as he leaned over. Killion walked around to her side.

"A tornado." She held out her phone, the person on the other end still talking. She looked at the device as though it was alien, not her own. "Easy Street Events was hit."

Chapter Forty-Nine

Beckman

They'd found Jonah and Ellie breaking down their tent. Their smiles fell away when Lucy informed them of the news. Ellie swayed before she shook her head as though to clear it.

Jonah pulled her to him, already turning them both toward the vehicle. "We'll leave now."

"Come with me," Ellie asked, reaching back and holding her hand out to him. Her face was as pale as Lucy's had been.

There was no way he could reject her plea. He reached forward, giving her hand a reassuring squeeze. "I'm coming."

As much as he wanted to be with Lucy, he knew that at this moment, Ellie needed him more. Jonah recognized it as well; they all did.

"I'll let the others know our plan and ask them to break camp. Then Killion and I will be right behind you," Lucy said quietly, the tears welling in her eyes not falling.

She was holding it together and taking charge.

"See you in a bit." Beckman walked over to her and dropped a quick kiss to her lips. Stepping back, he flicked his gaze to Killion. "Take care of her."

Killion would have countered with a snarky reply before last night, but this time, he simply nodded. Of course he would take care of Lucy, Becks knew that, but it was his way of expressing trust in the guy.

Then he, Jonah, and Ellie climbed into the Jeep. Considering the couple sometimes traveled on the motorcycle, it was prescient that they'd opted for the car. The drive was tense and mostly silent. Ellie's hand had rested on, occasionally gripping, Jonah's thigh. Beckman observed from the back seat, knowing every time her fingers tightened, she was fighting against panic or memories. Or both. Imagining the worst.

Jonah laid his hand over hers, his thumb moving back and forth, caressing. He regularly glanced over, taking stock of her stoic profile.

Beckman recognized her expression; it was the same one she'd had at Gage's funeral.

It was an exhausting three hours.

Then they were approaching the turnoff to the property. Trees—if they remained rooted—were ripped bare of their leaves and distorted. It was a spine-tingling sight to see dark, broken silhouettes that resembled winter. Signs and other landmarks were gone. If Beckman hadn't known the way so well—and Jonah, for that matter—he doubted he would have recognized their exit.

Jonah eased the Jeep down the extended driveway, swerving around fallen trees and piles of split wood that littered the ground. The crunching sound of the vehicle's wheels over the debris and mud accompanied the jostling as they crept down the long drive.

Beckman leaned forward, looking through the seats. The nothingness in front of him was surreal. When Jonah braked, he realized that they were in the driveway. His gaze landed on the fountain, which had been spared, but not much else appeared to be intact.

He shifted his attention from the destruction to Ellie. She stared ahead, her expression an indecipherable mask as she held her silence. They remained silent, the atmosphere shifting from anticipatory terror to how people behaved driving through a cemetery. In a sense, they were. The tremble of her bottom lip belied her stoicism.

The house was gone, having been ripped off its supports. From appearances, it was slammed into the event center, which collapsed under the weight of it. There was no withstanding the assault. The red door was either gone or buried in the rubble.

He fought hard to keep his emotions at bay as he surveyed the devastation.

He'd watched Ellie struggle to preserve the place, her link to her brother, determined not to let Gage's memory and efforts fade.

He'd fallen in love here, not realizing at the time the impact Lucy would have on his life. And it was in ruins. Gone. Lost to the whims of Midwestern weather. If he was feeling this way, he knew Ellie was screaming inside.

Beckman couldn't wrap his head around what he was looking at, even though he'd seen destruction in every sense of the word. This was different. He knew the man who'd built this place, had witnessed its rise, lending a hand now and then. He'd also watched that same man decline, eventually ending his pain with a rope.

He'd fucked, he'd fought, he'd almost lost this place years ago because of that devastating end. And Ellie. He'd almost lost her, too.

But they'd persevered.

Jonah turned off the engine. They looked everywhere, stunned. As if on cue, they reached for their doors at the same time. He slid out of the back seat. They met at the front of the vehicle. After five heartbeats, Ellie moved again, taking the lead. His eyes bounced from the scene to her, ready to go to her the instant she needed him, but he checked himself. Jonah was here, watching her intently, with only brief glances at the wreckage.

Ellie's footfalls crunched as she walked. She stopped by the fountain devoid of water, the tornado having taken that with it as well. The cacophony of birds—angry, confused, and equally displaced—surrounded them, disrupting the otherwise eerie silence. The afternoon sun had the nerve to power through, casting a bright glow, the water droplets from the recent rain and hail shimmering joyfully in the light, casting tiny rainbows over the scene.

The quiet reminded him of a similarly muted morning.

Ellie continued, stumbling over the large splinters and slipping in the mud. Pacing her, Jonah was quick to reach out, but she shrugged him off. Beckman hung back, hands shoved in his pockets as he watched them. Ellie was tense, waves of emotion washing off her and bathing them in her quiet pain. Jonah was on high alert, tuned in to her. Beckman could have been invisible, but maybe that's how it should be.

She stopped, crouching down to pick up a fragment of pottery. Head bent, she wiped it off as she turned it over in her hands as though trying to decide whether she knew this shard.

Jonah finally spoke, his tone low and gauging. "Kitten?"

She held up the blue and white pottery. "My coffee mug."

Dropping it, she stood again, wiping her hands on her shorts. She declared vehemently, "I'm never going on another of those canoe trips again. It only brings disaster."

Although she wasn't looking at him, Jonah's stare was unyielding.

Beckman rubbed the back of his neck. She wasn't wrong. Last year, the canoe trip ended with her motorcycle accident and the death of the driver.

"We weren't here," Jonah countered.

His meaning was clear, but it wasn't the answer she wanted to hear. She spun toward him, expression angry and accusing, as though Jonah himself had brought about this destruction.

"Being here wouldn't have made a difference," he pointed out gently. "Only, *we* might not be standing here right now."

She tilted her head, and her bottom lip quivered again. Jonah was in front of her in a flash, moving quickly, traversing the uneven ground with certainty. Framing her face with his hands, he lowered his forehead to hers. She grasped his arms, looking up into his eyes. His whispers were lost in the air, but Becks didn't need to hear them. It was an intimate moment, and he felt like an intruder witnessing it.

Looking away, he took better stock of the damage now that the initial shock began to dissipate. Ellie's sniffles and Jonah's rumbled words accompanied his scan. He walked away from them to better view the side of the property.

The warehouse next to the house—Lucy's office and Killion's home—was wiped clean off the concrete pad. The structure next to it partially collapsed, its contents sucked out and littering the ground. But the building at the end, the one where Gage had ended his life, was standing. Sheet metal was peeled aside, one of the front sliding doors was gone, but it remained relatively intact.

Ellie would take that as a sign. How she'd interpret it, he didn't know.

His shoes crunched over the glass, the splinters of wood and shingle, and god knew what else. Gage's cherry red Mustang was crumbled on its side. Jonah's motorcycle, which normally resided near it, was gone entirely. The heavy bag was in the drive, as though the winds hadn't wanted to bother with its weight and dropped it there.

Clothes, furniture, window screens, and toys were tossed about. The toys were from some other unfortunate home. They'd find more belongings of neighbors, just as the wicked wind would have carried off Ellie's, Jonah's, and Killion's things. The motorcycle, for instance, was probably in the next county. Tornadoes were fucking random like that.

When he glanced back at the two, Ellie was tucked in at Jonah's side, her mournful gaze wandering over her home. The sweep of her eyes landed on him. He hoped she could see his support, his love, in his expression. As much as he wanted to hold her and grieve with her, she belonged in Jonah's arms.

Her expression was a mix of yearning and sorrowful understanding. He knew she was recalling everything he was: the good, the bad, the nightmares. She shifted, appearing intent on heading his way, so they could share their grief and take comfort from someone who knew how deep these cuts were, slicing into the past.

The crunch of tires stilled her.

They turned to watch the arrival of Lucy and Killion. The truck hadn't come to a full stop when the passenger door swung open. Beckman could hear Killion chide her as he slammed on the brakes. But Lucy leaped from the vehicle, her eyes puffy and cheeks tear-streaked. Without acknowledging anyone, including Killion as he called after her, she stumbled toward the broken, twisted pile of wood and sheet metal that had once been her world.

"Gage! Gage!"

Her screams tore through him, the depth of her pain rending his heart. It propelled him into a run, to intercept her. But Ellie was already there, wrapping her arms around Lucy's waist, holding her back.

Above the sound of his shoes on the debris, and his pounding heart, he heard Ellie over Lucy's sobs.

"He's not in there. Gage isn't here. He's gone." Her voice broke. "He's been gone."

Lucy sagged, giving up her fight, and the two women fell against one another. Ellie finally let the dam break, sobbing so hard he knew it was more than the event center.

Beckman's heart broke, watching them struggle with the heartbreak, their tears. He knew Ellie's words cut her to say as much as they sliced Lucy to hear. Despite it, though, he'd never felt Gage's presence more than he did in this perfect crescendo of grief and pain. It was like the man ethereally hugged them both goodbye. Their hard, jagged sobs confirmed their recognition of the moment.

Lucy had fallen in love with a man she'd never known. Her heart was that big. It was why she could love both him and Killion without understanding how society dictated her love had to stop with one to begin with the other. Fucking bullshit, that mindset—one he'd admittedly shared until her—and he was one of the lucky recipients of her bottomless well of love.

But it was hurting her as well, and he hated her pain. He glanced at Jonah, who watched the scene with the same level of realization. Moving his gaze past Jonah to Killion, who was approaching them, the man nodded imperceptibly. He got it, too.

Chapter Fifty

Killion

"Hey, sunflower. We've got you."

He cradled her in his arms. After the women had parted, Elliott finding solace in Jonah's embrace, Lucy looked ready to collapse. Being closer, he leaped forward and grabbed her up, swinging her into his arms.

Beckman quickly made his way to them, pushing Lucy's hair from her face and drying her tears with his thumb. The two men exchanged a look, silently agreeing: Take Lucy home.

"Keys are in the truck," he informed Becks as they moved toward the vehicle.

Beckman glanced toward Jonah and Elliott before stepping back. Then he led the way to the truck and walked to the passenger door, opening it for them.

Killion carefully slid onto the seat, Lucy wrapped in his arms. Her hot tears coasted down his neck where she buried her face, sniffling. Beckman grabbed the seat belt and leaned over them, engaging the device.

The drive to her apartment was mostly quiet. The only sounds in the cab of the truck were her soft cries and their murmured words of comfort. Killion rocked her as much as he could, given the seat belt, and dropped kisses on her forehead. Beckman occasionally reached over and caressed her leg.

This ride to her apartment, however, felt as long as the one from the campsite. Hours of him trying to concentrate while Lucy frantically accessed the security system app, scrolled social media and newscasts, mumbling, "I need to see it. Why isn't anyone covering it?"

Her tears then had been of frustrated anger.

Then she'd attempt to calm herself. "Maybe it's not on the news because the tornado missed it. Close enough to disrupt the security feed. Right? I shouldn't panic and cancel the events we have planned, should I? Not until I know?"

He nodded, not wanting to feed her hope in the event it didn't turn out well, but also wanting to provide some comfort. As they'd approached the turn off to the property, she'd unfastened her seat belt and slid over to him. He'd carefully maneuvered around the debris.

"Killion," she whispered.

She dug her fingernails into his arm. Her voice held the fear he was also experiencing.

"I know."

"It's—"

"I know," he repeated.

His home. His job. *Her* job. But it was more than a place, a job. It was a year of happiness, security, family, and love. Ripped apart and strewn across Kansas City, discarded pieces like it meant nothing.

When they'd seen the destruction, she jerked away from him. "No!"

She'd been out the door before he could react.

But he had her now, and she was his sole focus. Despite the reason, he was glad for the excuse to concentrate on her instead of the fact that his home and belongings were gone. In comparison, it wasn't a lot to lose considering her dreams had been ripped from their foundation and scattered into the wind.

She'd held it together for hours—held onto hope for hours—so she'd earned this meltdown. He knew what Easy Street Events meant to her. This was deeper than a building and some land. Although he couldn't understand the depth of affection she had for a man she'd never met, he knew her pain was real. Therefore, it needed to be acknowledged and honored.

He gently rocked her as Beckman sped through the city once clear of the swath of devastation. Glancing over, he noted the focus of the other man, concentrating on not adding another tragedy to the day. No matter what Becks might be experiencing internally—concern for Lucy and Elliott—there wasn't a crack in the man's armor.

Once in her apartment, Killion headed for the bathroom while Beckman veered toward the kitchen.

He didn't know how they knew, but they did, that a hot bath and tea would comfort her.

When Beckman entered the bathroom moments later with a steaming cup, he blinked rapidly for two seconds, pausing, seeing Killion in the bath with her.

He'd run the water as he stripped them both, then wedged his ass in the standard-size bathtub, pulling her back in his arms. She'd sighed in contentment as bubbles rose around them.

After those blinks, though, Beckman continued in the room and knelt by the tub. "Earl Grey."

Lucy sniffled and reached out, taking the offering with a quiet "Thank you." She took a sip, sighed again, and handed it back. "Thank you both."

He and Beckman shook their heads at the same time.

"No need, pix."

"You don't need to thank us."

Her head rolled to the side, her attention on Beckman, who stared back with a mixture of concern and affection. Killion cupped handfuls of warm water and dribbled it on her, ensuring she stayed warm.

It was the only sound in the room beyond their breathing, the water he manipulated.

What was missing? Tension. Jealousy. Possessiveness.

Lucy needed them and they were there for her, without question.

Chapter Fifty-One

Beckman

If the past few days taught him anything, it was that he and Killion could function as a team. Where Lucy's well-being was concerned, the two of them found a balance.

Had he expected to step into the bathroom and find them in the tub together? No. But the dried tear stains on Lucy's face and her expression of exhausted contentment gave him pause. If she found peace in Killion's arms, he wasn't going to take it from her.

Nor did he take it from her later that night when she'd wanted to cling to them both, sandwiched between them in the bed. He and Killion exchanged a look, wondering who was going to argue her out of it first, but Beckman wasn't volunteering. Neither was Killion. So he'd provided Killion with a pair of his sweatpants, and they'd climbed in on either side of her. It would have been a similar sleeping arrangement if she'd stayed in the tent with them.

So they took care of her while she grieved for a man she'd never met, neither one questioning the depth of her pain. Instead, they strove to relieve her of it. Favorite foods, movies, and snuggles.

One stepped in where the other couldn't. Beckman resembled stability and safety for Lucy. Killion was more demonstrative and romantic in his gestures, feeding her need for pampering with an innate sense of what she wanted.

The hackles only rose when Killion had gone to the store to pick up basic necessities for himself. After all, the only belongings he had were in a duffel from the float trip. The moment he vacated the apartment, Lucy reached for Beckman, and he gave her what she—and he—both needed.

Killion immediately sensed, or perhaps smelled the musky air, and knew. His accusing gaze had flashed to Beckman. They'd stared off before Killion ripped his attention away, rubbing his bald head. The tensing of Killion's jaw let him know he was struggling with the realization he wouldn't be the only one having sex with Lucy.

They both knew, but there was knowing and then there was walking into it.

He'd squared his shoulders and moved on. Perhaps imagining the moment when Beckman was away so he could participate in the same activity with her. Of course, Killion hadn't waited for Beckman to leave if the sounds from the shower were any indication.

Did he like knowing that Killion was fucking Lucy? Hell no. But it was a shared experience that haunted Killion as much, knowing she preferred the safety, security, and comfort of his arms when she needed someone to share her grief.

And Killion wasn't going to deny her wishes any more than Beckman was.

It also drove home the reality that Lucy was fulfilled on a level she never could be with him alone. He'd venture a guess that Killion could sustain her, but *for her*, he was willing to sacrifice to ensure she had everything she needed.

And Beckman was someone she needed.

CHAPTER FIFTY-TWO

Lucy

Ever since Isaac, her childhood crush who'd provided her with a dose of romance—and she hoped wherever he'd ended up in life, he was as happy as she was—she'd wanted a grand, sweeping romance. She wanted to be the envy of all who witnessed her love story, the way she was envious of Jonah and Elliott's love story.

The silly thing was, while she'd been waiting for a cinematic happy ending, for the hunk to transform from a photo and walk into her reality, she'd found love.

It was evidenced by the box of cupcakes with the frosting removed, cups of tea brewed, the bubble baths, and rotations of human weighted blankets. They were supporting her and honoring her grief for a man she'd never met. They were doing that together, for her, not giving a damn if it was silly of her.

It was further evidenced by their cooperation and silent communication. They were respectful of the alone time she'd been able to experience with both Beckman and Killion. Like cuddling with Becks and sharing the losses they had in common: He'd seen Easy Street Events as it was built and was equally saddened by the end of Gage's dream.

Or more shared bubble baths with Killion as they quietly recalled disasters, successes, and the silliness they'd shared working together. And mourning the loss of jobs they both had loved.

Sex. There was also sex.

These things centered her, lifted her, and made her realize that her love story might look different, but it was as sweeping and cinematic. It was possible; this relationship with them both was possible.

Her depression over the event center—She wasn't kidding anyone. She was devastated that a connection to Gage, one she felt was a link to the man, was what had caused her to spiral. More than the loss of a dream job. Maybe.

Instead of judging her, they'd worked together to see her needs met. She was never alone. At one point, they'd both climbed into bed with her, one on either side, so when she turned in her sleep, she was able to nestle into a warm, comforting chest.

And they ensured one of her legs was uncovered at all times. They were a team, striving to give her everything she needed.

How they communicated with one another, she didn't know. One, she'd been too beside herself, and two, they didn't speak much. They both knew her so well that they were able to anticipate her.

If the horror of the loss of Easy Street Events had a silver lining, it was this.

Pastor Vanessa had been correct. She was their common ground. And they were her world. More than Easy Street Events had been.

This could work. She was determined that it would work, and she would do everything within her power to ensure they both knew the depths of her devotion, appreciation, and love for them.

It was time for her to suck it up, to give back what they had given her.

Although, as Killion had once pointed out, they weren't playing cards, it was their turn to feel the full force of support.

Killion lost his job and home. Well, he would live with her.

Beckman lost part of his past. She couldn't give any of that back to him, but she would be witness to his memories, listen to his stories, and give them back to him by sharing the videos she had of Gage, the photos she'd saved.

It was time for Gage to fade from her fantasies, to join the pleasant thoughts and recollections of the immature crush on Isaac Rice. A what-could-have-been replaced with the reality of what is: these men who loved her.

For them, she was determined to be their harbor, as they'd given her a place to grieve.

No, their love story wouldn't make for a good Hallmark movie, but it was hers, theirs. And therefore, it was epic.

Chapter Fifty-Three

Killion

Killion fiddled with his cell phone, watching Lucy and Beckman. She was leaning against the counter, sipping tea, listening as the other man explained he'd taken a short leave of absence. Lucy expressed concern for his job, but he'd downplayed it.

He didn't want to admit it, but he was glad Beckman would be around a few days—or weeks—longer. He was certainly glad he was here today, because Killion had been keeping something from everyone. But with Becks here, he could go do what he needed to do and hopefully return with good news.

He was fucking praying for good news. Considering the change in timing, he expected a good outcome. However, he also knew not to count his chickens and all that.

Pocketing his phone, he cleared his throat, gaining their attention.

"Do you mind if I take off for a few hours?"

Lucy tilted her head, curious. "You don't need to ask permission. Where are you going?"

She was doing much better. After the first few days of grief and crying, her sorrow transitioned, and she focused on them, acknowledging what they'd lost.

"I've been so selfish." She bemoaned.

They were both quick to deny it. For him, it was because taking care of her gave him purpose and took his mind off his losses.

Killion ducked his head, rubbing his scalp. He was afraid to say it out loud, that he would jinx any part of what was about to happen.

But Beckman answered her. "He has a special parole hearing today."

Killion's head snapped up. How the fuck did he know?

Beckman continued, his lips curved into a small smile. "He has an opportunity to be released from supervision early."

Lucy gasped, clasping her hands together as she turned toward him fully. "What? Why didn't you say something sooner? Do I have time to change?"

"Change?" he echoed.

"To go with you."

Killion frowned. "It's not a graduation. I don't think I can bring an audience."

Beckman interjected again. "You can."

"Then we're going," Lucy declared, setting her cup down decisively. "I'm so excited for you, Killion! The timing with everything else, this would be so awesome."

"It's not a foregone conclusion." Killion tossed a glare at Beckman.

He'd have preferred for it to remain secret until he knew the outcome. He didn't want his devastation doubled by Lucy's disappointment if things didn't work out.

Lucy turned to Beckman. "This is a good sign, though, right?"

He nodded. "It was a Class E felony, and he's been compliant with his parole terms." Beckman shrugged. "And there may have been a campaign of letters sent to encourage the parole officer to expedite an early release."

Killion's brows rose in surprise. But his surprise morphed to shame before he covered it up. Embarrassed, he asked, "Letters?"

"From friends. Family. Your congregation. Pastor Vanessa." Becks paused before adding, "Me." He shrugged. "It doesn't hurt to have a detective write an endorsement."

Killion was incredulous. Honestly, he was shocked that Beckman would be willing to vouch for him. A week or so ago, the man had cracked a joke that would have sent Killion back to prison, much less reducing his parole term. And this special hearing had been on the books for several weeks; what they'd done had been long before the float trip.

And it would have worked in Beckman's favor if the parole board hadn't bothered to hold this special hearing. Because when Lucy decided to go to DC to see Becks, he'd need permission from his parole officer to go with her. Hell, he needed to let his PO know when he went to visit his mom, or to cross over into Kansas to pick something up for the event center.

He was lucky Elliott continued to employ him—and intended to keep him employed—until the property was cleaned up. That could take weeks. He'd have needed to check in to change his job.

Today, all of that could disappear.

"Why would you do that?" Killion asked.

Beckman glanced at Lucy, and he had his answer. It was for her.

"We're going with you," Lucy repeated.

"I—" Killion started, then stopped when his phone pinged. His heart leaped into his throat, terrified the message would be a cancellation notice.

But it was worse.

"It's Mom's nurse. There's been an accident."

Fuck his life. But his mother took priority, no matter what. Torn, disappointed, and tortured, he looked up at the two people watching him. "I need to go to her."

Beckman shook his head. "This is one shot, and you aren't missing it. Lucy and I will go to Warrensburg."

"But—"

Lucy reached back and grasped Beckman's arm. "He's right. We'll go. The nurses know me. Your mom knows me. Let us do this."

Her blue eyes pleaded with him, mirroring his own devastation at what could be a lost—and last—opportunity if he didn't honor his hearing date. But he was torn. It was his *mom.*

As though reading his mind, Beckman asked, "What would your mom want you to do?" Sensing Killion's answer, he declared, "We're going. It's what family does for one another. We'll text you updates."

Chapter Fifty-Four

Lucy

Lucy rushed into Rachel's apartment without bothering to knock. The door was cracked open, which couldn't have been a good thing, so she barged in.

"Lord have mercy!" Rachel gasped, slapping her hand to her heart at the sudden intrusion. "Lucy, you almost gave me a heart attack."

She skidded to a halt, startled and alarmed. Killing Killion's mom wasn't anything she wanted to do. And Rachel's heart was already not good. But she was sitting in a wheelchair wearing a terry cloth robe, looking uncomfortable but fine. The oxygen tank and mask were missing, though.

"You're okay."

Fanning her cheeks dramatically, Rachel answered, "Yes, of course I am. Why are you charging in here with your hair on fire?"

Her gaze shifted, and her eyebrows hit her forehead. "And who are you?"

Lucy whirled, staring at Beckman wide-eyed. "Oh!" She hadn't forgotten him, of course not. But she'd expected to walk into a serious situation—maybe Rachel passed out, incoherent—but not this. "Oh."

"My eyesight isn't what it used to be, but I can always see a handsome man."

Beckman chuckled, sharing an amused glance with Lucy. "I appreciate that."

He reached up and caressed her arm as he passed her on his way to Rachel. He extended that same hand to shake. "I'm Elliott Beckman."

Rachel frowned. "I recognize that name."

"I'm Elliott Rork's namesake, I suppose you can call it." He squatted down, more on Rachel's level instead of standing over her.

The woman hummed, her assessment frank while bordering on curious suspicion. But whatever she was thinking, she kept to herself.

Looking at Lucy again, she asked, "Why are you here?"

"Killion said the nurse texted him about an accident." Lucy moved to the chair Rachel usually sat in. "He couldn't be here, so here we are."

"Yes, he had a meeting with the parole board." Rachel's contemplative gaze slid over to Beckman again. "And you two were with him before coming here?"

Lucy nodded. "Yes, of course."

"Of course," Rachel parroted.

"I mean, that's why we're here." Lucy cocked her head in confusion.

Had Rachel hit her head? Stroke?

"Yes. I understand that. But why are you here instead of there, with him?"

Lucy's mouth fell open, and she shifted her attention to Becks. "Killion said the nurse—"

"I fell. I fall all the time. I wish they'd stop notifying him of every little slip." She shifted the edge of her robe, revealing a large hematoma on her knee, the discoloration spreading down to her shin.

"Does it hurt?" Lucy asked, skating her fingers through the air above the bruising but not touching.

"Only when you bring gorgeous men in and I'm sitting here in a robe."

Beckman chuckled.

Lucy fought not to roll her eyes. Yep, she was Killion's mom. "Then may I assist you in getting dressed?"

"I'll step out." Becks stood.

He reached over and lightly squeezed Lucy's shoulder, winked, and walked out.

Lucy turned her attention to Rachel, who was eyeing her with a smirk. Killion's smirk, to be exact.

Ignoring it and the silent, knowing look in her eyes, Lucy popped up to her feet. "Let's get you dressed, shall we?"

And she proceeded to fill the air with conversation in an effort to avoid and forestall Rachel's questions. She talked about the tornado, Killion's new lease on life, "fingers crossed," and the comfort of a good sweat suit, which Lucy was assisting her don.

After getting Rachel settled in her armchair, she called Beckman back into the room. He reentered, glancing up from his cell phone where he was texting.

"I sent an update."

Rachel's expression shifted, her concern evident. "How long until we know?"

Beckman shook his head. "It depends on what time the hearing was scheduled for and how many people are in the queue."

Lucy shared Rachel's concern. Waiting was a special kind of hell. Killion had earned this. If anyone deserved a break, he did. And to think he'd almost passed this chance up to come to his mother's side—who was okay, all things considered—gave her heart a panicked squeeze.

But he was there, and she and Beckman were here, and Rachel was fine.

"What do you want to do while we wait?" Lucy asked.

She needed a distraction. And Rachel was looking between her and Beckman, those questions silently floating around them. She needed Rachel to be distracted, too.

But Rachel wasn't having it. "So, you two are friends?"

Lucy wrinkled her nose. Technically, yes, but that wasn't the question Rachel was asking. She also didn't want to be dishonest with the woman—her other boyfriend's mother.

"More than that."

"Dating?" Rachel looked to Beckman for the answer.

"Yes." His answer was firm and sure.

Meanwhile, if Lucy wasn't sitting, her knees would be knocking. She watched Rachel closely, bracing for the affronted assault on her son's behalf.

Attention returning to Lucy, she asked, "And you and Killion?"

"Still together."

Had she squeaked? Her answer sounded like a squeak.

Rachel nodded. "Well, look at you."

Was that good or bad? Look at her like she was a whore? Or look at her like she could successfully pull two ridiculously handsome men at the same time?

"How about we watch a movie while we wait?" Rachel suggested, motioning to the television.

Lucy's eyes widened. Had she been dismissed?

Beckman gave her another wink as he walked over to the old TV-VCR combo. "Well, at least I know how to work one of these."

The movie ran its course. Lucy couldn't have named what it was to save her life. She was twisted up inside with worry about Killion and trying not to stare at Rachel, wondering what she was thinking.

Dinnertime came along, and Beckman escorted Rachel to the dining hall while Lucy followed. The staff provided them with a meal. Rachel assured them that guests were always welcome, as so few family members visited a majority of the tenants.

That depressed Lucy. And it made her fall in love even more with Killion for spending the amount of time with his mom that he did. Doubly so, because he'd needed to check in with his parole officer every time he left town.

Hopefully that ended today. But where was he? And why hadn't he at least texted an update?

They ate, chatted with Rachel's neighbors, and thanked the staff for the meal. Beckman once again offered his arm to Rachel for their stroll back to her apartment. Lucy didn't pay attention to their quiet conversation, walking behind them as she checked the signal on her phone. Nope, it was working.

"Baby!"

Lucy almost walked into their backs when they suddenly stopped at the door.

"Hi, Mom."

Lucy gasped, ducking around Beckman. Killion was leaning back against the window well he normally perched on when they visited. His arms were folded over his chest, and he was smiling wide.

Rachel released Beckman and rushed forward, her arms thrown wide. Killion met her in two steps, sweeping her into a fierce hug. Like a little boy, he buried his face in her neck.

Lucy slapped a hand to her heart, reaching for Beckman at the same time. She was going to cry. Rachel had already started, from the sounds of it, despite Killion's quiet assurance.

Looking up, Killion gave her a sheepish smile. "I'm no longer under supervision."

Lucy squealed. Beckman congratulated him. Rachel cried harder.

"Ma, calm down." Killion pulled back and started wiping her tears away, his smile intact. "It's all good."

"I know. I know." She grasped his hands and kissed them, looking up at him. "You've made mistakes, son, as we all do. But I am so proud of how you accepted responsibility and reacted to it. I'm proud that you're my son."

Killion swallowed hard, casting an embarrassed glance their way before returning his attention to his mother. "I'm sorry I let you down."

Rachel playfully smacked his chest. "You never did."

"May I...?" Lucy hesitantly asked, edging forward.

It wasn't that she wanted to deprive them of their moment, but she was dying to wrap her arms around this incredible man she was lucky to have in her life.

"Of course, of course, dear." Rachel stepped back. "After all, we're... what, exactly?"

"We're a family," Beckman said.

Lucy gauged Killion's response to the declaration that the three of them were together. He smiled and opened his arms to her. She flew into them, covering his face with little pecks.

"Oh, isn't that lovely," Killion's mom said. "And you make a beautiful family."

Killion pulled away, narrowing his eyes at his mother, suspicious. "Do you know what he means by that, Mom?"

With a playfully beleaguered sigh, Rachel nodded. "You treat me like I'm eighty. Of course I understand what he means. The only thing that matters, my beautiful boy, is that where there's love, there's family."

That was too easy. How was it so easy that everyone around her—around *them*—was so quick to accept the unusual relationship? Except for the hiccup with Elliott and Jonah, this was easier than she'd have imagined.

The answer came quickly. It was because she surrounded herself with good people. Accepting and supportive people, who loved and cared for her, for them. Who were rooting for their success despite any reservations because her happiness—their happiness—overrode any concerns.

She hoped her parents were understanding. Then again, she was raised to be as accepting as she had been accepted. Jonah's parents were the same; the two of them were shaped by their love and guidance.

They'd understand. And not because they would expect it of their silly goose, but because they loved her.

The when and how this was going to work out was a challenge to attack tomorrow, or the next day. She had her job ripped away. Killion had both his job and home disappear in the same moment.

They could take a minute to exist, to breathe. They were safe and together. For now, that's all that mattered.

Chapter Fifty-Five

Beckman

Beckman watched Killion and Lucy through the glass door of her balcony. After returning to the apartment, he'd made the excuse that he needed a cigarette. He didn't, nor did he light one up. He simply wanted to watch.

They sat on the sofa, reflections from the TV occasionally splashing across their faces, a bowl of popcorn between them. When their fingers clashed in a grab for the treat, they smiled. They pretended to have finger fights over the snack, not looking at one another, their gazes riveted on the television screen.

Killion surrendered every time so Lucy could fill her hand.

The evening was a quiet continuation of their earlier celebration. They'd gone out for ice cream at Rachel's insistence; she wanted to mark the occasion with her son. After negotiations and pleading with the staff, they were able to make the proper assurances for Rachel's safety and return.

The outing was brief, regardless, because it had worn Rachel out quickly. He and Lucy waited out in the hallway while Killion remained with his mother, getting her ready for bed and saying goodbye.

They'd driven back to Kansas City separately. Lucy rode with Killion, and Beckman followed them. Alone, his gaze trained on the truck ahead of him, he'd experienced the familiar panic usually reserved for the Rorks.

Instead of dwelling on the fear despite his clenching stomach, he decided to do something about it so he wouldn't have to worry again. The leap was bigger than he was ready for, but that was the whole point, wasn't it?

You made sacrifices for the one you love. Only, it didn't feel like a sacrifice to give Lucy everything—and everyone—she wanted. And she wanted more than him. She deserved more.

Were he and Ellie in the place he needed to be—where *they* needed to be—after one conversation? Was he prepared for life to move this fast after the night he and Killion came to an agreement in the tent? Had he foreseen a speedy pace when they'd told Rachel about the relationship?

No, to all. He'd expected time for them to ease into this dynamic. But Mother Nature, the universe, whatever it was, had other plans for them.

Ellie and he had taken huge steps forward, and they would continue to do so.

But Lucy and Killion? Like he'd told Rachel, and Killion had backed him up, they were family. He would take care of them.

Beckman left his perch on the balcony and went inside. Both sets of eyes turned to him. Lucy smiled, a touch of curious concern evident by her creased brows. He had been outside for a while.

Killion merely watched, bringing a handful of popcorn to his mouth.

"I saved you a seat." Lucy patted the sofa.

Beckman nodded once in acknowledgment but opted for the ottoman in front of her. She stared back quizzically. Killion slowed his chewing, his expression turning wary, guarded.

Whatever the fuck was happening on the screen behind him no longer held interest. He had their undivided attention.

"Move to DC."

Well, that wasn't how he'd wanted to approach it, blurting it out, but there it was.

Killion stiffened, darting a look over at Lucy. She looked confused, like she hadn't heard him correctly.

"Come back to DC with me. Permanently."

Their stunned silence overpowered the action on the television. Killion's gaze ping-ponged between them, looking to Lucy for her reaction while sizing him up and his sincerity. There was a hint of anger in his eyes.

Worry.

Defensiveness.

Amending, Beckman added, "I meant both of you."

Killion finally swallowed, but his expression didn't change much. It was obvious he was waiting for Lucy's response before he said anything.

Lucy shook her head. "I don't understand."

Beckman's heart was pounding so hard he was sure they could see the pulse in his neck. Maybe even hear it over the laughter on the screen. Preferring not to compete with it, he grabbed the remote and hit the mute button.

"It's a conversation we haven't had yet, how this plays out in the future." He glanced at Killion. "Now seems like the right time."

"It sounded like an order," Killion pointed out.

Fair. He'd been clumsy. "A request. A plan."

Lucy placed a hand on Killion's thigh. It was a gesture to soothe, as though she could sense his unease, but her attention stayed on him. "Where is this coming from?"

"Recent events, pix. You're out of a job." He shifted his gaze to Killion. "A job and a home."

Stating the obvious.

"Yeah, but you can't expect to snap your fingers and we'll fall in line. Move several states away at the drop of a hat?"

"Elliott might rebuild."

Beckman understood she was hopeful more than certain. "If she doesn't?"

Lucy shrugged, looking lost. She didn't want to contemplate it, and he hated pushing their reality to the fore.

He addressed Killion. "Not today. Like I said, this discussion would have taken place at some point. Am I right?"

Killion's jaw tensed, but he nodded.

They were quiet again. Contemplative. Understanding they were on the precipice of the unknown and the next words spoken would plunge them forward or force a step back. Seconds ticked by. Minutes.

Beckman watched them as they mulled, considered. Took his offer seriously. Lucy's eyes roamed around her little apartment. Killion rubbed his hand over his scalp, his gaze downcast.

It wasn't like they weren't aware—of course they were—but they'd all been reacting to the now instead of looking ahead. Some of that might have been denial, but Beckman guessed it was largely survival mode.

"My mom."

Beckman shifted his attention to Killion. "There are facilities in Arlington and DC."

"I've lived in Kansas City since I was a kid. And my apartment is so cute."

What she wasn't saying gave him hope. She wasn't digging in her heels. In fact, her statements were those of bidding another goodbye. She had lived here most of her life, and her apartment was cute, but truthful statements weren't a refusal.

"It's not safe to live here without a working smoke detector." He winked, trying to lighten the somber mood.

Grabbing at the bit of humor he displayed, she matched him, dramatically throwing herself backward against the cushions. "Oh my god, I'm losing my deposit."

Beckman smiled. She was in.

Chapter Fifty-Six

Killion

Beckman's offer of his home was humbling. For Lucy, Killion expected it, but Becks included him. And offered reassurances about his mother. His initial delivery had been shit, but he'd also been thoughtful.

Killion wasn't sure he would be as magnanimous as Beckman if their roles were reversed, which was why it was humbling. There was also a part of him that was embarrassed he *couldn't* do the same, offer the same. He was always depending on someone else's charity. First Lucy's, through the church program, then Elliott, giving him a job and home.

Now Beckman.

He loved Lucy. They both loved Lucy. She loved them. Making her choose a state, a home, a man, wasn't fair to her. Or to them, either.

When Beckman had told his mom they were a family, a unit, Killion had agreed. Not because he was completely sold on it—nor, he suspected, was Beckman—but because it was a goal.

Now, he saw the foundation of that family unit being poured. And he was ready and willing to make that jump with them. As uncertain as the future may be, he knew he didn't want to face it without Lucy beside him.

Chapter Fifty-Seven

Beckman

Ellie stood next to him as they considered the only building left standing on the property. Demolition had started on the destroyed structures. Large dumpsters were strategically placed, filled with the remnants of Gage's work.

Except this building. The place where Gage had discovered Beckman and Ellie. Where Gage had held a gun on him and threatened to kill him, severing all familial-type strings, a scene that had broken them all differently.

Beckman knew Gage had been struggling to maintain his hold on life. They had all been aware of the silent phantom that stalked them when they sang around a campfire to Gage's covers of country songs, joked over morning coffee and eggs, and as Gage kept perfecting the event space. Ellie stubbornly ignored the apparition, as though wishing it away would make it disappear. Beckman tried to gauge the intensity of the specter.

But that day. Those few days after. Not even Beckman had seen it coming; or maybe he'd simply grabbed onto Ellie's denial and cloaked himself in it. He'd been cocooned until he'd heard her screams. Until he'd placed

Ellie in a chokehold so he could drag her away from her brother's hanging body.

He'd clocked it when initially discovering that this was the only building unscathed: Ellie would take it as a sign. Hard not to. It was how she'd interpret it, he'd imagined. Now he knew.

"He'll never forgive me."

Beckman tapped out a cigarette, shaking his head.

"This one," she said quietly. "This is the one he left for me, mocking me, blaming me. Condemning me."

He lit up, taking in a calming draw and pushing it out. "It was a fucking tornado. This is random."

She turned toward him, angry disbelief on her face. "Random? Weirdly fucking random, Becks. Why *this* one?"

"It's the farthest out. Physics. Fuck, I don't know, but this isn't about you, us. Nothing supernatural occurred here." He didn't fully believe his own words because it was really freaking creepy.

A flicker of amusement briefly permeated her sadness.

At his questioning look, she answered, "Jonah and I have an inside joke about physics."

The moment was short-lived.

"He's forcing me to tear it down. That feels like a punishment, a further punishment. Tear it down, the last place I'd seen him—both alive and then dead—the place where I'd pushed him over that line."

"Or maybe he's asking you to say goodbye. Clean slate, Els. Knock it down, don't get tethered to a *fucking building* and move on with your life. If you want to go supernatural, it's symbolism, I guess. Lay our shit to rest—including his—by you swinging the hammer. So to speak. Instead of seeing it as a sign of doom, maybe it's a gift." He pointed toward the woods. "A bigger lesson than his stones: What gets built gets destroyed.

Rebuild."

Her gaze swung back to the structure, contemplating.

"I'll be right here with you when you do it." He added, "And Jonah. He'll want to be here."

A small smile made an appearance at the man's name.

"He will. And Lucy."

Now Beckman smiled because the thought of Lucy made him smile, and knowing Lucy would want to say goodbye, too. Yeah, she'd lost her dream job, but it helped her heal and move beyond the man's ghost. To that end, he added, "And Killion. This was his home. He knew every nook and cranny as well as Gage, or you."

Beyond the fact that Lucy would want Killion here as well, it was something Killion would want to take part in simply to support Lucy and Ellie.

She nodded. "Our family."

His heart tumbled. Gooseflesh rose on his arms. He sniffed hard so he wouldn't gasp out a sob. He didn't know how much he'd needed that from her, the acknowledgment and acceptance. The reassurance.

Yeah, Gage—or nature—had given them a gift. This building, this property, was a tie that bound both he and Ellie to their guilt, shame, and grief. It was high fucking time that bind was severed. And their family would cut the invisible cord with them.

Chapter Fifty-Eight

Lucy

Cleaning up Easy Street Events was an exercise in torture. There wasn't anything left to salvage, yet her romantic heart felt sentimental about every shingle and shard of glass thrown away. Day after day, they were out here, placing their home, their job, their memories, into dumpsters.

Small equipment, mowers and other tools, trellises, party tents, and the like were undamaged in the last building. Before it was torn down—after Beckman and Elliott had a go at it with sledgehammers first—Elliott suggested, "Maybe the church will have a use for these things. Or know what to do with them."

Jonah and Killion had turned disbelieving eyes to her.

Noticing, she shrugged. "What?" She moved past them, wiping her hands on her blue jeans. "If they don't take it, call Disabled Veterans."

A whisper of a smile on his lips, Jonah answered, "Nothing. I'll make some calls."

Of course, it was too big a job for the five of them alone. Members of the church did show up, and the warehouse items were hauled away to find use elsewhere. After a couple of weeks, though, the real contractors were scheduled to arrive. Other than overseeing the clearing of the property, there wasn't much left to do.

Elliott wasn't rebuilding. Lucy was sad about that, but she knew the event space had been Gage's dream, not Elliott's. It was right that she moved on to pursue something of her own.

As dusk gathered, Jonah, Beckman, and Killion reluctantly left them. She and Elliott had assured them that they would meet up at the pizza shop in Parkville. Kisses, hugs and final assurances were made before the men left.

Alone, she and Elliott sat on the concrete rim of the empty fountain. Elliott reached into a cooler and pulled out two beers, handing one to her. In silent contemplation, they sipped their brews and stared at the scene.

For Lucy, it would be the last time. She and Killion would be going to DC with Beckman. She had an interview lined up as a hotel event coordinator. Killion found a spot as an apartment maintenance man. She would put money on the fact that Beckman facilitated both of those interviews—and Killion's resulting position—considering how many people he knew, and how fast it happened.

Would it be as wonderful as Easy Street Events? Most likely not, but she would be with Beckman and Killion. That made up for the loss of the best job she'd ever had.

"I'm glad you put the pictures on the website."

Lucy nodded, knowing Elliott was referring to the photos of the construction of Easy Street Events; the ones she'd scanned, along with the architectural designs, and uploaded to the event space website. Some were from a computer file, but the drawings in Gage's own hand hadn't been.

"It wasn't enough," she said quietly. "I didn't have enough time here. Then again, it was so much."

Elliott nodded.

Lucy assumed it wasn't because she agreed—not wholly, anyway—but more of a gesture to acknowledge Lucy's words.

"I don't mean to be selfish, but I want more time. I love this place."

"I know." Elliott sighed, turning the beer bottle in her hands. "More time would have been nice."

With Gage.

Lucy didn't need her to say the words to hear them.

"What are we supposed to do now?" Lucy asked.

It was rhetorical considering they'd made plans, but it felt like the right thing to ask.

Elliott was quiet for a minute. Then she chuckled softly as she nudged Lucy with her shoulder. "We live, Lucy."

Epilogue

*B*eckman

Lucky seven. Who the fuck would have thought they'd last so long?

For the first couple of years, he and Killion were laying bets on who would bounce first or which one of them Lucy would finally choose. But neither he nor Killion walked away, and Lucy never chose.

The adjustment to Arlington—the three of them cohabitating—hadn't been easy. Watching Killion and Lucy together in close quarters, the displays of affection, knowing when she wasn't in his bed, or hers, that she was in Killion's, struck harder than he'd anticipated. He knew Killion experienced the same reaction judging from the initial glares and expressions of possessiveness.

Did they sometimes share a bed? Yes. Did they fuck her at the same time? No. Did she want that? Maybe, but she'd never asked for it. If she had? Honestly, he was sure that would be the first time they disappointed her, so he was grateful when she hadn't requested it. Beckman was confident, however, that she craved intimacy more than the sex. And both men were on board with providing that.

It took time for them to achieve the balance and symmetry they'd briefly experienced after the tornado. But they got there. And a year after relocating, they'd returned to Kansas City for their wedding.

Pastor Vanessa married them in the church. Although not legally binding, his and Killion's commitment to Lucy deserved a ceremony amongst their family and friends. The congregation gathered to witness Lucy's start of her happily ever after. Of course Rachel attended, along with both Lucy's and Jonah's parents.

"Your love and commitment to each other is more powerful than any one of man's laws." The pastor assured them, speaking loudly for everyone to hear.

The place had erupted in cheers and applause.

If he were honest, in the beginning, he and Killion were only committed to Lucy and her happiness. Over the years, though, they'd formed a friendship and a bond. Mutual respect and an appreciation for what the other brought to Lucy's life—and by an extension, their own—cemented that commitment. So they'd hung in there, the three of them, through growing pains, endless compromises, fights, and a fuck ton of love. All their experiences—good, bad, and downright ugly—kept them on track.

Jonah and Ellie assisted in keeping the peace when needed, even if from a distance. Those two remained in Kansas City after flirting with the idea of moving to Oregon, but KC was their home. They bought the space next to Jonah's shop, where Ellie taught kickboxing. They remodeled the upper floors of the shops, converting it into their home.

But the best addition to his, Killion, and Lucy's unconventional life was their kids. Two sassy, cheeky, rambunctious girls with dark hair and Killion's features.

When Amber was born, somber and looking pissed off at being forced out her mother's womb, he'd fallen as hard as Killion. There'd been no doubt that she was Killion's child, but it didn't matter. Both dads and mom sobbed with joy. Eleven months later, their little monster, Ria—*definitely* Killion's daughter—provided the same experience.

Lucy's babies were his babies; the tumble into parental love was instant.

Killion hadn't missed a beat while beaming at his firstborn. He kissed Amber's head and whispered, "I'm Daddy." Then he'd passed her to Beckman, making the introductions. "And this is your Papa."

And he was; he was their Papa. They were a unit, a family, the five of them.

They'd moved Rachel to a facility close by. Before she died, she'd met her first granddaughter. Holding the tiny bundle, she cried happy tears, declaring to her son, "You're okay now."

He'd laughed. "I'm fine, Mom."

Two days later, she'd slipped away peacefully in her sleep. They'd all understood her words then, recognizing, after the fact, that she'd been waiting to release her hold on life. Killion was happy with a family of his own; he was okay.

Not that they weren't devastated, himself included. Rachel had become a good friend. They'd grieved together, supporting and comforting Killion where and when he needed it. Lucy's second pregnancy eased the pain as they focused on welcoming another life.

Although distant geographically, Ellie and Jonah were there for every win, loss, and fight. The connection ensured memories and traditions were passed on—except for Charlotte's lasagna recipe. Ellie held that one close.

But there had been that time over the holidays when Amber started calling him "Papa Becky." Beckman had side-eyed Killion, but it was Ellie who'd snort laughed, giving away the culprit. The cycle continued. He didn't give a fuck; he loved the mischievous look in Ellie's eyes.

With Lucy's third pregnancy, they prepared for another daughter. They had previously agreed that any and all babies' genders be a surprise, and no paternity tests were to be taken. Looking at Amber and Ria, however, there was no need for tests. Lucy once chortled that their natures were also a dead giveaway.

But as Beckman stared in awe at the wrinkled red face of the boy he held, twenty minutes into life, the world cemented for him. For the first time, he had a *family*. He wasn't on the periphery, wishing and wanting more even though he was already so fucking fulfilled. Amber and Ria were his daughters, and he'd rock anyone's world who dared to hurt them. There was a sense of peace when he read them bedtime stories, or when he watched Killion and Lucy carrying them on walks, or trying to control tired temper tantrums at the zoo.

But there was no experience that could have prepared him for the earth-shattering feeling of holding his son. The babe had a sprinkling of blond hair, like both he and Lucy. But Luce had taken one look at her newest child and mockingly wailed, "None of my babies look like me!"

And then she'd beamed at him despite her exhaustion.

Killion smacked him on the back. "Congratulations, Dad."

He'd blubbered, he'd bawled, and he'd been directed to a chair so he could receive his son without collapsing to the floor. Lucy was being put through her postdelivery paces, but she'd waved him off. Killion was taking care of her, and she swung from crying happily to wincing in pain.

The fucking weird thought that raced through his brain as he'd stared at the fourth most perfect child he'd ever seen (fourth, because Ellie had been the first)? He was glad Killion was young enough to take care of his son. At fifty-nine, Beckman never felt his age more than in this moment, a sharp terror gripping his heart. But the fear was soothed because he knew his son would have Lucy and Killion and his sisters.

The hustle and bustle subsided, the hospital staff leaving them. Lucy was sitting up in bed. "I only picked out girl names."

He heard the door swish open.

"It'd only be fair to name him Kristine."

Hearing her voice, Beckman looked up, smiling through his tears. Ellie grinned back at him, peeking her head in the door. Killion, obviously having beckoned them from the waiting room, moved to hold the door open wider. She slipped inside, Jonah sidling in next to her; he looked to Lucy first, ensuring she was okay, before turning his attention to father and son.

"Why Kristine?" Killion asked, returning to Lucy's side, taking her hand.

"It's my middle name. I was named for him, so he can name his baby boy after me." Her expression was mischievous.

Beckman breathed deep and looked into the face of his boy—his *son*—again.

"There is one name." Lucy said it quietly, and it was like she'd conjured the man into the room.

"*No.*"

Shocked by the word adamantly spoken, everyone turned to Ellie, but she was focused on Beckman. Moving across the room, she knelt beside the chair. Her expression mirrored love, pride, and a plea.

Glancing over at Lucy, she explained. "I love you for thinking about it, but no. Gage's legacy isn't one this child should bear. I love my brother. There won't be a day I don't grieve for him, but Gage needs to remain that: a memory we recall with love." She looked at Beckman. "And for me, regret."

Beckman gave her a chiding look before he glanced across at Lucy and Killion. Tears were falling down Lucy's face, but she nodded. He shifted his gaze to Killion.

"No, don't look at me. Luce and I've named two girls."

Lucy added, "Can we at least call him Elliott? His middle name? I'd like for that name to continue."

Ellie burst into tears.

With a playful groan, Jonah crossed the room to them. He pulled Ellie up into his arms, hugging her. "Okay there, kitten."

She sniffled, wiped her nose on his shirt, then turned in his arms to lean back against him.

Beckman noted Jonah's hand slid to her abdomen, and she melted, covering his hand with her own. Beckman flicked his gaze to hers in serious assessment. "Are—?"

With a slash of her hand, she cut him off. "Quit stalling, Daddy."

But her eyes were soft and answered with a quiet *yes.*

The day couldn't get better. He was holding his son while Ellie was holding a secret of her own. He cleared his throat; they would tell their news when it suited them.

"I'm not Daddy. I'm Papa." He smiled at Killion. "*That's* Daddy."

Killion couldn't have looked more shocked. "Wait—"

"We have two girls at home who I don't want to confuse."

Lucy dramatically threw her head back against the pillows. "Oh my god, do you understand now why I love these two men?" With a laugh, she rolled her head on the pillow, seeking out her best friend. She looked so fucking exhausted and goddamn beautiful at the same time. "Hey, Jonah?"

Jonah softly responded, "Yeah, Lucy?"

"All the love. Overwhelmed by it. It wasn't too much to wish for."

***

Beckman pushed the cash across the counter, trading the dollars for cigarettes.

"Those things'll kill ya."

Beckman nodded. "Maybe I should quit." He smiled at the older man and grinned. "After all, my son was born today."

Fishing in his pocket, he produced his phone. Lucy holding their child was already set as his lock screen. He was looking forward to having all three of his children represented. He tilted the device to share the photo. "Kristopher Elliott."

He and Luce had taken Ellie's "Kristine" comment to heart, but not too much to heart. The look on Ellie's face—worth it.

Glancing briefly at the phone, the old man shook his head, taking the money. "No better reason, then."

Beckman stared down at the pack. The old man was right. He pushed the cigarettes back across the counter. "How about replacing these with one of those cigars?"

Like a double celebration of life: the birth of his child and a healthier future so he could watch his son grow.

The cigarettes were swapped out for what was probably a stale cigar, but Becks waved off the few dollars the man tried to return to him. He stepped outside the convenience store and paused, looking around. As late as it was, the downtown neighborhood where the hospital was located bustled with activity.

He walked over to a filthy, dented trash can and removed the plastic. His eyes scanned the windows in front of him, lingering in the area where he imagined his family was ensconced, happy and tired and safe.

Lucy had been lightly snoozing when he'd left. Killion had been in the corner, cell phone pressed to his ear as he quietly checked in on the girls. Ellie had been snuggling with the baby, cooing and grinning while Jonah watched with pride and anticipation—no doubt imagining their own bundle in her arms.

He'd caught Ellie's admonishing look when he'd opened the door.

Winking, he slipped out.

His family. Like Lucy had said, it wasn't too much to wish for.

Two pops exploded behind him from inside the store he'd just vacated, snapping him to attention. And when the kid with stringy blond hair came charging from the shop, Beckman gave chase.

It didn't matter that this wasn't his jurisdiction.

It didn't matter that he wasn't armed.

His training kicked in, and he chased. After all, his son was born today. He was invincible.

Killion

Two pops made him jump and instinctively reach over the bed in a pathetic attempt to protect Lucy, who remained oblivious as she slept.

"This fucking town."

The hospital had a great reputation; it was tied to Lucy's ob-gyn. But it wasn't located in the best area.

"That was close." Elliott's tone was hushed, a natural level when a baby and exhausted mother were sleeping.

She cast a concerned look toward the windows, holding Kristopher closer, her hand covering his head.

Jonah left her side where he'd been sitting and walked to the window to peer out.

"Jonah!" she whisper-yelled.

"We're too far away to be a target." He scanned the outside.

Curiosity getting the best of him, Killion started around the bed to join

Jonah at the window. Three more shots rang out. As he had moments earlier, he lunged over the bed even as Jonah stepped to the side, away from the glass.

"What the hell?" Killion demanded, more irritated by his lack of cool than fear of being harmed.

Kristopher started fussing, the newborn's cry adding to the tension.

But it was Lucy who gained his attention when she jerked, eyes fluttering open, disoriented and alarmed. "Beckman!"

Epilogue 2

GAGE

Jonah once pointed out that I was the most present absent person ever.

Hey there. Yes, the ghost speaks.

You've read my sister's story, and now you've read my uncle's. I'll keep this short because he just arrived. Don't be upset, he's okay. He went out in action, doing the right thing, and on the top of the world; the happiest he'd ever been. What better time to go? Opposites, we are. He went out on a high, and I went out on the lowest of lows. I'd have taken his exit over mine any day.

I wanted to tell my own story in the first book, but it wasn't deemed necessary, so you heard my story from Ellie's point of view. That means something got left out, so let me set the record straight: My leaving was never her fault. It wasn't Beckman's fault. Their guilt made my afterlife suck, knowing I couldn't relieve them of that.

The letter? Yeah, in hindsight, maybe not the best idea. I wasn't myself, and I didn't want to *be* myself. Els handed me an excuse, and I used it, damning her as I did so. That's not to say I wasn't fucking livid to find out what they'd been doing—I was. But that wasn't what ended me. *I* ended

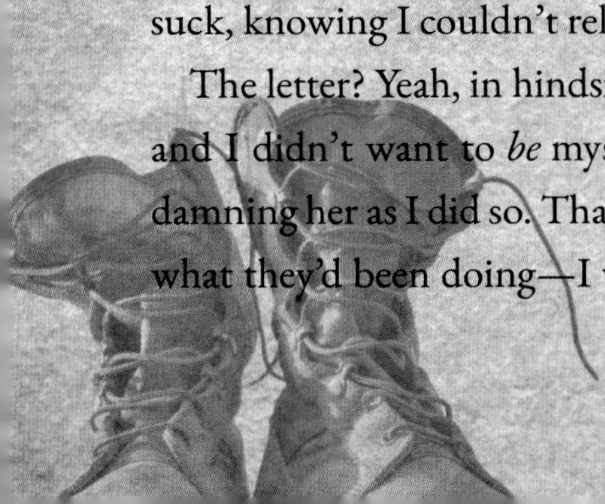

me.

I got to a point where the music no longer had rhythm; I didn't care if I finished reading the book. Hell, nothing tasted good. Everything that'd gone wrong was my fault—that's the perception. I literally had zero fucks left to give. That's where my head was when I found them together. I was already there, in that hole.

What took me so long after I found them? My pussy ass was afraid that people would think I was weak. I'm not weak. Planning your death is fucking hard. Paperwork, wills to make sure the people you cared about were taken care of—it was all in place. Lucy pointed that out in the beginning.

I did this. Me, alone. I hate that she was too twisted up to realize it was never about her, or about how much she loved me. Was her love enough? It is—it was.

Lucy. Fuck, that woman would have had a chokehold on me. A pretty woman with a prettier heart. Could she have saved me? No. Only I could have, and I didn't want to. I was tired.

Is she going to be okay? Yeah. Killion will make sure of that. He's a solid man whose happiness comes from making those around him happy. And she has their three babies. She's going to hurt for a long time, but that's life.

And death.

So why am I riding the coattails of their story? Because I need Ellie to know it wasn't her fault.

Love you, sis. I want you to have the best fucking life possible. And you will. You all will, despite everything, because you're surrounded with love.

Now, I'm going to welcome my uncle.

Peace out.

XOXO.

Bonus Scenes

B1: Lucy

She'd had a dream once, as she lay in Beckman's arms, that he'd disappeared. He reassured her that he wouldn't leave her.

But he did.

How was she going to explain to Kristopher his father's choice that took him away from them on his birthday? How could she look into his eyes and take away his innocence? To tarnish the grin that reminded her so much of Becks?

How could she provide him with answers she didn't know?

She tried to fool herself that the love he was surrounded by would be enough. And he was desperately loved. By her, Killion, his sisters, Jonah, and Elliott.

Who would have imagined that she and Elliott would bond the most over the death of Beckman? Before Lucy had been released from the hospital, Elliott climbed into the bed with her, and they held each other, inconsolable, knowing only the other understood the depth of the other's pain.

They rallied for Kristopher, the only connection left to a man they both loved.

When they left the hospital, they planned a funeral. Although, to be fair, it was Killion and Jonah who worked with the MPD regarding the ceremony. As much as the community attempted to support her, her devastation was so great that she couldn't focus.

She knew it was about respect and honoring his service to the community, but she was in too much pain to notice or care how he was buried. He wasn't here with her, and that's all she wanted. Him.

Elliott and Killion rode with her, their vehicle following the procession that led the hearse, which had its own escort of four motorcycles. Jonah stayed behind to watch the children, not because he didn't want to be there for them, but because she didn't want to leave Kristopher with a stranger. And she didn't want her newborn's first outing to be his father's funeral.

After the ceremony, she and Elliott lay in bed and cried. They shared memories. They cooed and fussed over Kristopher, neither one of them voicing their devastation that Kristopher would never know his father.

Then one day, Jonah entered the room and took Elliott away.

Shutting everyone out hadn't been intentional but she knew Killion was taking care of the girls so she could fall apart. It was when she dragged herself into the kitchen late one night to get a drink of water and she found him crying at the kitchen table that she realized she'd been selfish long enough.

Since that night, she hobbled forward, determined not to let her broken heart wipe the smiles off her little girl's faces any more than they had been. And when they cried for their Papa, she comforted them. She didn't try to put on a brave face when confronted with their grief because she wanted them to feel safe expressing their feelings.

But she also wouldn't mope around her girls, fearing her depression would frighten them.

And she took immense joy in them, basking in their light for a moment.

Both she and Killion marveled over their wonderment of their little brother, the demands to hold him, their guesses at what his cries meant.

Even Ria's dramatic grumbling over Kristopher's nighttime crying—"Daddy, can you turn him off? I'm losing beauty sleep"—had her parents laughing.

Lucy was trying, she was. But she wasn't succeeding.

A few months after Kristopher was born, she was feeding him, gliding back and forth in the rocker. She looked up at Killion. He was leaning against the jamb, watching, arms folded over his chest. Her favorite pose, his sexy man lean.

"I want to move back to Kansas City."

He hadn't answered, but his attention didn't waver.

"There's been too much death here."

And although she loved Beckman beyond measure, his ghost in this house was too much.

Killion nodded. "Let's go home."

She loved Killion for many reasons. At this moment, it was because he felt it, too: Without Becks, Arlington was no longer home.

B2: Killion

Killion gently bounced Kristopher in his arms as he paced the darkened hallway. The ritual was familiar, one he'd done for the past eleven months. He'd performed the same rites with Amber and Ria. The difference with Kristopher, besides the hallway of their new Kansas City home, was the sting of resentment that continued to accompany his steps.

He wasn't upset with Kristopher—that would be fucked up—or with Lucy, who was still struggling to find her footing because her heart had been shattered. Her sunny smiles were reserved for the children. In his arms was where she had permission to fall apart.

No, he resented Beckman.

Killion had looked forward to relinquishing night patrol when Kristopher was born. Although Becks had helped with the girls, Killion didn't sleep much when Beckman had taken his turn. He was an anxious father even though he trusted the man implicitly. The need to be the one to care for the girls had been consuming. Despite being exhausted, there was a thrill that'd run through him taking care of his daughters. He'd ceded the responsibility to both Lucy and Beckman because he could, but he'd wanted to spare Lucy the task because middle-of-the-night feedings had kept her from a full night's sleep. It wasn't fair to further deprive her of sleep.

So this late-night attempt to soothe Kristopher back to sleep should have been something Beckman experienced with his son. Walking the halls, exhausted, the joys of parenting entwined with the sheer work of it. Beckman should have been the one to wonder, and attempt to answer, why his child consistently woke up at eleven every night and fought returning to slumber.

The time Kristopher chose to jolt from sleep was disconcerting. It was close to when his father had been shot. Killion refused to think about the coincidence as he walked a darkened hallway, only because he didn't want to freak himself out.

Which he'd done plenty of times since bringing the child home.

After almost an hour of bouncing, walking, and low humming, Killion sensed victory. He cautiously made his way to Kristopher's little room. A tiny barely illuminating lamp was on the dresser—next to the boy's birthday photo with his father—but it was enough to light his way, guiding him to the crib where he deposited his precious bundle.

He watched for a few seconds to ensure Kristopher remained asleep through the transfer. Satisfied, Killion sidestepped and collapsed into the rocking chair. He rocked himself back and forth, an automatic motion once seated.

It was moments like this, late at night, that he gave in to his fears and his tears.

The overwhelming loss, still, almost a year later.

He preferred to grieve alone. Lucy wouldn't begrudge him, of course not, but he didn't want to contribute to her heartbreak. He wanted to be strong for her.

They'd been a team, the three of them. A tripod relationship. Where one faltered, the other stepped in. It'd taken them a while to find that balance, but they'd achieved it. Now, a very important part of them—a critical piece—was gone.

And Beckman had missed out on so much already. His son was speedily crawling, pulling himself up, and shuffling along furniture. He was babbling, earnestly attempting conversations with his older sisters. He threw kisses with his hand.

The first time he'd called Killion "Dada" had devastated him. Not for any other reason than Beckman should have heard his son say those words to him.

His panicked and guilty gaze had shot to Lucy to gauge her reaction, as though he'd done something wrong to bring on the identifier.

Her eyes had watered, but tears didn't fall. Instead, she let out a soft laugh. "His first word." She'd caressed his arm and beamed up at him. "Congratulations, Dada."

Killion hadn't known it was possible to be honored and gutted at the same time.

How was he supposed to raise the man's son? How would he know if Beckman would approve? It was a terrible burden to thrust onto someone, the responsibility to get it right, for both father and son.

Becks assisting with the girls was different. Then, the man had two guides: Killion and Lucy. It'd never been discussed, but Beckman had quietly deferred to them, following in their parental footsteps.

It wasn't how he and Luce had meant it to be; it hadn't been intentional. Killion had been certain that the three of them played equal roles in raising the girls.

But as he watched Kristopher sleep, he realized that hadn't been the case at all. He knew that, because he was lost. He didn't know how to be a dad to this child, despite his desire to do so, because this wasn't supposed to have been his alone to figure out.

"Fuck you, man."

Those words were also familiar.

He daily cursed Beckman's decision to leave the hospital room that night.

Explaining to the girls that Papa wasn't coming home had been the hardest thing he'd done. They hadn't fully comprehended what it meant, and in the weeks since Beckman died, they'd ask when he was coming back. And then the tears started again at the loss. They missed him. Of course they did. Everyone did.

It'd been equally hard explaining why Mommy cried and slept all day, and why Aunt Ellie was allowed to sleep in the bed with Mommy but not them.

That only lasted a few days, the cocooning of the women. Jonah had broken into their grief and taken Elliott home. A few months later, Lucy asked to move back to Kansas City.

"There's been too much death here," she'd said quietly.

Two. His mom and Beckman.

And because he'd do anything for her, he agreed. Kansas City was where their support system was now that Beckman was gone. Remaining in Arlington didn't make sense.

They found a cute home in Kansas City. Four bedrooms, which was an easier find than the five bedrooms they'd had in Arlington: one each for he, Luce, and Beckman. They would have had to move again in the DC area, regardless, once the girls got older.

But this house provided a room for each child. He and Lucy shared a bedroom now.

Their timing had been such that he'd been able to step in as a trainer for Elliott's kickboxing classes. She was too upset—Becks having been the one to teach her to kickbox—to resume the demanding schedule. Eventually, she was too pregnant.

Then baby Elizabeth Lucille was born.

Although only five months old now, the child was a stunning replica of her mother with a hint of green invading her otherwise blue-gray eyes. And she was a giggling baby, quick to burst into laughter. Infant giggles were the best.

So he joined the staff at Trek Gear, Jonah's sporting goods store and Elliott's kickboxing studio. Lucy was able to transfer within the hotel chain she worked for.

They had a home, jobs, the children, and their extended family. They were luckier than most, and he knew it. But he'd have given anything to watch Beckman walk the halls in an attempt to coax his son back to sleep.

B3: Lucy

Jonah sat next to Lucy on the park bench as they watched the antics in front of them, a small smile on his lips.

The girls—Elliott included—scream-laughed as Killion chased them, hands up imitating claws, growling fiercely. They scrambled to escape the tickle monster. Amber and Ria had begged Aunt Ellie to play with them, and although Lucy could tell she was reluctant to leave her daughter's side, Elliott couldn't resist the girls.

Elizabeth slept in her stroller parked beside Jonah. Her pink lips moved in and out as she breathed with her mouth open. Similar to her mother, the child liked to sleep. Elliott was thrilled to discover her daughter was a great sleeper.

"Sweep, Beff."

Kristopher leaned closer to her and patted her head gently. He critically eyed her blanket, finding the need to adjust it and tucking it under her chin. Kristopher was captivated by the baby.

Elliott and Jonah, while they called their daughter by her full name, had once wondered if she would use Eliza or Beth as a nickname when she got older. Kristopher decided it for them when he naturally shortened it to

Beth.

"Six months apart," Jonah said.

Lucy nodded in response to Jonah's observation.

He nudged her with his shoulder. "We get to watch us grow up together."

She smiled. "Best friends."

"I'm out!"

Elliott's declaration, her hands raised in front of her to ward off Killion's loping approach, caught their attention.

Killion nodded, hands up in surrender. The girls started to protest, but Killion shook his head. "Water break."

The girls grumbled good-naturedly, but they obeyed, racing to the bench where Lucy held out their water bottles for them along with a baggie of grapes.

"Grapes!" Ria squealed. "Thank you, Momma." She and Amber plopped down in the grass and giggled over their treat, chattering with each other in a language all their own.

Elliott knelt next to Kristopher. "Are you keeping an eye on my girl, little man?"

Kristopher nodded solemnly. Lucy's heart twisted. So many of his expressions mimicked his father.

"Sweep." He held a finger to his lips, frowning. "Shhh."

Elliott grinned over at them. "The cheekiness is from Killion."

Jonah chuckled.

Killion shook his head. "Of all the things he picks up from me..."

"Thank you, by the way," she said. "I don't think I've said it, but thank you for being his dad. Beckman would be so proud of you."

Lucy's eyes watered as Killion's did the same. His breath caught on a sob, but he held it together, staring at Elliott with a mixture of gratitude and relief. For some reason, they were words he'd needed from her, and Lucy was grateful he got them.

He already knew Lucy was proud of him, that she loved him. But Elliott's stamp of approval would relieve any lingering fears or doubts he had about measuring up to Beckman. She hoped so, at least, because Killion was an amazing partner and father.

Ducking his head, he peeked up at Lucy, his hazel eyes twinkling with unshed tears and happiness. "I guess the B side isn't so bad after all."

No, it wasn't. Her B side was perfect.

Afterword

Beckman's story brings me full circle in my publishing adventures. I don't know if there is anything else in me—he fought me every step of the way writing this—and that's okay. My people have said what they needed to say. Does it mean other characters aren't bouncing around my head? No, it only means I don't feel a driving need to write down their stories yet. Maybe one day, I will.

This story is a departure from my other books. I joke that *Those Who Are Bound* is my light and fluffy read, but it is a darker-themed romance. *The B Side* is my lightest one, and connecting with Lucy was difficult. She's optimistic, happy, and somewhat sappy—she has emotions and a relationship with the world that are foreign to me. But it's her sweet goofiness that I eventually fell for. Her empathy is her gift. Her love for love is endearing.

The words at the beginning are true, at least for me: It's not your fault. The moment of despair that Mac (*Holding on to Day*) saved me from hadn't been triggered or caused by anyone other than myself. Gage's words echo my suicide note I'd written years ago. Giving Gage ownership of the words, however, releases me from their power. It's out there, I'm okay, and he sacrificed himself for me. Mac saved me. Gage freed me.

My best resource during the rough patches was my therapist, Kevin. For those without their own Kevin, please see the below resources, and know that it's okay to not be okay, and to reach out:

Suicide and Crisis Hotline (USA): 988 or 1-800-273-8255

Veterans Crisis line (USA): 988, Press 1 or 1-800-273-TALK (8255), Press 1

Acknowledgments

Jess Elizabeth said—over two years ago!—that Beckman needed his own story. This one might not have been the one she'd imagined, but here it is. Writing this story—while an absolute struggle—proved to me that I can still write after therapy (although the readers will be the judge of that, lol). So thank you, Jess, for wanting Beckman's story, although there was no way for you to have known this wee bit.

I had a great group of beta readers for *The B Side* who provided insightful feedback and made the story better for you, the reader.

Simoné. You hold the record for the *fastest* turnaround on a beta read. And although you didn't know it at the time you wrote it, you contributed to the blurb. As most authors will tell you, the blurb is the hardest part of writing a book. But when you pointed out that one story couldn't exist without the other: bam-o. *The B Side* of an album can only be possible when there is an A-side. So, thank you!

Alexis Crotty. Thank you for providing the welcomed and needed feedback of someone who went into this story without the benefit of reading *Those Who Are Bound*. I am so happy you enjoyed these characters on their own merit.

Nikki Winkler. My heart dropped when I read your experiences, but I am grateful for the perspective that it brought in how you approached the story. Your suggestions allowed me to provide deeper insight to Killion's relationship with this mother. And I'm sorry the men didn't perform properly, as expected. ;-)

Jess Elizabeth. Sorry I didn't let you—or anyone—see the epilogues. You now know why. Don't hate me, lol.

Once more, a shout out to my BFAM, Jay-Vincent, for giving me the male perspective. And to our dear Panda, for being so awesome listening to your husband consider the poly angle when it's not your dynamic. I love you both for your openness and acceptance. You two are the embodiment of love. Hugs and kisses.

Jeanine, what an interesting journey we've been on with *Those Who Are Bound* and now *The B Side*. You were a beta reader for the first, and now the copy/line editor for this one. How much is it killing you to edit this wee paragraph? Haha. I appreciate that you took this story to heart. So much so, you remembered details from *Those Who Are Bound* that I'd forgotten or overlooked, and you made sure the stories remained consistent. A thousand thank you's for going that extra mile.

Thank you, Nay, for the final proofread. Sorry (not sorry) I made you cry. It's Beckman's fault.

And thank you to my readers! Thank you for taking another journey with me that veers from the norm of what I write. *Prize* was definitely a departure, and now *The B Side,* as I step away from romance and dip my toes into simply a love story. But Beckman wanted to make an impact. I hope he did. XXOO.

Also by Lilly...

Audiobooks
Duet or multi-cast

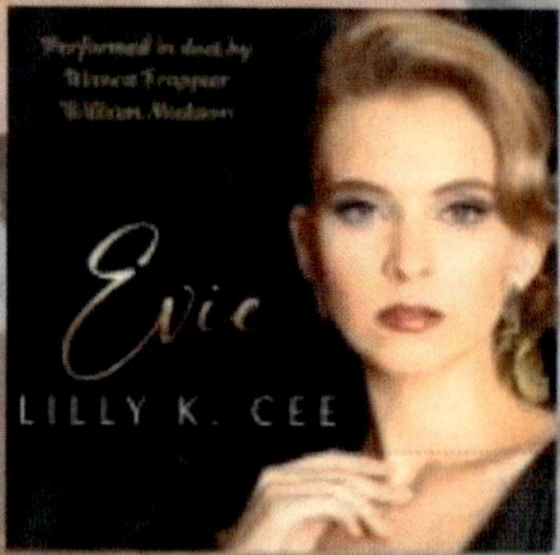

About the Author

Photo credit: In Her Image Photography

Lilly is a Kansas City native who currently resides in sunny California. She has a degree in English (emphasis on literature) from The University of Kansas and an incomplete degree in medieval history, so does that count? The tuition bills say it does.

She is a frequent traveler with a soft spot for Ireland, but Puerto Rico is her favorite destination. Alaska has joined the list of favorites. No matter where she is in the world, however, coffee is a need, necessity, addiction, and obsession (one that she shares with most of her FMCs.)

All of Lilly's books have a playlist on Spotify. Follow the link in her LinkTree: Linktr.ee/LillyKCee

Made in the USA
Coppell, TX
28 January 2026

70260090R00217